HUSBAND, FATHER ... AND MURDERER?

What kind of a man was Dennis Price? What was his reputation? To Janice Hale, Price was a fortune hunter, a gigolo, a parasite. To Fowler, Price was just another play-boy, another city slicker, posing as something better.

To his wife, in her last moments, Dennis Price might have been a murderer.

And John? At age seven, the only son of star-crossed parents, how did John fit into the puzzle? Had John been a witness to his mother's murder...?

"The man to watch ... Wilcox's work boils with life."
— Ross Macdonald

Alan Bernhardt mysteries by Collin Wilcox

Bernhardt's Edge
Except for the Bones

SILENT
Witness

COLLIN
WILCOX

TOR

A TOM DOHERTY ASSOCIATES BOOK
NEW YORK

SILENT WITNESS

A Tor Book
Published by Tom Doherty Associates, Inc.
49 West 24th Street
New York, N.Y. 10010

Cover art by Stephen Peringer

ISBN: 0-812-51149-2
Library of Congress Catalog Card Number: 90-38892

First edition: November 1990
First mass market printing: January 1992

Printed in the United States of America

0 9 8 7 6 5 4 3 2 1

With Love from Us All, This
Book Is Dedicated to Marie

SILENT
Witness

FRIDAY
June 16

11:45 P.M.

The sounds were animal: wild sounds in the savage darkness, sounds of ragged, tortured panting. Fingers had crooked into claws, flesh tearing at flesh, fists flailing. She saw the clenched flash of teeth, lips drawn back, human no longer. And their eyes: predators' eyes, killers' eyes. Human killers, more dangerous than animal. She heard a scream: her voice, her scream. But the sound was lost, only a whimper, stifled in her throat. Strangler's fingers, his flesh on hers: murderer's flesh, no longer a lover's. She must break free. Legs thrashing, arms lashing, she must—

The first crash, metal on bone, ignited the kaleidoscope, an incandescent shower cascading through the darkness behind her eyes. She'd seen these lights cascading through this same darkness only once, when she'd fallen from her horse. She'd—

With the second crash, perspectives were changed. She felt sensation leaving, felt herself falling away—slowly at first, then faster, a sickening spiral, accelerating.

With the third crash, the incandescence flickered, faded, finally failed. Her last moment of consciousness registered the particular smell of the rich, loamy earth—and the sound of her horse's hooves as he trotted away, riderless.

3

THURSDAY
June 22

4:15 P.M.

On his shoulder, John felt his father's hand tighten. Was it a signal? Was he meant to move, say something, do something special? Slowly turning, he looked up at his father. But his father stood as before, chin lowered, staring down at the coffin. In the corner of his father's eye, John could see a tear, one single tear, glistening. But in his father's face, in the well-remembered pattern of the lines and the creases and the angle of the mouth, something had changed. It was the eyes that were different. Even with the single tear, the eyes were a mystery.

The cemetery was on a hill that overlooked the ocean. When they'd driven up the curving road to the cemetery, following the huge black car with the coffin and the flowers inside, he'd looked out the window of the limousine to see the crescent of the Santa Barbara yacht harbor, below. When he and his mother had visited Disneyland, about a week and a half ago, they'd stopped in Santa Barbara, to see Aunt Janice.

Aunt Janice lived in the same house where his mother had grown up, the house where his grandparents had lived before they died. It was a large white stucco house with a red tile roof and a big, heavy front door. When his Aunt Janice had opened the door for them she'd given him a big hug, and asked how it felt to be a second grader, no longer a first grader. "The graduate," his aunt had said. Then she'd laughed. And then she'd hugged him again, harder.

Every day, for three days, they'd gone sailing in Aunt Janice's sailboat, just the three of them. While he'd fished, anchored in the shallows, his mother and his aunt had taken sandwiches and potato salad and cans of 7-Up and beer from the cooler. Aunt Janice's face was tanned a deep brown, and when she laughed at something his mother said, he'd seen white foam on her upper lip, from the beer. He'd always liked to hear Aunt Janice laugh.

His mother hadn't laughed that day. Not once, had he heard her laugh.

Had she laughed when they'd gone to Disneyland? Could he remember?

Why did he remember his aunt laughing, and even remember the white foam of beer on her upper lip, when he couldn't clearly remember his mother's face?

His aunt was standing beside him, as close as his father was standing, on the other side. He realized that, now, he was turning toward his aunt as, yes, she lowered her gaze to meet his.

Even dressed all in black, with a black hat he'd never seen before, his aunt's face looked the same. Someday, he knew, someday soon, she would laugh again, the same laugh.

But his father's face had changed.

Forever.

FRIDAY
June 23

2:15 P.M.

Janice lifted her foot from the accelerator, waited for the pickup truck beside her to draw ahead, then eased the Toyota into the right lane as they passed beneath the airport turnoff sign.

It had been less than a day—twenty-two hours—since the undertaker had touched the button that began lowering Connie's coffin into the ground. As the coffin had been covered over by the earth, so the psyche would begin to scab over.

But beneath scabs, wounds could fester.

At the cemetery, they'd stood together: she and Dennis, with John between them. Once—only once—she'd torn her eyes away from the coffin to look at them: Dennis, the perfect personification of grief bravely borne, holding John's hand as if the flesh felt nothing. John, only seven, numbed, his eyes so large, fixed on the coffin.

Aware that stress had dulled her driving acumen, she guided the Celica with particular care around the semicircular driveway that led to the airport terminal.

In less than an hour, Dennis and John would be airborne, bound for San Francisco. It was a short flight, a little more than an hour. For Connie's last birthday, her thirtieth, the big three-oh, Janice had flown up to San Francisco for the party. "It's a semisurprise," Dennis had said. "She's expecting a few people for dinner. But there'll be fifty people, minimum." On the phone, Dennis had sounded excited, pleased with himself. Dennis had always enjoyed a party.

He sat beside her now. In her peripheral vision she could see his profile: eyes front, patrician nose in perfect alignment, impressive chin lifted, hair impeccably styled. Connie had always appreciated men with handsome profiles.

And now Connie was dead. For six days, dead. Leaving behind a husband, a son—and a sister.

It had happened late Friday night, early Saturday morning, actually. Janice had been at Gordon's house, Friday night. They'd done what they'd done every weekend for more than two years, she and Gordon. They'd gone out together. That was the operative word—out. Sometimes it was a movie, followed by a snack—out. Followed by the drive to Gordon's house, usually driving slowly along the shoreline, comfortably aware of the surf's eternal presence.

Followed, after the preliminaries, by their weekly night of love. Followed, next morning, by breakfast, probably at Jessica's, sometimes at the Neptune.

Last Saturday—only six days ago—they'd walked to the wharf, and had breakfast at the Neptune. Then, even though the fog was still in, they'd walked along the beach for a mile or two before returning to Gordon's house. She'd gone inside, used the bathroom, kissed him goodbye. As she'd driven the three miles to her house, she'd planned the day. First she would shower, and get into fresh clothes. Then she would shop. Once Gordon had suggested that she leave some clothes at his place, so she could shower and change there. She'd responded that then she'd have to take her discarded clothing home to wash, a non sequitur. Gordon hadn't mentioned it again.

It had been almost noon, when she'd arrived home. The mail had come, and she'd spent a minute or two sorting through the envelopes, to be opened and read later. She kept the answering machine in her studio, in the back of the house, on the first floor. Since she didn't paint on weekends, and was therefore half-reluctant to enter the studio, her work space, she'd been tempted to first go upstairs, and shower, and change, and do something with her hair before she checked the machine. But, thank God, curiosity had been stronger than work place reluctance.

The first two messages had been good news. Don MacLean, in Phoenix, had sold the "roof tops" painting. And the Tolls had invited her for cocktails the following Wednesday, to meet a "darkly handsome capitalist," Lillian Toll had said, her voice burbling with casual good humor.

Dennis's voice had been the third one on the tape. "Call me, Janice," he'd said. "It's Connie. Something terrible's happened."

Fumbling at the machine, she'd played the message again. Then she'd—

". . . can just drop us off, if you like," Dennis was saying.

She'd expected him to say it, and had decided what she would say in return: "I'll drop you off, then I'll park, and come in."

"But that's not—"

"I want to do it," she answered. "I want to see you off. The two of you."

She knew he wouldn't protest further, and he didn't. She looked in the mirror. John was staring pensively out the window, his chin cupped in his hand. As they passed a bicyclist, a young man, pedaling hard, John followed the rider with his eyes. Had it only been a week since she'd last seen him? They'd gone to Disneyland only last week, John and Connie. They'd come to Santa Barbara Thursday, and stayed overnight. They'd left bright and early Friday, for San Francisco—for Saint Stephen, actually, fifty miles beyond San Francisco.

Friday night, Connie had been killed. Murdered.
Murdered . . .

The word had a leaden resonance, like a muffled bell tolling in the dark of night. There was a name for words that sounded like the things they described. Lessons from freshman English, long forgotten.

Ahead, the road forked: right for the terminal, left for the parking lot. She signaled for the right turn, took her foot from the accelerator. "Let the engine slow you down," her father had said. "Save the brakes." He'd only given her two driving lessons, before he died. But she still remembered the advice.

Murdered . . .

If she repeated it often enough, would the word lose its dreadful finality, its terrifying aura of infinite doom?

No. Never.

Only time could help. She was thirty-six years old; she was just beginning to realize that, yes, time was the only balm that eased the pain.

Ahead, two cars were stopped in front of the terminal, unloading passengers and baggage. One car was the standard Santa Barbara Mercedes. The terminal, too, was standard Santa Barbara: a cluster of low, mission-style white stucco buildings with vine-shaded patios and low, red-tiled roofs. She'd lived here all her life. Sometimes, seen through a certain unpredictable prism, Santa Barbara seemed too good to be true: too picturesque, too affluent, too removed from pain and poverty.

As they rolled to a stop, Dennis unbuckled his safety belt, swung the door open, put out his hand, for the keys. "I'll get the bags. Sit tight." Typically, his voice was clipped, flattened with bogus authority. Many men who lived off their wives acted like that, she'd discovered. Santa Barbara was loaded with men like Dennis Price. "Fortune hunters" was the archaic phrase.

She took the keys from the ignition, dropped them in his palm. Let him figure out which key opened the trunk. It was a small, petty barb, but gratifying. She knew he wouldn't ask her which key fitted the trunk. Not Dennis. He'd try them all, before he'd ask.

She twisted in the driver's seat to face John. In all the world, this was the only mortal left with whom she shared a blood kinship. John Hale Price, seven years old. He'd been in the house the night of the murder. He could have heard his mother screaming.

One week ago tonight, he could have heard her screaming.

He was looking at her with round, solemn eyes. What secrets lay locked in violent memory behind those soft brown eyes?

"John—" She reached out her hand, to touch his shoulder. Through the rear window she saw the trunk lid come up. Dennis had found the right key. "I want to see you soon, John. Later in the summer, before you start school, I want to see you. I'll come up and get you. We can go to Disneyland again. Would you like that?"

The solemn eyes did not change. Had it been a mistake to mention Disneyland, where he'd just gone with his mother?

"Or we could—" The trunk lid slammed down. Only seconds remained. Life, she'd learned, was measured in seconds—seconds for a young mother to die, seconds for connections to be made, for love to find fragmented words: "We could go fishing, out in the ocean. We could—"

"Okay, John—" Through the open door on the passenger's side, Price handed her the keys, then folded the front seat forward, for John to get out of the car. At the sound of his father's voice, the boy's eyes changed. Had he flinched?

"He can come with me," she said quickly. "We can park the car while you check in."

Decisively, Price shook his head. "No. He's got a bag,

he can carry it. Come on, John. Bring your bag. We don't
have much time."

"You've got a half hour," she said. "At least."

Price looked at her: a quick, hard glance. Then he
turned to his son. "Come on, John. Please." To Janice, the
last word sounded like an exasperated afterthought.
Plainly reluctant, the boy took hold of his bright red nylon
satchel, lifted it, and climbed out of the car.

"We'll see you inside, Janice," Price said. "Thanks."
Abruptly, he closed the door, lifted his two suitcases and
walked up the flagstone sidewalk to the terminal's arbored
entrance. Shoulders rounded, head bowed, John followed.

2:25 P.M.

The check-in line was abnormally long, even for a Friday.
With twenty minutes remaining before departure time,
there were eight San Francisco–bound passengers standing in line ahead of Dennis and John. While she was still
several paces from him, John turned toward her. He'd obviously been watching the entrance to the terminal, waiting for her.

Smiling, she spontaneously held out her hand to him.
"Come on, John. I'll buy you an ice-cream bar while your
dad's checking the suitcases."

The boy stepped quickly toward her, his satchel on the
floor, forgotten. But, just as quickly, Price frowned,
dropped a hand to his son's shoulder. "Let him stay here,
Janice. He doesn't need anything to eat after that lunch.
Especially ice cream."

16

2:50 P.M.

Standing on the lawn in front of the low adobe wall that bordered the tarmac, she watched the airplane's door close, watched the motorized ramp move back. Should she wave? She always felt faintly foolish, waving at faces she could never recognize behind the airplane's small windows. So she simply stood in the bright June sunshine as the 737's engines started, rose to an ear-piercing whine as the airplane began to move slowly across the tarmac. Automatically, she glanced at her watch. Ten minutes until three, exactly the scheduled departure time.

In half an hour, she would be home—the home of her childhood.

She'd been six years old when Constance was born. Old enough to realize that the tiny baby lying beside her mother in the hospital bed had come from inside her mother's body.

She'd been sixteen that Sunday afternoon when the sheriff's car had pulled into their circular driveway. She'd been in her room upstairs, watching tennis on TV. She'd heard the car's engine, and gone to the window and looked down. When she'd seen the light bar on the car's roof, and the number, she'd experienced a momentary titillation, the involuntary response to the presence of the police. But the next moment she'd experienced the first small, sharp stab of fear. Had something happened to her parents? To Connie?

As she'd watched, the car's rear door had swung open, and Connie had emerged. It was all right, then—it would be all right.

But then she realized that Connie was wrapped in a

17

blanket. And, in that moment, she'd known. Her parents were dead. Connie was alive. But their parents were dead.

The 737 was at the far end of the airport. Soon, she knew, the airplane would turn onto the runway. Moments later it would begin its takeoff roll, blasting into the bright blue sky, bound for San Francisco.

Dennis and John had arrived yesterday, on the ten o'clock United flight from San Francisco. She'd debated hiring a car and driver to take the three of them from the airport to her home. But unless the car was a limo, the driver would have been party to their bereavement. And a limo would have been too ostentatious. So she'd picked them up in her bright red Toyota Celica, the best car she'd ever owned.

From the very first, as she and Dennis exchanged their ritual phrases of hushed condolence that instantly lost all meaning, she'd been aware of the underlying tension that inexplicably centered on John. Whenever she sought to draw John aside, even for a moment, Dennis intervened. At first she'd thought her brother-in-law was being overly protective, compensating, belatedly playing the role of father. But when she'd drawn Dennis aside, and suggested that perhaps John should stay at home with her rather than attend the funeral, Dennis's reaction had been almost hostile. "Of course John'll go to the funeral," he'd said, loud enough for John to hear. "That's why he's here." And last night, after the funeral, while John was preparing for bed, Dennis had been careful not to give her a chance to talk with John alone, even for a moment.

Why?

Was Dennis afraid?

Of what?

What could John tell her that Dennis was so determined she should not hear?

As she watched the 737 begin to move, gathering momentum as it hurtled down the runway, she was aware that, whatever the cost, these were questions that must be answered.

MONDAY
August 14

5:15 P.M.

Aware that fate could hang on the moment, yet wryly amused by the melodramatic thought, Janice lifted the phone and punched out the number. After four rings, Paula's recorded voice came on the line: "You've reached the residence of Paula Brett. I'm not able to answer the phone now, but if you'll leave your name and number at the beep, I'll get back to you. Thanks. And remember, wait for the beep."

"Paula," she said, "this is Janice. I'm sorry I haven't called you since—"

"*Janice.*" It was Paula's voice, live.

"Ah—so you monitor your calls, one of those."

"I was in the kitchen." A moment's hesitation, a drop in the timbre of the other woman's voice, registering compassion: "How are you, Janice? I've thought about you every day since the funeral. But somehow—" Another moment of hesitation, as Paula searched for the phrase. "Somehow it—it's hard to know when to call and when not to call. If that makes sense."

"It makes perfect sense, Paula."

"So—" Another hesitant beat. "So how *are* you?"

She drew a long, ragged breath. "I miss her. I miss her a lot. But—" She was aware that in the empty room, in the empty house, she was shrugging. There was no one to see, but she was shrugging. Why? "But I'm taking it one day at a time. So far, it's working."

"Is there anything I can do?"

"As a matter of fact," she said, "there is. That's why I called."

The other woman's response was prompt and fulsome: "Whatever it is, you've got it."

"Are—" Her voice caught. She'd known Paula Brett since childhood. In all her life, she'd never had a better, more generous friend. Irrationally, the thought threatened to bring tears.

"Are you still seeing the man you told me about—the private detective who's also an actor?"

"And a director, too. And a playwright."

"I don't have to ask whether you're still seeing him. I can hear it in your voice."

"No . . ." It was a half-shy response. "No, you don't have to ask." Janice could visualize Paula as she said it: the perceptive warmth of the dark eyes, the pensive mouth up-curved in a very private smile. It would be a smile that, to a friend's eye, revealed a latent vulnerability. For ten years, at least, Paula had been trapped in a bad marriage to a cruel, narcissistic screenwriter, a sadistic predator who had systematically preyed on her sense of self-worth.

"I'm envious. God knows, you're entitled. But I'm still envious."

"Nothing's—settled. We're just—" She was uncertain how to finish it.

Janice let a beat pass, to change the mood. Then: "Listen, Paula, is he—what's his name?"

"Alan. It's Alan Bernhardt."

"Is he a good private detective?"

As if she'd divined the reason for the question, and was carefully considering, the other woman paused thoughtfully before she said, "I think he is. If I had a problem, I'd hire him." Another pause. Then: "Have you got a problem, Janice?"

"It's about Connie—about the way she died. I've got to talk to someone about it."

"Alan?"

"Yes, Alan. I'm sure. Almost sure, anyhow."

"Shall I tell him? Or would you rather—?"

"I think I'm going to come up there, and stay for a few days."

"When?"

"Tomorrow, probably. Or the day after. Will you be in town?"

"Of course. I'll pick you up at the airport. Have you got a flight? I can put you up on the couch, that's the best I can do."

"No. I'll find a hotel. And I think I'll drive up. I'll call you back, when I've figured it out. Can you call Alan, in the meantime?"

"No need. He's coming over for dinner."

"I'm glad, Paula. I'm very glad."

"Thank you, Janice. I'm glad, too."

WEDNESDAY
August 16

1 P.M.

"I'll have the Kung Pao Chicken," Janice said. "And rice. And we'll start with the shark fin soup."

The waitress nodded, wrote the order in Chinese characters on her order pad, and turned to Paula Brett. Sipping tea from a porcelain cup, Janice watched Paula frown at the enormous red menu with its two golden tassels. Even when they were little girls, and had ridden their bikes to McDonald's during the long vacation days of summer, Paula had always been slow deciding what to order.

How reassuring it was to be with someone whose presence brought back those youthful memories. Their fathers had been classmates at Yale, lifetime friends. Paula's father had taken a Ph.D. and gone on to teach at UCLA, a professor of sociology. Her own father had gone into banking, then into finance, finally founding his own venture capital business, based in Los Angeles. He'd specialized in electronics, and had prospered: a millionaire at thirty, a multimillionaire ten years later. The family had moved to Santa Barbara soon after Connie was born, when Janice was six, and just beginning first grade. The Bretts always spent a week or two each summer with them, either in Santa Barbara, sailing and swimming, or at the Hales' ranch in the San Ysidro Mountains behind Santa Barbara, riding and hiking. The three girls had always been required to do regular chores. Chester, the ranch foreman, had been a stern taskmaster. Her father and mother had never failed to

27

back up Chester's work schedules—and the penalties he imposed, for work done badly. At the funeral service for her parents, she had insisted that Chester sit in the same pew with her and Connie and their Aunt Florence, the first pew, ordinarily reserved for family. At first Florence had objected, but only briefly.

At Connie's funeral, in the family pew, there had only been her and John—and Dennis. Chester had died, and Florence was infirm.

Having finally ordered, Paula handed the menu to the waitress, who bowed ceremoniously and withdrew.

"This is a beautiful restaurant," Paula said. She pointed to a nearby four-panel screen, carved teak, and jade. "Look at that screen. It's a museum piece. And the food's famous. Really famous."

"Santa Barbara has one decent Chinese restaurant. San Francisco has a hundred. More than a hundred, probably."

"It's a wonderful city, really," Paula said. "I like Los Angeles. Malibu will always be home. But San Francisco's something special."

"You didn't talk like that when you first came here."

Paula shrugged. She was a small woman, slim and full-breasted, almost perfectly proportioned, still—at age thirty-four. But Paula was a woman who chose not to put her body on public display. Even as a teenager, when the world revolved around the appreciative appraisal of the male, Paula had dressed as she was dressed now: in clothing calculated to suggest the body beneath, but not to flaunt it. Some women dressed for men. Some dressed first for themselves, then for men.

"It was hard, when I first came here," Paula was saying. "I guess I felt pretty sorry for myself."

"Most people do, after a divorce."

The other woman nodded, but made no reply. In her eyes Janice could see the shadow of a sadness that, during the last years of Paula's marriage, had revealed a wound to the spirit that her family and friends had feared might never heal. Her husband had been a screenwriter: talented, successful—and utterly amoral. Would Alan Bernhardt, the playwright, fit the same description? Had one mistake compounded into two? Such things happened, Janice knew.

The waitress arrived, and served their soup. The waitress's smile was delicate as the porcelain she handled with such gentle deftness. They sampled the soup, and judiciously approved. Then they exchanged a smile, signifying that the time had come to discuss the matters at hand.

Janice spoke first: "So tell me about Alan Bernhardt." She pitched the question casually, lightly matter-of-fact. The other woman's reaction was a small, subtly playful smile.

"Bernhardt the detective?" The smile widened. "Or Bernhardt the love object?"

"Do I have to choose?"

Appreciatively sipping the soup, Paula shrugged, a burlesque of maidenly coyness. "Actually," she said, "he's got an interesting history. His parents were Jewish, both of them from New York, that hard-core Jewish middle-class intellectual stock. His father was a bombardier in the war. He got killed before Alan was born."

"So Alan's—what—forty-five?"

"Forty-three, I think. Maybe forty-four. Anyhow, his mother raised him. His mother and his mother's parents. It was one of those real—" Even though it was Paula's nature to keep her enthusiasms private, treasures unto herself, she nevertheless allowed her enthusiasm to show through as she said, "It was one of those real vintage New York Jewish families, apparently. His mother was an only child—a much-loved only child, the way only the Jews can love their children. Alan was the only grandson. His grandfather was a small clothing manufacturer. He wasn't very successful. He was always more interested in playing chamber music and fly tying than in making a fortune, I gather. There was always enough money, though. The grandparents took care of Alan's education. A good education, private schools in New York and Ohio."

"The grandfather sounds wonderful."

"I know . . ."

"What about Alan's mother. What'd she do?"

"She was a modern dancer and an activist. You know—women's lib, ban the bomb, human rights. Marching and meetings and dance recitals, that's what Alan remembers most about his childhood."

"His mother never remarried."

Paula shook her head. "No. She danced and she marched and that was it, apparently. They lived in a loft, in the Village. Alan could fly model airplanes in it."

"A happy childhood, then." Approvingly, Janice nodded. "Like us."

"Yes . . ." As if the thought was new to her, Paula spoke thoughtfully, reflectively. Then she nodded. "Yes. Like us."

"So why'd he come to San Francisco?"

"The truth is, he was running away. That's why a lot of people come to San Francisco, I've decided. San Francisco—California—it's the promised land. Or so people think."

Ruefully, Janice smiled. "Sometimes I think about running away to Manhatten. Or Taos. Or San Miguel."

"I know . . ." Paula finished her soup, and nodded appreciatively. "Excellent. I've never had shark fin soup before. Now I know what the shouting is all about."

"Are you going to tell me what Alan is running away from?"

"When he was in college," Paula answered, her voice measured, her manner grave, "he got hooked on acting—on the theater. He married a girl who also wanted to act. After they graduated, they went to New York and started making the rounds—trying out. They lived in the Village, not far from Alan's mother. It was an idyllic life, really perfect. After a year or two, both Alan and his wife started to connect, to get small parts. Then Alan had a play produced off Broadway.''

"A play he'd written?"

Paula nodded. "He wrote it while he was in college. He wrote three, actually.''

"I'm impressed." She nodded to the waitress, who cleared away the soup dishes. "Very impressed.''

"He directed, too, off Broadway. He was a comer, no question. A rising star. And his wife was starting to do well, too.''

"So what happened? Divorce?"

"No," Paula answered, her dark eyes solemn, her voice subdued. "No; not divorce." She drew a long, deep breath. "In the space of a year and a half, his wife and his mother and his grandparents all died.''

"Jesus Christ. How?"

"His grandfather had a heart attack, they think, while he was driving. His wife was with him. In any case, their car crossed over the center divider of an expressway, and hit a tanker truck head-on. Alan's mother already knew she had cancer, when her parents died. She died less than a year later. And then—" As if she could still hardly believe the story she was telling, the other woman incredulously shook her head. "And then, Jesus, his wife was killed. She was mugged. She hit the back of her head on a curb." As she told the story, Paula's voice had dropped to a low, leaden monotone, as if she sought to distance herself from her own words.

"My God, no wonder he had to leave New York. There wasn't anything left for him." As she spoke, their entrées arrived. After they'd been served, Janice asked, "So how does his being a private detective fit into all this? He sure doesn't sound very hard-boiled.''

Paula's smile was indulgent. "That's mostly a myth, you know. Two of Alan's good friends are private detectives. One of them was a tenured professor at Berkeley. The other, a lady, used to do film reviews for the *Los Angeles Herald*."

"You're kidding."

Instead of replying, Paula smiled, using ivory chopsticks to sample a vegetable dish. "This is excellent. Really excellent."

"So what about the theater—Alan's plays, his acting?"

"He still acts, and still writes. He's with the Howell Theater, which is probably the best little theater in San Francisco—and that's saying a lot. But it isn't a living. He's one of the owners of the theater, but it still isn't a living. For years, he worked part time for Dancer and Associates. They're the biggest firm of private investigators in town. They specialize in high-ticket divorces, plus a little child-stealing. About the time I met Alan, he had a big argument with Herbert Dancer, and Alan quit. He's been free-lancing ever since."

"How do I get in touch with him?"

"I thought you'd never ask." Paula took a business card from her purse, and slid it across the table.

Janice looked at the card, slipped it into her own purse. "I'll call him when I get back to the hotel."

"Good." Another smile: Paula's pixy smile. "You can use my name. You can also come to dinner. Name the day."

"Thanks. I will. Let me talk to Alan, though, first."

As they appreciatively ate, they allowed a companionable silence to fall. Then Paula asked, "What's it all about, Janice? You said something on the phone about the way Connie died. What'd you mean?"

Having expected the question, she was ready with a response: "You've been in San Francisco—what—six months?"

"More. Eight or nine months, now."

"How many times did you see Connie, in that time?"

"Four times, I think. Three times for lunch, in the city.

And once for a day at the winery—swimming, and a barbecue."

"Have you spent much time with Dennis?"

"No. Except for their wedding, I only saw him once. That was at the barbecue. It was a big party, though. I hardly talked to him."

"What'd you think of him?"

"The truth?"

Decisively, Janice nodded. "Definitely, the truth."

"I thought he was a—" A short, animated pause, searching for the phrase. "I thought he was a phony. A stuffed shirt at best, a gigolo at worst. Handsome, but that's all. I was always afraid Connie would marry someone like him."

"Really? How come?"

"The truth?"

"The truth."

"Well," Paula answered, her voice heavy with regret, "we all pick our own ways to make ourselves suffer. And, let's face it, Connie always picked the wrong men, even when she was a teenager. She was—what—four years younger than me, so I didn't really know her all that well. But—" Paula shrugged. "But let's just say I wasn't surprised, when she married someone like Dennis."

"When you saw her here—those lunches, you had—did she say anything about him, about her marriage?"

"No, nothing," came the prompt response. "But I wouldn't've expected her to say anything, not really. We just weren't that close." A pause. Then, earnestly: "Why, Janice? What's it all about?"

Her lunch forgotten, she instinctively lowered her voice, leaned closer to the other woman. "You know what happened—how she died."

"I know there was a prowler, a burglar."

"Dennis *said* there was a burglar."

"Janice . . ." Awed, Paula's voice, too, was lowered. "Christ, what're you saying?"

"I'm saying that I think Dennis knows more than he's telling." Her voice was firm, her eyes steady. "A lot more, maybe."

"My God . . ." As if she suddenly needed a stimulant, Paula drained her teacup. "Are you serious?"

"I'm very serious."

"You mean that—that—" She was unable to say it.

Speaking slowly, in a calm, measured voice that suggested she had thought so often of the events she described that the facts were rote, she recited: "On June ninth, a Friday, Connie and John drove down to Santa Barbara. They'd been here, in San Francisco, at the townhouse, so they left from here. They stayed with me through the weekend. On Monday—that was the twelfth—they drove down to Los Angeles. They did Disneyland and the Spruce Goose and the Q.E. II, and came back to Santa Barbara on Thursday. They stayed overnight, and left Friday morning. Connie told me they were going to San Francisco, but she apparently decided to go to the winery instead. Except for what Dennis has told me, that's all I know. The next day—Saturday—Dennis called to say Connie was dead. She'd surprised a burglar, he said, and she'd been killed. It had happened in the master bedroom, at the winery. There's a big fireplace in the room. Apparently there was a struggle. Furniture was overturned, things were broken. She was hit with a poker. Or, rather, fireplace tongs. It—" She broke off, bit her lip. Then: "It crushed her skull on one side, at the temple. It happened about midnight, Dennis said."

"Where was Dennis when it happened?"

"He said he was asleep in the spare room." Bitterly, she grimaced. "He said he couldn't sleep in the master bedroom, in their bed, without her."

Paula frowned. "Dennis didn't strike me as that sentimental. Or that lovey-dovey with Connie, either."

"Well, that's what he said." She drank the last of her tea and nodded to the waitress, who cleared away the lunch dishes, leaving only the teapot and cups. "I'm sure that's what he told the police."

"But you don't believe him."

"At first I believed him. It's a perfectly plausible story, if you accept his statement that he was sleeping in a spare room. But then I asked him about John."

"I was wondering. Where was John, that night?"

"He was downstairs in the living room. 'On the couch, Dennis says. 'Asleep.'"

"Don't you believe that?"

"I *do* believe that. They got a late start leaving Santa Barbara, and the winery is at least fifty miles north of San Francisco. Connie would've stopped for dinner, so I'm sure they didn't get to the winery until late at night. And John, I'm sure, would've gone to sleep in the car. Connie might've been able to carry him inside. She's—she was—an athlete, as you know. A tennis player, and a swimmer. I used to tease her about her muscles. But she wouldn't've carried him upstairs, I don't think. She would've gotten Dennis to do that."

"What does John say happened?"

"I don't know, Paula. Dennis won't let me talk to him." Paula frowned. "I don't understand."

"He says he doesn't want John questioned. He says it's doctor's orders—that a child psychiatrist doesn't want John reliving the trauma."

Still frowning, the other woman considered. Finally, tentatively, she said, "That makes sense, of course. It's only been two months since Connie was killed. I can see that John needs time to heal. But you have to wonder why Dennis took John to the funeral, if he was so concerned about trauma."

"He says he hadn't consulted this child psychiatrist at that point."

Judiciously, Paula shrugged, then spread her hands. "I

have to say, it all seems to add up, Janice. What is it, exactly, that's bothering you?"

"What's bothering me," she answered, speaking quickly, decisively, "is that, ever since Connie died, Dennis hasn't let me spend a single minute alone with John. Literally, from the time they arrived in Santa Barbara for the funeral until the next day, when they got on the plane to go home, Dennis didn't let John and I exchange a single word out of his earshot."

"Well—" Still judiciously, Paula considered, then shook her head. "I don't know, Janice. I doesn't seem to me that he's being—"

"He's hiding something, Paula. I *know* he's hiding something. I'm *sure* of it."

"Are you saying—" Involuntarily, the other woman dropped her voice, moved closer across the table. "Are you saying that you think Dennis killed her? Is that what you're saying?"

"I'm saying," she answered, "that the only thing I know about Connie's murder is what Dennis told me—what he wanted me to hear. And that simply isn't good enough, Paula. It just isn't."

"Have you called John since the funeral?"

"I call once a week, at least."

"And?"

"And Dennis stays on the line." As she spoke, the waitress arrived with the check. Firmly, Janice placed her credit card on the elegant red lacquer tray. "My treat."

"Thank you. Would you like to come to dinner with Alan?"

"I'd love to. But I'd like to talk to him, first."

"Of course. You talk with Alan, then give me a call. Okay?" Across the carved black teak table, Paula smiled. Then, seriously, she said, "If you need anything—anything at all—give me a call. Promise?"

"Promise."

"I know you, Janice. I know you value your autonomy.

And I can relate to that, as they say. But everyone needs friends once in a while. Maybe this is one of those times, for you."

As Janice smiled at the other woman, images came back: Paula standing in front of a horse she yearned to ride, solemnly staring the horse straight in the eye—Paula on the beach at night, one of a circle of teenagers, experimenting with beer and the beginnings of sex—Paula at Connie's funeral, stricken.

"Definitely, this is one of those times," she answered softly.

THURSDAY
August 17

2:30 P.M.

Placing the yellow legal pad on the marble coffee table, Bernhardt wrote *Janice Hale* on the first line, followed by the date. They'd been talking for almost an hour: a long, hard hour filled with this woman's strong emotions, always rigidly contained, yet constantly boiling just beneath the surface. Now it was time he began taking notes. On the second line he wrote *Constance Hale Price, disc. Friday, June 16th., age 30.*

"You say the Prices had a house in San Francisco. Do you know the address?"

"Yes. It's 2784 Broadway."

Bernhardt nodded approvingly as he made the note. "Pacific Heights."

"Yes."

"Do you know the phone there?"

She recited the number.

"And the winery. It's about ten miles west of Saint Stephen, you said."

"Yes. It's the Brookside Winery."

"That's in—what—Benedict County?"

"I think so, I'm not sure. They've only had the winery for two years. I've only seen it once in that time."

"Do you know the phone number?"

"Sorry, no. But the Dennis Price number is in the book. And—yes, you're right—it's in Benedict County, I remember now. The area code is six-four-seven." Then:

41

"Are you sure you won't have some coffee? Wine? It's no trouble to send down for it."

Smiling, Bernhardt shook his head. "Thanks, no. I'm cutting down on caffeine." The smile widened. "I'm also cutting down on booze, come to think of it."

She answered the smile—successfully, she knew. Since Connie had died, almost exactly two months ago, she couldn't remember smiling, not really smiling, with genuine pleasure. Perfunctorily, yes. Dutifully, yes. Sadly, certainly. But, until now, she hadn't really smiled. For this small boon, she realized that she could thank Alan Bernhardt. He was one of those quiet, perceptive men who could help the healing process. He listened. He considered. He thought before he spoke. She remembered Paula's account of his life: everyone close to him dead, beginning with the father who was killed before Alan was born. And ending with his wife, a victim of random street violence.

She watched him as he bent over his yellow pad, earnestly frowning as he wrote. He was a tall, lean man, slightly stooped. His complexion was dark, unmistakably Semitic. The nose was long and slightly hooked, the forehead and cheeks were furrowed, prematurely aged. It was a thoughtful face, a reassuring face—a face deeply etched by both pain and compassion. There was sadness in the face, but no bitterness—anguish, but no anger. His dark eyes were expressive, his mouth firm. His dark hair was thick and only casually combed. The glasses went with the face—serious, horn-rimmed glasses; but they were high styled, suggesting that, yes, appearances counted, yet another hint of the man behind the face—and the actor behind the man.

Would they marry, Paula and Bernhardt? *Should* they marry? When she saw them together, perhaps she would know.

"What's the name of the winery again?" Bernhardt was asking.

"Brookside."

"Is it a boutique winery?"

She nodded. "Exactly. It's the trendy thing, you know, to have a winery. A wonderful spot for weekend parties."

"Was your sister trendy?"

She hesitated, then decided to say, "Connie wasn't really sure what she was, I don't think. 'Trendy' doesn't fit, though, not really. But—" She dropped her voice. "But Dennis is trendy. Definitely trendy."

Bernhardt nodded, reflected for a moment, then said, "Does Dennis know you're hiring a private investigator?"

"No."

"When's the last time you talked to him?"

"A little less than a week ago. I call once a week, to talk to John. Dennis always answers the phone—and listens in."

"Paula told me a little about your family history. John is your only blood relative."

"Yes. Except for an aunt, who has Alzheimer's."

"And you and your sister were very close."

"Our parents died when Connie was only ten. I was sixteen. Our aunt came to live with us, my father's sister. But I really raised Connie. Florence—our aunt—" She shook her head, shrugged.

Bernhardt's nod was sympathetic, but his next question was professionally matter-of-fact: "You haven't seen John since the funeral. Dennis won't let you spend any time alone with him. Is that right?"

"Yes."

"I can understand how that would be painful for you. But—" Bernhardt hesitated, choosing the phrase. "But I'm not sure it's necessarily suspicious. If he says he's protecting John from pain, maybe you should give him the benefit of the doubt."

She decided to smile. This time it was a humorless smile, the hallmark of her life since her sister's death. "You don't have a very strong profit motive, do you?"

He guffawed, then shrugged. It was a reprise of a sheepish, small boy's shrug. "Touché."

They sat silently for a moment, each regarding the other with growing trust. Finally Bernhardt said, "Give me a rundown on Connie and Dennis. Start as far back as you can. I've discovered that helps—the histories, the bios. I know a little of Connie's story, from Paula—and your story, too. Your father was rich. You grew up in Santa Barbara, in Montecito. I know your parents died when Connie was only ten." He broke off, gestured that the story was hers to finish.

As she nodded acknowledgment of her cue, Bernhardt saw a shadow of sadness remembered darken her eyes. "That's part of it," she said, speaking softly. "Psychologically, my parents' death was certainly part of it—the start of it, maybe. They drowned in a boating accident—a freak wave. That was bad enough. But, worse than that, Connie was with them. Connie was wearing a life jacket. My folks always did that, always made us wear life jackets, even though they didn't. So when the Coast Guard arrived—" She shook her head, lowered her eyes. "Connie was the only one they found."

"Christ—" Bernhardt, too, shook his head. "That's terrible. The guilt, for Connie. The loss must've been bad enough. But the guilt—" Eloquently, he let it go unfinished.

"I've always thought—I've always known, really—that the accident marked Connie for life, psychologically."

"In what way was she marked?"

"The usual way, for a girl. Getting involved with the wrong boys—and then the wrong men. Letting them walk all over her, victimize her so she could expiate the guilt she felt for living. Psychologically, it's pretty open and shut, really. But that doesn't make it easier, when it happens to someone you—" Suddenly her voice caught, choking off the rest of it.

"And Dennis is just like the rest of them—the wrong man."

"Definitely, Dennis is just like the rest of them. The old-fashioned word was 'gigolo.'"

"'Fortune hunter,' too?"

"Definitely, 'fortune hunter.'"

"Tell me about Dennis."

"The truth is," she answered, "that Dennis is a Los Angeles type. His father was a supporting actor in Hollywood—not much more than a bit player, really. He's one of those men who was born with a handsome face but not much else. And Dennis is just like him, really. Except that Dennis has pretensions. And ambitions, too. Dennis is greedy."

"What're his ambitions?"

"He wants to be one of the beautiful people," she answered promptly. "Which is exactly the life he's living, at least superficially. He's a gentleman vintner, which is currently the with-it thing to be doing, as you know. And, of course, there's the townhouse in Pacific Heights. And, yes, he has an airplane, too."

"Did Connie go along with all that?"

"Connie fitted in. She had the looks, and the money. For the kind of life Dennis wants, that's all you need—as long as your forehand is acceptable."

"Does Dennis inherit everything?"

"He inherits a third of her estate. I get a third. And John gets a third, when he's twenty-one."

"Who administers John's third?"

"Dennis does. And there's a provision that John gets an allowance until he's twenty-one, administered by Dennis."

"What's the total value of the estate?"

"We won't know exactly until the will's actually probated."

"What d'you estimate?"

"I'd estimate at least twenty-five million dollars." She spoke calmly, without visible emotion. The message: for Janice Hale, wealth was synonymous with ordinary, day-to-day life. The moral: the rich *were* different.

Twenty-five million divided by three. More than fifteen million for Dennis Price—plus access to his son's allowance, plus an administrator's fee for the son's share of the estate.

"How soon will the will be probated, do you know?"

"The time for probate is six months, if there aren't any complications. That'd be four months from now."

"Do you have the name of Connie's lawyer?"

"Yes. It's Albert Fink. He's in San Francisco. I haven't found him very helpful, though."

"Is it all right if I talk to him?"

"Yes. And when you do, tell me what he says." As she said it, Bernhardt heard the hard edge of resolution in her voice, saw the muted flash of determination in her clear blue eyes. Janice Hale spoke softly, but she knew what she wanted—and knew how to get it. She was a slim woman, economically proportioned. Beneath a casually worn cotton fisherman's sweater, her breasts were small. Beneath loosely cut slacks, her legs were slim, her buttocks firm. If she was six years older than her sister, then Janice was now thirty-six. Worn short, her brown hair showed streaks of gray she'd disdained to have retouched. Her features, too, were unretouched: the face of an intellectual, unmistakably a member of the privileged class.

"Does Dennis know you're here?"

"No. Do you think I should tell him?"

"Probably not, at least for now. You'd better give me a chance to ask a few questions."

"We'll be in touch, won't we?"

"Certainly. I'll call you every day. Here—" He slid a business card across the table. "I've got a machine, so you can leave a message. I'll need a letter from you, identifying yourself as Constance Price's sister, and authorizing me to investigate the circumstances surrounding her death." He gestured to a nearby writing desk. "You can write it now. Mention that, aside from Dennis and John, you're Constance Price's only blood relative. When it comes to the legalities—things like authorizing funeral arrangements, swearing out complaints—a blood relationship is what it's all about." He let a beat pass. Then, conscious of his own awkward discomfort, he said, "I charge—"

Quickly, she raised a hand. "Please. I've known Paula all my life. Let's not talk about money. Just send me a bill. Will you?"

Gravely, he nodded. "Of course."

"Good." With an air of someone releasing energy, she rose to her feet and strode across the large, ornately furnished hotel sitting room. When she returned to sit across from him, Bernhardt watched her cross her legs, lean forward, prop an elbow on her knee and cup her chin in her hand. It was a classic finishing school posture.

"What'll you do first?" she asked. Her eyes were brighter now, more sharply focused. "Is there anything I can do?"

"I don't think so," Bernhardt answered. "Not now. Of course, I'll be calling you, for instructions. For instance, when I talk to Price, should I say that you've retained me?"

Considering the question, she frowned. "Yes, I see." She uncrossed her legs, thoughtfully tapped a fingernail on the arm of her Regency chair. "I see what you mean. Strategy."

"Exactly."

"Will you talk to Dennis first?"

"To be honest," Bernhardt answered, "I haven't figured it out. But I think I'll talk to the police first, find out who handled the murder investigation, and talk to him. Do you have any idea whether the authorities have a suspect?"

"As I said, I only know what Dennis told me. But somehow I don't think there was a suspect. I think Dennis would've mentioned that."

"What about John? Was he questioned by the police?"

"I don't know."

As Bernhardt nodded, he capped his pen, put it in his pocket, and slipped the yellow legal pad into the briefcase that rested beside him on the floor. Now he glanced at his watch, and moved forward in his chair. "I'd better run. I think I can start on this tomorrow."

She nodded. "Good."

"But first—" He gestured to the writing desk, a reminder of the letter she must write. Obediently, she rose, went to the desk, began writing.

FRIDAY
August 18

2 P.M.

Bernhardt rose to his feet, stretched, walked to the water cooler for his second drink of water in the last forty-five minutes. Pantomiming a basketball star, he balled up the paper cup and lobbed it into the wastebasket. Coming out of his pirouette, he stole a glance at the uniformed woman behind the desk. The lady was not amused. She was almost certainly a spinster, he'd decided. Her soured, down-curved mouth, her worst feature, was sharply drawn in bright red lipstick. Like her mouth her eyes were soured, a chronic condition, Bernhardt suspected.

Bernhardt strode to the large window that offered a view of the Saint Stephen village square. The vista evoked a calmer, gentler era: a city hall built of stone, a life-size verdigris statue of Saint Stephen, the town's namesake. And, yes, there was a muzzle-loading Civil War cannon. The pyramid of cannon balls beside the cannon recalled one of Bernhardt's earliest frustrations. His grandfather had once rented a house in Bucks County for the summer. On their first trip to the village for groceries, his mother had taken him to the town square. Transfixed, he'd stared at the cannon, which had symbolized, perhaps, his first realization that, yes, might made right, like it or not. He'd turned to the cannon balls stacked beside the cannon, and tried to dislodge the topmost ball, unsuccessfully. He'd never known why the moment of sharp disillusionment had remained in his memory, but he suspected it had to do with an early loss of innocence. His mother had—

He heard an intercom buzzer. Expectantly, he turned, watching the sour-mouthed lady officer lift her phone, listen, nod, say something cryptic and replace the phone in its cradle. As she frowned at him, Bernhardt realized that, without the generous application of black eyebrow pencil, her eyebrows would not exist. Or, if they did indeed exist in their natural state, they would have softened the face, doubtless an undesirable option.

She gestured to the frosted glass door marked SHERIFF FOWLER, and nodded. Bernhardt's patience had been rewarded. Plainly, his pleasure caused the lady officer mild consternation.

Dressed in a tan uniform, Sheriff Fowler sat behind a large steel desk that was strewn with piles of papers, each pile secured by a paperweight. Grossly overweight, Fowler's body bulged on either side of his swivel chair's armrests. As Bernhardt introduced himself he stepped forward, signifying that he sought to shake hands. Ignoring the gesture, Fowler grunted once, wetly, and gestured to a chair placed beside his desk. As Bernhardt took his seat he played the secret game he always played when he met a fat man: mentally stripping away the fat from the face and neck to divine the true nature of the face beneath. The younger Fowler, he decided—the much younger Fowler—must have had a choirboy's face. His lips were pursed in a cupid's bow, his china-blue eyes were round and guileless, his nose was cherubic. Even in this overweight incarnation, the flesh that covered the fat was smooth and clear and pink. Even Fowler's bald pate was a glowing pink, fringed with finely spun brown hair.

Bernhardt opened his wallet to show his license, then took Janice Hale's letter from an inside pocket. He unfolded the letter, leaned forward, placed it on the desk. Before he turned his attention to the letter, Fowler let a long moment of silence pass as he stared at Bernhardt, playing the eye contact game. Finally, inscrutably, Fowler grunted again, then took a pair of heavy black-rimmed reading glasses from his center drawer. As he read the letter, his lips moved. Finally finished, he pushed the letter across the desk to Bernhardt. After another round of hard eye-contact, another draw, Fowler shrugged his large, pudgy shoulders. "I guess," he said, "that we can start by you asking me questions. I'll tell you what I can. What I can't answer, I won't." His voice was thick, clogged with phlegm. Sunk deep in the porcine face, his eyes were small and shrewd. Plainly, Fowler was nobody's fool.

A disarming aw-shucks approach, Bernhardt decided, was the only tactic that could possibly succeed. Playing the big-city private detective role would never work, not with the taciturn, Buddha-size despot across the desk, bulging in his chair. Although sparsely populated, Benedict County included dozens of rural retreats owned by the idle rich. Saint Stephen, population six thousand, was Benedict County's only town of any consequence. Earlier in the day Bernhardt had called Lieutenant Peter Friedman, co-commander of San Francisco's homicide detail, Bernhardt's indispensible law enforcement mole. Friedman confirmed that Fowler had presided over Benedict County for almost twenty years. In that time, Friedman said, Fowler had learned all the tricks the rich can play—and had devised some tricks of his own. No one messed with Fowler, Friedman said. His power was absolute.

"I guess," Bernhardt began, "that I'm only looking for two things—how the murder came down, from your point of view, and whether you have a suspect."

Fowler's sparse eyebrows drew together, affecting a tactical puzzlement. "When you say 'my point of view,' what's that mean, exactly?"

"It means what you think happened," Bernhardt answered. "And why."

"Well, now, I have to tell you, Mr. Bernhardt, I don't go in much for theorizing. That's uptown stuff, according to

53

my way of doing things. I just try to stick to the facts and leave the theorizing to others, if they're so inclined."

"Of course," Bernhardt answered. "I—obviously, I go along with that." Aware that, already, he was on the defensive, he cleared his throat, began again: "What I meant was that—"

"We got the call about one-thirty on Saturday morning, June seventeenth, if I recall correctly," Fowler said, smoothly interrupting. "Maybe it was quarter to two, I'd have to check. It was Dennis Price, and he said he thought his wife was dead, that someone had killed her. I was home at the time, of course, sleeping. Time I got dressed, and called Roy Parker, who's my captain, and got out to the Price place, it was probably two-thirty. Roy was already there, and so was an ambulance, from Santa Rosa General, that's the closest hospital. Roy was outside the house, waiting for me. Price and Al Martelli—he's Price's foreman, at the winery—they were inside the house, downstairs, in the living room. John—that's the Price's little boy—he was with them. Both Price and Martelli had guns—a rifle and a shotgun. Are you familiar with the layout, out there?"

"No. I thought I should come here first, check with you."

"Ah—" As Fowler nodded approval, his chin disappeared in rolls of flesh. "Yes. So noted."

Bernhardt was careful to smile, an exercise in calculated self-effacement. Thank God for all the acting lessons.

"The way it's laid out," Fowler said, "the main house—a big, three-story redwood-and-shingle house—is back maybe two hundred feet from the county road. There's a garage, and a couple of outbuildings there, all very nice, very rustic. The house was built by Avery Weston, the writer. There's a rise in back of the house, and that's where the winery is, behind that rise. It's not much of a winery. They do maybe ten thousand cases a year. The vineyard itself is about forty acres, if I'm not mistaken.

Mostly chardonnay grapes. Al Martelli's house is behind the rise, about a quarter mile from the main house, I'd say. You can't see the winery from the house, and you can't see the house from the road, either, because there's a screen of trees planted beside the road. Well—'' Suddenly Fowler coughed: a hard, wracking cough. Was it a smoker's cough? Bernhardt looked for ashtrays, saw none.

"Well," Fowler continued, "Roy gave me the rundown, and I put in a call for the coroner to come out, and Cliff Benson—he's our D.A.—I called him, too, of course. Cliff and I decided we'd talk to Price, while Al Martelli looked after the boy. Roy, meanwhile, was seeing to the pictures, and fingerprints, and all those things. Preserving the chain of evidence, in other words.

"It all seemed pretty straightforward, what happened. And the physical evidence—forensics, et cetera—all pretty much tell the same story. Mrs. Price and the boy had been down south, visiting relatives and going to Disneyland. They got home at maybe eleven-thirty or twelve, we never were able to determine the time for sure. Apparently Mrs. Price took the bags out of the car, and put them in the entry hall of the house. Then she got John out of the car, probably. Price speculated that John fell asleep in the car, and Mrs. Price carried him into the living room, and put him down on the couch. She probably intended to go upstairs where the bedrooms are, and wake Price up, and get him to carry John upstairs, to bed. Anyhow, she obviously left John downstairs, asleep on a sofa, while she went upstairs, to the master bedroom. Price wasn't there, he was sleeping in another bedroom. Al Martelli was in his house, in bed with a lady friend, as it turned out. And Maria— that's the Prices' Mexican cook—she was asleep in her room over the garage, which is a good distance from the main house. So the rest is pure speculation, since Price didn't wake up until after the murder was actually committed, apparently, and neither Martelli nor the Mexican woman heard anything. But it seems pretty obvious that

Mrs. Price surprised a burglar. There was a struggle—a sizable struggle by the look of the room. Mrs. Price was apparently an athlete, a first-class tennis player, and swimmer, by all accounts, so she would've been capable of putting up quite a fight. But when it was over, she was dead. Whoever it was hit her with the fireplace tongs, and she probably died within a few minutes, the coroner said."

"And Price didn't hear a thing?" Deliberately, Bernhardt gave the question a skeptical accent.

Fowler shrugged, then glanced pointedly at his watch. As if he'd lost interest in the proceedings, he allowed his voice to go flat, his eyes to wander to the littered desk and the work that awaited. "He heard something, no question, but he didn't know what it was he actually heard; that's the way it seemed to me. He's a real heavy sleeper, he says. But, of course, he *did* wake up, eventually, and he investigated."

"And you believed him, accepted his account of what happened."

Fowler shrugged again, obviously a chronic habit. "There's nothing to contradict what he said. Still isn't, as far as that goes."

"Was anything stolen?"

"No," Fowler answered. "Nothing."

"Were the drawers ransacked?"

"No."

"So if it was a burglar, Mrs. Price must've surprised him when he'd just gotten there."

Fowler nodded.

"But—" Pretending puzzlement, Bernhardt frowned. Speaking hesitantly, as if he would certainly need help to finish the thought, he said, "But this doesn't sound right, Sheriff. I mean, first, we've got a burglar—or a prowler, whatever—who's just broken in, for whatever reason. He's upstairs, when he hears a car drive up, and hears someone enter the house, downstairs. Wouldn't it be logical that he would have gotten out then? It sounds like he'd've had plenty of time, seeing that Mrs. Price probably made a couple of trips to the car."

Projecting long-suffering patience, Fowler grunted. "When you say 'logical,' you blow the whole thing. Prowlers—burglars—don't do things logically. Some of them, for instance, get their rocks off hot-prowling—running the risk that someone'll wake up, and catch them. That's why they're so dangerous. They work so close that when they get caught, they're all ready with the knife—or the fireplace tongs. Same thing with sex offenders. It isn't the sex per se they're after. It's the high they get when the victim struggles."

"Was there any indication that the killer might've been a rapist?"

Fowler shook his head. "Nope. All the victim's clothing was intact. It was torn, because of the struggle. But it was intact. There wasn't any semen, either. Not inside her, not on her clothes. Whatever it was, it wasn't sex."

"What'd you think it was, Sheriff?" Bernhardt asked quietly. "You, personally?"

Fowler sat silently for a moment, staring at Bernhardt. For a moment it seemed that he might be willing to speculate, one-on-one. But the moment passed, punctuated by another grunt, this one more decisive, signifying that the conversation was almost finished. "I already told you I don't deal in theories. It's a sucker's game."

Accepting the autocratic disclaimer, resigned, Bernhardt nodded. Then: "Have you turned up any suspects?"

"Afraid not. We talked to a couple of drifters, and a few local characters who're mean enough or crazy enough to've done it, but we didn't turn up anything."

"What about fingerprints? Blood types? Any match-ups from the computer in Sacramento?"

Fowler shook his head. "There was lots of blood, but it was all the victim's type. As for fingerprints—" He shook his head. "So far, nothing. There wasn't any flesh under her fingernails, either, nothing easy like that."

"So—" Deliberately, Bernhardt let a calculated beat pass. Then, deftly planting the barb, he said, "So are you pretty much waiting to see what happens next?"

Fowler's china-blue eyes seemed to grow visibly smaller. Sunk in the smooth pink flesh of his cheeks and chin, his cupid's mouth stirred, gently up-curving. Except for the coldness around the eyes, it might have been a smile. Fowler's voice was very soft. "We plan to find the killer, Mr. Bernhardt. We aren't waiting. We're watching."

Signifying that he was about to leave, Bernhardt moved forward in his chair as he said, "I just have one more question, Sheriff."

"Oh?" Grunting, this time with the effort it required, Fowler leaned forward to grasp the contents of his "in" basket, which he began spreading out on the littered desk.

"Is Dennis Price a suspect?"

"Naturally," Fowler answered. "The husband's always the number-one suspect."

"But you aren't—" He hesitated, once more searching for the phrase. "But you aren't leaning on Price, I gather."

"As to that," Fowler answered, "I have no comment." He forked the black-rimmed reading glasses to his temples. Mouth pursed, eyes even smaller behind the glasses, he began reading. As before, his lips moved.

3:30 P.M.

With the sun sinking toward the ridge of hills to the west, the light was softening. Between the pines and the oaks that shielded the Price home from the two-lane macadam county road that bordered the property, the late afternoon sunlight was slanting golden through the tree trunks. As Bernhardt down-shifted the Corolla, a fragment of memory flashed: summer camp in the Berkshires: the long, fragrant summer evenings, the mountains to the west turning purple as the sunset above them turned golden. Were those the best times of his life? Sometimes he thought they were. Every summer, the same group of noisy kids clustered around the Camp Chippewa sign in Grand Central Station. They piled into a decrepit train and began the journey to the Berkshires. With every mile, as inhibitions fell away, the volume of youthful voices rose. Camp Chippewa . . . his mother with her dancing . . . his grandparents with the big house in Jersey . . . his own huge room in his mother's loft . . . *The Nutcracker*, during the holidays . . . they all defined him. Several times he'd tried to write about it all, a one-act play, a slice of life, maybe beginning at Grand Central Station, maybe on the train, to save a scene change, all those raucous kids, most of them Jewish. Even so young, some of them only seven or eight, they played the "What's your father do?" game. He'd felt uneasy, somehow, that his father had been a bombardier, killed in the war. All the other kids had fathers who went to offices and had secretaries.

It was his third time, driving slowly past the entrance to the tree-shaded lane that served both the house and the winery buildings. Decision time, the first decision of many, he suspected, in the matter of Janice Hale versus Dennis Price. Should he opt for the high profile, flashing the plastic ID, watching the eyes flicker when the words "private investigator" were spoken? Or should he pose as a tourist, ostensibly sightseeing while he learned all he could before he finally confronted Dennis Price?

It was, he knew, a pointless speculation. As always, he would improvise, making up the script as he went along.

He checked the mirrors, made a U-turn, drove back to the entrance to the property, and drove slowly between two pillars made of fieldstone. A large bronze plaque was fixed to one of the pillars: BROOKSIDE WINERY, ESTABLISHED 1941. It was a touch of class, a claim on history. The winery's vineyard, someone had said, was forty acres. How much had it cost, to buy a winery almost fifty years old? A million? Two million? More?

The lane forked just ahead. A sign and arrow directed winery-bound traffic to the right fork. He let the Corolla coast to a stop at the fork. To the left, across a broad green lawn dotted with lawn furniture and croquet wickets, shades of English country living, he saw the house. It was three stories, vintage redwood and weathered cedar shingles, just as Fowler had described it. The verandahs were broad, the generous bay windows were multipaned, the massive chimneys were fieldstone. Beyond the rustic wonderment of the house he saw the sparkle of sunlight on the surface of a large swimming pool. A visitor to the house would turn left, toward a redwood-and-shingle garage and a collection of small outbuildings, then turn left again, into a circular gravel driveway that served the house. The gravel of the circular driveway was a sparkling white, enhancing the white of the lawn furniture and croquet wickets. When they played croquet, Bernhardt wondered, did the men wear white flannels and the women pleated white skirts?

He put the car in gear, and turned right. Matching Fowler's description, the terrain rose behind the house, so it was not until he topped a low rise that he saw the winery buildings clustered picturesquely together in a hollow between the house and the surrounding vineyards. One of the buildings—obviously the original—was made of rock, with small windows, a low shingled roof, and a wide iron-studded, wood-planked door. The other buildings, of recent vintage, were made of wood, with black asbestos roofs. Behind one of the buildings, Bernhardt saw three cylindrical stainless-steel tanks. Several trucks and cars were parked at random among the buildings. A small bungalow, white clapboard and ornamental green shutters, was set apart from the winery buildings. This, Bernhardt knew, would be the winery foreman's house. Al Martelli.

Another sign and another arrow directed him to visitor parking, a small gravel lot defined by large redwood logs laid directly on the ground. There was only one vehicle in the visitors' lot, a custom painted boss four-wheel-drive pickup with four lights clamped on a big black roll-bar mounted behind the cab.

He parked beside the pickup and switched off the Corolla's engine. It was decision time. Improvisation time. He'd been doing investigations part time for more than three years, at first working for Herbert Dancer, then for himself. For six months, he'd been on his own. *Alan Bernhardt, Private Investigations.* Yet, every time out, it always came down to this: improvising as he went, catch-as-catch-can. Pick a role. Any role. For the Fowler interview, he'd chosen to play the part of the earnest amateur, seeking wisdom. But what now? Another situation, another persona. It was both the actor's fate and the detective's dilemma.

To select from his actor's bag of tricks, he must first decide on the mission. Why, precisely, was he there? Primarily, he was looking for background on Dennis Price. What kind of a man was Dennis Price? What was his reputation? To Janice Hale, Price was a fortune hunter, a gigolo, a parasite. To Fowler, Price was just another playboy, another city slicker, posing as something better.

To his wife, in her last moments, Dennis Price might have been a murderer.

And John? At age seven, the only son of star-crossed parents, how did John fit into the puzzle? Had John been a witness to his mother's murder?

As if the thought had materialized into substance, he saw a small boy on a bike. Riding fast downhill, coasting, feet off the pedals, head gleefully flung back, abandoned to the thrill of speed, the boy came whizzing down the narrow macadam access road that led from the surrounding vineyards to the winery buildings. The road dipped at the winery buildings, then rose to join the graveled road that led to the Price family home, over the low crest of the hill. As he began to lose speed on the upgrade, the boy lowered his feet to the pedals, lowered his head, and began pumping. The boy was about seven, a classic Tom Sawyer boy: towheaded, freckle faced, blue eyes, pug nose, slim of limb and torso. Without doubt, this was John Price.

Bernhardt swung open his driver's door and stepped out into the warm August sunshine. The boy was abreast of him now, pedaling harder, losing speed to the rising road. Should he call out to the boy, pretend to ask directions, hopefully to strike up a conversation? No, it would be a bad beginning. If the boy braked he would lose momentum, lose his contest with gravity. To a bike rider, stored downhill momentum was precious.

The boy was standing up on the pedals now, working hard. As, yes, he made the crest of the rise. Watching the towhead disappear, Bernhardt heard closeby voices. Turning, he saw three men approaching the candy-striped boss pickup. The man in the center was taller than his two companions, and plainly exercised a kind of freewheeling authority. Dressed in tight blue jeans and a tight red T-shirt, the tall man had the muscles of a weight lifter and the dark, snapping eyes of a lead tenor: *Carmen*'s Don Juan, incarnate. His thick black hair was curly, another operatic cliché. And, yes, the phrase that best described the tall man's features was ruggedly handsome. His manner, the restless energy in his voice, and his pattern of movement all suggested the final cliché: animal magnetism.

As the three men came closer, the sound of the tall man's voice separated into words: "I think you'd better figure it both ways, Cal. Give me a flat quote, then give me an estimate on the materials, if we decide to do it time and materials."

"Right." One of the men nodded briskly. He carried a clipboard with an air of authority.

"You understand," the tall man said, "that you've got to work the numbers out tonight, and bring them by tomorrow morning. And you've got to be ready to start Monday, first thing. We've got to have that press working by this time next week. There's no other way. None."

"Jesus, Al—" The shorter man shook his head. "Five days—" Sighing, he swung open the driver's door of the pickup as his companion got into the truck on the other side. "I can *try* for Friday. But I can't guarantee it, not a hundred percent. I mean, things can happen, you know, on a job like this."

As the car's engine blanked out the rest of it, Bernhardt considered. "Al," one of the men had said, suggesting that this handsome man with his stuntman's muscles and his rich, restless voice could be the foreman, Al Martelli, the man who had been present at the murder scene when Sheriff Fowler arrived.

As he thoughtfully listened to the three men say their country-style good-byes, Bernhardt decided on his tactical persona: the brisk, bluff, savvy, completely self-assured detective who, nevertheless, knew enough to mind his manners. When the pickup began to back away, he stepped forward: three long, firm strides, setting the tone. His voice, too, was firm as he extended his outstretched hand, confidence incarnate.

"Mr. Martelli?"

Half-turned away, the tall man turned back to face him. "That's right . . ." Martelli's face was noncommittal as he grasped Bernhardt's outstretched hand. Predictably, the other man's grip was solid muscle.

"I'm Alan Bernhardt, Mr. Martelli. I'm a private investigator. I've been retained to, ah—" Momentarily the words came abruptly to an end. But then, surprise, the flow returned: "To clarify some of the details surrounding

63

Mrs. Price's death. It has to do with, ah, her estate." Hearing himself say it, the first improvisation, Bernhardt was gratified. A mention of the dead woman's estate smacked of musty law libraries and stooped, fusty clerks, an inspired Dickensonian fillip.

"I've just come from Sheriff Fowler," he said. Leading into the second improvisation: "He mentioned your name, suggested I contact you—" As he spoke, Bernhardt gestured to a nearby picnic table and benches placed beneath a huge oak. "Have you got a few minutes?"

Coolly, Martelli gave himself a long, deliberate moment to look Bernhardt over—twice. Then he gestured for Bernhardt to precede him to the picnic table. "I suppose," Martelli said, "that you've got credentials."

"Of course." As they sat facing each other across the table, Bernhardt passed over his ID. Martelli studied it with interest, returned it, and slowly shook his head. "It's incredible, you know. I mean—" He spread his muscle-bulged forearms. His dark, bold eyes were softened with the pain of recollection. "I mean, a couple of minutes—a few seconds—and everything changes. Not too long ago—six months, I guess it was—my sister's daughter was killed by a drunk driver. She was twelve. She was in the crosswalk, had the green light. But this goddamn drunk—" As he shook his head, anger shown in Martelli's eyes. It was a helpless anger, doubly embittered by deep loss. "And then, a couple of months ago, Con—Mrs. Price."

As he noted the quick shift from the familiar to the formal, perhaps a clue to some secret liaison between this handsome hired hand and the mistress of the manor, Bernhardt decided on another gamble with names and faces: "I saw John, a few minutes ago. He seemed happy enough."

Martelli shrugged. "Kids change every few minutes, in my experience. At least—" Another kind of pain shadowed the dark eyes. "At least, that's how it is with my kids."

Aware of the other man's new moment of sadness, Bernhardt forbade inquiring about Martelli's family. Instead, speaking conversationally, he said, "I understand from Sheriff Fowler that John was there when—" He let a beat pass. Then, suitably solemn: "When Mrs. Price was killed."

Heavily, Martelli nodded. "Yeah . . ." As if to blind himself to the memory, he momentarily shut his eyes. Then, more softly: "Yeah, he was there. At least, he was in the house."

"I gather that Mr. Price called you immediately after he discovered that his wife was murdered."

"Yeah. Right." Martelli drew a deep breath. Repeating: "Right."

Bernhardt gestured to the small white frame-house. "Is that your place?"

"Yes."

"Were you there when she was killed?"

Silently, Martelli nodded.

"Did Mr. Price knock on your door?"

"No. He phoned. He told me to bring a gun. He said there'd been a prowler, that Con—that Mrs. Price was dead."

Again, the false start, the shift from the familiar to the formal. *Had* Constance Price and Martelli played the mistress and the handsome servant game? She'd been desirable; Bernhardt had seen the pictures. And Martelli's muscular persona was a metaphor for male virility, almost a stereotype.

"Did you see anything suspicious? The prowler, for instance, escaping?"

"No. Nothing."

"When you got to the Price house, where was Mr. Price?"

"He was downstairs, in the living room. He was sitting on a sofa, and he had a shotgun."

"He was worried that the prowler was still around. Is that why he had the gun—why he told you to bring a gun?"

"Right."

"Had he called the police, by the time you got there?"

"He must've. Fowler arrived maybe ten minutes after I got there, no more."

"Was John with Price, when you got to the house?"

"Yes. They were both sitting on the sofa, I remember that."

"How was John acting, when you saw him?"

"Well—" Considering, Martelli frowned. "Well, he was—I guess you'd say he was stunned. He didn't say anything, didn't move. He just sat there with those big round eyes, staring. I remember thinking that it seemed like his face had gotten smaller, because his eyes looked so big. And he was pale. Very pale."

"It sounds like he was in shock. Mild shock, anyhow."

"I suppose he was."

Bernhardt let a beat pass, then decided to ask, "Do you see much of John?"

"Oh, sure." The answer came quickly, suggesting a fondness, a comaraderie. "He's around here almost all summer. The rest of the year, they come up for weekends, from the city. So I see a lot of him."

"What kind of a kid is he?"

"He's a nice kid." Approvingly, Martelli nodded. "He's very imaginative. And cheerful, too. Very cheerful. He's no crybaby, either. I wouldn't say he's a tough guy, or anything. But he's got spunk."

"You have children." Bernhardt said.

Martelli's face fell, revealing an instant's vulnerability, a sadness. Clearly, Martelli's emotions lay close to the surface.

"I've got two kids," he answered, his eyes downcast,

his voice low. "A boy and a girl. They live with their mother." He let a moment of silence pass. Then, raising his eyes to Bernhardt, Martelli smiled: a wry, quizzical smile. "How about you? Do PIs get married and have children?"

At the question, Bernhardt felt the vulnerability revealed in his own expression, felt his eyes fall, heard his own voice drop huskily as he said, "My wife died, a long time ago."

"Ah . . ." Martelli nodded. The single syllable was expressive, all that was required to signify the beginning of an understanding, one man to another. "Sorry."

They sat silently for a moment, each one evaluating the other. To Bernhardt, the silence was evocative, signifying that possibly—just possibly—Martelli could help him, might even want to help if the right words were spoken, the right questions asked.

But it was Martelli who asked the lead-in question: "You seem to be very concerned with John. Why's that?"

This, Bernhardt realized, was his opening, his time for decision. How much information could profitably be passed on to Martelli? How much must be kept back? Could he trust Martelli? Up or down, decision time; could he trust Martelli?

The answer, he decided, the bird-in-the-hand decision, must be yes.

"The reason I'm concerned with John—the reason I want to talk to him—is that Janice Hale believes Mr. Price is keeping John away from her. And, among other things, John is her only living relative. She loves him. She thinks she can help him."

Martelli's expressive brown eyes sharpened slightly as they exchanged a long, silent look. Was it suspicion that Bernhardt saw in the other man's eyes? Caution? Calculation?

"How does that tie in with what you said originally?" Martelli asked bluntly. "You said you were investigating the murder for financial reasons. What's that got to do with John?"

Holding the other man's gaze, Bernhardt decided to push all his chips into the pot. "What I said originally," he said, "was mostly a con. That's what this business is basically all about. It's like politics. There's no way—no way at all—that you can tell the whole truth, if you're a private detective. At least, not at first."

"Hmmm . . ." As if he'd suddenly experienced a jolt of energy that must be dissipiated, Martelli rose abruptly to his feet, strode a half-dozen paces across the parking area, then returned to the picnic table. He drew a deep breath, leaned across the table, and let his voice drop. "So what *is* the truth?" As he said it, his eyes moved instinctively in the direction of the Price house.

This time, Bernhardt was ready. Also leaning forward, also dropping his voice, he said, "Janice Hale says that from the time of the murder until right now, Mr. Price hasn't allowed her to speak with John alone, even on the phone. Price's excuse, she says, is that he doesn't want John reliving the night of the murder."

"But she thinks there's more to it than that." Martelli's eyes lost focus as his thoughts sharpened.

Gambling that his man was now fully engaged, Bernhardt flattened his voice to a matter-of-fact pitch as he said, "Do you think John actually saw the murder?" Carefully watching the other man's face for a reaction, Bernhardt let a beat pass. Then: "As I understand it, the supposition is that Mrs. Price arrived here from Santa Barbara sometime after eleven on the night of Friday, June sixteenth. Maybe it was midnight. She unloaded the car, put the bags in the living room. She got John from the car. Maybe he was asleep, and she carried him into the living room. Or maybe she woke him up first and he walked into the living room, and then he fell asleep while she was getting the bags out of the car. Anyhow, she went upstairs to get her husband, ask him to carry John upstairs. At least, that's the way Mr. Price thinks it happened. He was sleeping in the spare bedroom, which he apparently did when his wife was away. But she apparently went into the master bedroom. Maybe she heard suspicious noises, and went to investigate. Anyhow, she was attacked and killed in the master bedroom. Shortly after it happened, her husband discovered the body. Then he discovered that John was asleep in the living room, downstairs. He got his shotgun, and had a look around. Then he called Sheriff Fowler—and you. At some point, he woke John up. You arrived, and the sheriff arrived about ten minutes later."

Bernhardt let a long moment of silence pass as he watched Martelli think about it. Then he asked, "Is that the way you think it happened?" He let a beat pass before he said softly, "Is that what you think *really* happened?"

Slowly, heavily, Martelli shook his head. "I have no idea what really happened." Martelli, too, let a short, significant beat pass as he fully met Bernhardt's eyes. Then: "All I know is what I was told. As for what John saw, or didn't see, I have no idea about that, either. Like I said earlier, the whole time I was in the house, there, waiting for the police to come, John didn't say a word. He just sat and stared."

"You've talked to him since the murder."

"I've talked to him almost every day. We do things together. Like I said, he's a great kid. We get along."

"But you've never talked about the night his mother died?" Asking the question, Bernhardt let a hint of skepticism show.

Martelli met the muted challenge squarely, defiantly: "No. Never. He didn't offer, and I didn't ask."

"You say he's a cheerful kid. But is he ever sad? Moody?"

Martelli shrugged. "I wouldn't say so. No more than any other kid who's lost his mother. That's about the worst thing that could happen, 'specially the *way* it happened. He—" Martelli broke off, looked beyond Bernhardt toward the house. He spoke cautiously, moving his head in the direction he was looking. "Here he is." Martelli rose from the picnic table, beckoned for the boy riding his bike to join them. Also rising, Bernhardt faced the boy as he braked to a stop. Still astride the scaled-down mountain bike with one foot braced wide, John Price looked expectantly at Martelli. The boy wore sneakers and cutoff jeans, no shirt. He was deeply tanned, slim, and graceful. Squinting against the sun, freckled nose wrinkled as he looked up at Martelli, his blue eyes clear and innocent and true, the boy epitomized the clarity of youth that every man must leave behind.

"This is Alan Bernhardt, John." Making the introduction, Martelli spoke laconically, as if introducing two men. "He's a private eye."

"A—" The boy frowned, puzzled. Then, as recognition dawned, he swallowed. "A detective?"

"That's right," Bernhardt answered, smiling. "I was hired by your Aunt Janice. I'm working for her for a while."

"Do you have a gun?" John dropped his eyes to Bernhardt's waist, searching for the bulge of a holster.

"I do have a gun. But—" The smile widened. "But I didn't think I'd need it, today."

"How many people have you shot?"

"I've never shot anyone, John." But as he said it, an instant's flash of memory seared his consciousness: the figure of the black man, his body flaming, running through the night until he finally collapsed, screaming as he died.

"Oh." The disappointed monosyllable was eloquent.

"But I haven't really been at this business very long," Bernhardt added. "It takes time, you know, to find some guy bad enough to shoot. Years, sometimes."

"Oh." Diffidently, the boy nodded.

He'd made it worse, then. Not better. Now John was shifting his feet, ready to ride away. "I'll tell you what, though," Bernhardt said, "next time I come, I'll bring my gun. Okay?"

The boy visibly brightened. "Can I hold it?"

"We'll see, John."

Just as visibly, the anticipation dimmed. At age seven, John Price had plainly heard "We'll see" before. He put a scuffed sneaker on a pedal, cast a meaningful glance at Martelli, and pushed off. As the boy pedaled away on a narrow dirt road that led to a cluster of trees bordering the vineyards to the west, the figure of a man appeared on the crest of the rise that separated the winery buildings from the main house. Dressed in running shoes, fashion-faded blue jeans, and a regimental khaki shirt, his blond hair stirring in the light breeze, the man stood motionless, looking down at them. He was medium height and weight, athletically built. He carried himself with the calm arrogance of the privileged class. As the newcomer began walking toward them, the details of his deeply tanned face resolved into their separate parts: clear gray eyes, bleached-blond eyebrows, a mouth that was slightly too tight, and a nose that was slightly too long. It was a lean, aristocratic face, overbred, overindulged. Now in his early forties, the pattern of the man's facial lines and creases were pleasing to the eye. In later years, Bernhardt suspected, the effect would be less pleasing.

"If you're looking for Dennis Price," Martelli said, sotto voce, "there he is. Handsome devil, isn't he?"

A quick glance at Martelli's sardonic expression clearly revealed that Martelli's opinion of Dennis Price closely matched Janice Hale's.

"Lots of luck," Martelli murmured. "If I can help, let me know. I'm in the phone book."

With his eyes innocuously fixed on Price, Bernhardt whispered, "Thanks. I'm counting on it." Then, hastily, he took a business card from his pocket, surreptitiously slipped it to Martelli.

"Gotcha." Martelli palmed the card, waited until Price

had joined them, performed the brief introductions, mentioned a matter at the winery that required his attention, and precipitously walked down the pathway toward the vintage winery building constructed of old stone.

Leaving Bernhardt once more forced to improvise: "I—ah—was going to knock on your door, Mr. Price." His smile, he hoped, was disarming.

"What's it all about?" Pointedly, Price did not return the smile.

"I—ah—I've been retained to clarify some of the facts surrounding the death of your wife, Mr. Price. Specifically, I—"

"Retained by who?" It was a truculent question. Price's clear gray eyes were hostile, his stance had turned aggressive.

"Sorry—" Diffidently, Bernhardt shook his head. "I'm not at liberty to say. All I need, though, is—"

"I've already talked to the sheriff, and the DA. They've got everything they asked for. And it took us a goddamn week to clean up that goddamn black fingerprint powder. So I'd suggest, whatever you're trying to *clarify*"—the word was bitingly emphasized—"that you start with the sheriff. Fowler. There's no reason for you to—"

"I've already talked to Sheriff Fowler." He allowed his diffident smile to fade. "He's given me some valuable information." Covertly watching the other man, he paused. No reaction was visible on Price's lean, improbably aristocratic face. "But I really feel that I need more." Another pause. Then, quietly: "And so does my client."

"Well—" Price began to turn away. "I'm afraid, Mr. Bernhardt, that you'll have to—"

"Actually, it's not so much your testimony I need. It's John's. You see, since—"

Glowering, Price angrily turned to face him fully. "John?"

"Yes. You see, since you and John were the only two witnesses to the—"

"John wasn't a witness. Neither was I, not to the murder. I found her. But John was downstairs, the whole time. And he—"

"What I meant to say," he said, "is that the two of you were both in the house, when it happened. I gather she was killed in the master bedroom, on the second floor. Is that right?"

Plainly enraged, Price advanced a furious half-step. With an effort, Bernhardt stood his ground. Price's eyes, he saw, were blazing, a good reason to be careful. But, even though Price's mouth was angrily clamped shut, the muscles of one cheek were beginning to twitch. And now—yes—Price was beginning to rapidly blink. Did the twitching and the blinking reveal a fear that bluster couldn't conceal?

There was only one way to find out: "The reason I ask," Bernhardt said, "is that, since the murder was committed on the second floor, it's obvious that the murderer had to've gone down to the first floor to escape. And since John was down there, asleep on the couch, as I understand it, then I thought that—"

"I'm going to the house," Price said, his voice shaking, "and I'm going to call the sheriff. I'm going to tell him that I ordered you off the property, but you refused to go. And then I'm going to get my shotgun. And then—" With a trembling forefinger, he pointed to Bernhardt's Toyota. "And then I'm going to start shooting out your tires. Then I'll start on the windows. Do you understand, you son of a bitch?"

Hearing a telltale unsteadiness in his own voice, Bernhardt tried to speak calmly, keep the muscles of his face from twitching, keep his eyes steady as he said, "It seems to me, Mr. Price, that you're off the deep end, concerning John. All I want to do is—"

With outrage tearing at the ruins of his overpriviledged face, Price's voice rose beyond his control: "We're talking about doctor's orders, asshole. Do you understand?"

Price's stiffened forefinger dug into Bernhardt's shoulder. "John's been to a psychiatrist. Dr. Wolfe in San Francisco. And the orders are no talking to anyone about how his mother died. *No one.* Especially not two-for-a-dollar private detectives."

With his whole body braced against another finger jab, Bernhardt felt his jaw tighten, his fists clench, the rush of adrenaline. But, the next instant, Price turned away and began stalking toward the house. Bernhardt relaxed his fists, drew a deep breath, and turned toward his car. The time was almost five o'clock. At seven-thirty, Paula was expecting him for dinner at her place: salmon steaks, a gift from a satisfied client.

5:30 P.M.

Using both hands, bowing his back and digging his feet into the soft earth, John tugged at the huge wooden door, sagging on its rusty hinges, each hinge as long as his arm. The door was more than twice as tall as he was, and wide enough to take a wagon load of hay, Al had once told him. A horse-drawn wagon, Al had said, in old-fashioned times. Scraping in the dirt, the door came slowly open, just enough for him to squeeze through.

Inside the barn now he stood still, looking and listening. If he kept quiet enough, if he paid close attention, and just listened, he'd learned that he could always hear something inside the barn. Small sounds, sometimes mysterious sounds. Animals, scurrying. Things tapping, things rustling. Invisible things. Outside, the sun was sinking in the sky, almost gone behind the ridge that bordered the vineyard to the west. Inside the barn, the narrow lines of light that shone through the cracks in the barn's old boards were turning golden. Bits of dust and tiny winged insects were suspended in the narrow shafts. Hundreds—thousands—of tiny specks, some of them alive, some not. Some of them just floated, some of them flew, circling in the sunlight.

Everywhere, on the ground and in the air, there were insects. Millions of insects. Flying insects, crawling insects. Some of them buzzed, some stung. Some of them even lit up in the dark: lightning bugs, almost the first miracle he'd experienced.

There was no floor in the old barn, only dirt. The dirt wasn't really dirt, more like the sand and shavings and whatever made the ground of playgrounds, deep and soft, if someone fell into it: dirt that didn't get you dirty, dirt that felt good.

Walking in the deep, soft, fragrant earth with its hay and everything else mixed together over so many years, even before he was born, horses with their shoes and their manure, big tall wagon wheels with wooden spokes and narrow iron rims, he let his feet drag, toes digging in. He could feel the earth inside his sneakers, a particular pleasure. The ladder was ahead: wooden rails and crosspieces nailed to a post that showed the ancient marks of ax and saw. He began climbing: cautiously, two feet to each rung, hands gripping the rails hard. He didn't like to climb. He liked to be high up in the loft above him, or in the tiny attic room in the house, looking out across the vineyards. But he didn't like to climb. Ladders, trees, even jungle gyms, they were all the same, tests he could hardly pass.

This ladder, though, was only eight rungs. And even if he fell the ground below was so deep, so soft, it would be all right.

He stepped from the ladder onto the floor of the hayloft. It was here that the feeling of things began to change, in this one special place. He could sense it in the rough-cut wood, and the pegs that secured the beams and planks and the crisscrossed braces that angled high overhead. He could see it in the narrow shafts of sunlight between the boards that fell across the floor, magic from the sun. He could hear it in the buzz of the insects, and the sound of the wind, like a soft sigh from far away. And he could smell it in the air, heavy with time and place and ancient memory.

The barn hadn't been used for years, Al had once told him, maybe twenty years. So the hay, that vast, fragrant mound that tumbled together with him when he jumped and rolled and wallowed, was older than he was. The barn and the hay and the smells, everything he saw or touched, had been there before he was born.

As he began to climb the mound of hay he sank almost knee deep, the hay prickling the bare skin on his legs. If he'd known he was coming, he would have worn jeans. And a shirt, too. Farmers always wore jeans and shirts and hats, even when the weather was hot. And now he knew why.

At the top of the mound, his own secret mountain, he raised his arms wide, threw back his head, and let himself fall forward—falling free, sinking, tumbling, hearing himself laughing as he rolled down the other side, cradled in the hay. He rose to his knees, shook his head, brushed the hay from his hair, stood up, stepped close to the edge of the hayloft, where he gripped the ladder to steady himself. Overhead, among the beams and rafters, birds flew busily, darting and swooping and then disappearing, returning to the sky while other birds swooped in through the gaps where boards were missing. Many gaps, many birds. Barn swallows, Al had called them.

Down below, he saw the rusted farm machinery, all tumbled together along the wall to make room for the truck. Except for the loft and the secret room behind it, the truck was his favorite place to play. Sitting on the split-open black leather seat with its springs showing through, gripping the big wood-rimmed steering wheel, just touching the pedals with his feet, he could almost hear the roar of the engine, feel the wheels thumping on the road as he traveled far, far away.

But now, so late, he had only time enough to check the secret room, make sure nothing had been disturbed.

Three paces took him to the wall of the secret room. The door to the room was padlocked: a huge, rusted lock that would never be opened. A narrow flight of stairs led up from the sagging wooden loading platform below the door of the secret room. But the stairs were rotted. No one would ever climb those stairs again. For as long as the world went on, no one would ever climb those stairs. So only he could enter the secret room. John Price, Explorer. John Price, Special Agent.

Yes, Special Agent . . .

Everyone—the good guys and the bad guys—they'd all searched for this place, all tried to find out what was inside. Because long ago, enemy agents had been here, planning how to blow up the whole country, one big mushroom cloud, everything turned to cinders. But then they'd been killed by the FBI, somewhere else. So nobody knew what they'd hidden here, the plans to blow up the whole world.

Nobody but him.

So it was all up to him.

Only he could save the country. As if the spies had somehow returned, not really dead at all, he thought he heard a noise—a scurrying, a scuffling. Holding his breath, he stood perfectly still. Was someone down there, down below? If they were, they'd never see him, not as long as he stayed behind the great mound of hay, higher than his head. He could stand up, even, and no one could see him.

As he listened, he realized his mouth was open.

"You mouth is open, John," his mother sometimes said, smiling, teasing him. "Do you know you open your mouth, when you listen very hard?" Smiling. Still smiling.

With the memory of his mother, everything changed: a shifting of sight and sound as the possibility of danger from below faded.

Then, as it always did, the memory of his mother faded.

Leaving him alone.

Once more, alone.

Aware that his legs had grown heavy, his arms listless, he moved to the secret board, known only to him. The board was loose at the bottom. When he'd discovered it was loose, nails rusty in the rotting wood, he'd found an old piece of rusted iron, and pried the board free at the top. With the board laid aside, he'd been able to squeeze through the opening, to find himself in the secret room. The room had once been used to hang bridles and harnesses, for horses. There were racks for saddles, and bits of broken equipment. There was even a saddle hanging on one of the racks, with only the stirrups missing.

With a rock, he'd been able to bend the nails that held the board so that he could always remove the board, as he was doing now. Allowing him to squeeze through, as he was doing now. When he left, he would replace the board so that the bent nails held it firmly in place, the secret entrance to his secret place.

The floor was littered with cans and bottles and buckles and bits of metal the first time he'd come. But he'd found a broom in one corner, and he'd used the broom to clean up, especially the cobwebs. There'd been boxes, too: three large boxes, with hinged tops and rope handles. How clearly he remembered the moment he'd pried the hasp free on one of the boxes, and lifted the lid. Would he find a treasure: sparkling jewels and bags of golden coins? And guns, maybe? Like *Treasure Island*?

There'd been no treasure, no guns. But there were tools, and strangely shaped pieces of metal, all rusty.

And then he'd found the knife: a big old sheath knife, in its leather sheath.

His knife, now, kept in the chest.

His secret. His weapon.

He could still remember the feeling in his stomach when he'd pulled the blade of the knife from its sheath. He'd felt like he'd become another person. In that instant, he'd known how it must feel to be a man.

Cowboys carried knives on the same belt with their guns. The real cowboys, the ones in the books his mother read him, they always carried knives. Just in case.

Brushing cobwebs aside, he went to the small window. He climbed up on a chest, and looked out. He was careful to keep his head back, so no one could see him from the ground. He scanned the clearing far below, and the line of trees that bordered the clearing. Nothing stirred. Not even a squirrel, or a jackrabbit.

He stepped down, opened the chest he'd been standing on, took out the knife. He'd found an old oil can on the shelf, with some thick, gummy oil in it. He'd oiled the blade of the knife, and with some steel wool he'd gotten from Al, he'd worked on the oiled blade until it shone. There'd been a whetstone on the shelf, too, and he'd tried to sharpen the knife, the way he'd seen Al do it.

Closing the lid of the chest, holding the sheathed knife, he sat down with his back to the wall, his bare shoulders resting against the rough wood.

The time, he knew, must be almost six o'clock. Yesterday he'd lost his watch, somewhere in his room, he thought. It was because he was so messy, his father had said, that he'd lost his watch. And Maria, their cook, had agreed: "You make a mess, you lie in it," Maria had said, "like a pig." And she'd frowned: a dark, hard frown. Sometimes, when she talked, Maria spat. When he'd asked Al why Maria spat, Al had smiled. "It's because she has false teeth," Al had said, "And they don't fit very well." Maria was Mexican. After Maria had lived with them for a while, cooking and cleaning, he'd decided he didn't like Mexicans.

He held the sheath with his left hand, and drew out the knife with his right hand. The handle of the knife was wood and felt smooth and powerful to his hand. He knew he would always have this knife.

From overhead, he heard the sound of a jet airplane: a faint, woolly, rolling sound, like thunder faraway.

How long had it been, that he and his father had gone to the airport, and made their way through the crowds in the terminal, and walked through that last long tunnel to the door of the airplane, and sat strapped into their seats, waiting for the airplane to take off? He'd never before been in an airplane, never heard the engine screaming, never felt himself pressed back in his seat as the airplane hurtled down the runway, then lifted into the clear blue sky.

His Aunt Janice had met them at the airport in Santa Barbara. When she met him, she'd smiled: a small, sad smile. Then she'd hugged him, hard. While she held him, he'd felt her sob.

That night, the night before the funeral, when his aunt tucked him into bed and then kissed him on the forehead, he'd felt her sob again. She'd whispered to him, very softly: "You'll always have me, John. Always."

Then she'd said good night, and left him in the dark room with the door half open. From the hallway, on its wooden floor, he heard two pairs of footsteps, going toward the stairs. His father had been out there in the hallway, listening.

He'd lain in the darkness a long time, eyes open, staring up at the ceiling. He'd never known when his eyes had closed, and he'd finally fallen asleep.

He couldn't remember.

But he would never forget.

Because somehow, as he'd lain in *his* bed, in *his* room, the room in his aunt's house meant only for him, with his toys, and his clothes, and posters of airplanes and lions and sharks in the sea, it had seemed as if he was back in the house at the winery. It had been dark then, too. Something had awakened him. The sound of voices, the sound of something crashing. The sounds—the voices—had come from upstairs. His father's voice, and another voice. His mother? Someone else?

Had he been awake? Or still asleep, and dreaming?

His eyes, he remembered, were closed. Was he pretending sleep, or was he really asleep? If he'd been awake, really awake, wouldn't he have opened his eyes when he heard the footsteps on the stairs? Had there been whispers, too? Soft, urgent whispers?

Had he opened his eyes? Had he seen them?

Sometimes he had dreams. And sometimes, when he woke up, it seemed like he was still dreaming. Sometimes, when the dreams were bad, he'd still been frightened, even when he was awake. So when he felt his father's hand on his shoulder, shaking him, he hadn't known whether he was awake or asleep. Not until he saw his father's face, so close, and smelled his father's breath, and heard his father's voice. But it was a harsh voice, a stranger's voice. And his father's face had been twisted into a stranger's face. The face of fear, fugitive from nightmare memories, one face beneath another face, one of them hidden.

The same face he'd seen at the funeral. A stranger's face, beside him.

11:30 P.M.

"So what'd you think?" Paula asked.

In the bedroom darkness, his naked body touching hers, both of them companionably sated—erotically sated, in passion's afterglow—Bernhardt chuckled.

"What do I think about what?

"About Janice's—" She hesitated. After their six months together, Bernhardt thought he could account for the hesitation. Paula was searching for a less dramatic word, to finish the sentence. Whenever possible, Paula opted for understatement. But the word she sought failed to materialize. So: "About her suspicions."

"I've no idea. She's right about Price. He's a horse's ass, no question. And Price definitely doesn't want anybody questioning John. But whether there's any more to it than that—" He moved closer to her, put his hand on her stomach, just below the rib cage. It was a good stomach, a flat stomach. Like everything he'd discovered about her body, he approved.

Had it only been six months since they'd first met?

"If there's more to it than that"—he stroked her stomach, felt her navel beneath his fingertips, felt himself quickening—"I've got no idea."

"Janice is pretty level-headed. Pretty smart. Very smart, in fact." Unlike Bernhardt's voice, lowered to a huskier, intimate note meant to suggest that, since it was Friday night, they might consider making love for a second time, her voice was clear and starchy. Paula wanted information.

"Janice doesn't imagine things," she said.

"I'm sure she doesn't."

"You sound—" Once more, she paused. Then: "You sound condescending."

"That's not true. Or, at least, I certainly don't feel condescending. She's obviously an intelligent, effective person. I'm surprised she never got married."

"It's a soap opera plot," she answered. "Sad, but true."

"How do you mean, 'soap opera plot'?"

"Did she tell you about their parents—how they died?"

"It was a boating accident, she said. Connie survived—and felt guilty about it, ever since. A classic case of childhood guilt that never went away, apparently."

"Their parents were wonderful people," she answered,

her voice softened by the recollection. "It was one of those—those perfect families. And then, in seconds, it all ended."

In seconds . . .

Suddenly the images returned: the policeman's knock at their door. Jennie's body, on a stainless-steel tray, her shattered head wrapped in green cloth.

Perhaps because she sensed his sudden pain, Paula went quickly on: "Connie was ten years old when it happened, and Janice was sixteen. Connie was in the fourth grade, still a little girl. Janice was a junior in high school, just beginning to bloom, really. I used to spend a lot of time with them in the summers. Our families were friends, you know. Old, old friends. The Hales had a ranch, near San Ysidro. I was two years younger than Janice. And I can remember envying her so much. She was so—so assured. She was never beautiful, not really. But, every day during those summers, there were boys around. Wonderful-looking boys. They all seemed to have sports cars. And they all liked Janice. Everyone liked Janice. And, when you're a teenager, that's the most important thing of all—simply to have your contemporaries like you." He heard her sigh. It was a soft, nostalgic sigh, filled with nameless regret.

"So Janice devoted her life to her young orphaned sister, and never married. Is that how it went?"

Another sigh. "That's how it went."

"And Connie turned into a beauty."

"Connie turned into a beauty. An unhappy, neurotic beauty who was always—*always*—picking the wrong guy."

"Including Dennis Price."

"Definitely, including Dennis Price." A moment of pensive silence passed. Then: "Connie was rich and she was beautiful. So she always thought men either wanted to get in her pants, or else her checkbook." Paula moved closer, as if he could offer her solace from her own thoughts.

Then, softly, she said, "Connie was a victim type, I guess you'd say. She had no sense of her own self-worth. None."

"The dilemma of the beautiful woman . . ." A playful pause, for timing. "Present company excepted, of course."

"Of course." She chuckled—but stubbornly returned to her subject: "You're right, though. Connie never had a chance. And Janice only had half a chance, really. Their only living relative was an aunt, and she went to live with Connie and Janice after their parents were drowned. But the aunt was always a semi-invalid. So it was up to Janice to raise Connie. And now—" She sighed. "And now Janice is thirty-six."

"The numbers game."

"We all play it, though. And for a woman—a thirty-six-year-old woman—the biological clock is ticking, too."

"Mmmm . . ." It was a purposely disinterested response, signifying that, for him, for now, the subject of the Hale family's soap opera problems was closed. The longer they talked, the less likely they were to make love. He moved his hand from her stomach to the curve of her thigh, then to the first swell of her buttocks. Yes, her breathing was deeper, responding. And, yes, he felt her hand on his thigh, an interested overture.

But, still, there was more. Perversely, more: "Janice is a good artist, you know. A very good artist. She even shows in New York galleries. Fifty-seventh Street, the big time."

"Hmmm . . ." Then, curious in spite of the rising sexual heat they were generating, Bernhardt asked, "What does she paint? What kinds of things?"

"Landscapes, mostly. They're sort of semiabstract. I've got one, in my living room. That landscape over the couch."

"Ah!" The monosyllable registered recognition, and approval. Vividly, he could recall the painting. It was so compelling that he'd thought it was a print of a major artist's work. Clearly, the lady could paint. Talented Janice Hale. Rich, intelligent Janice Hale.

Sad Janice Hale.

"So what'll you do?" Paula was asking. "What happens now?"

"I'm not really sure," he admitted. "Keep the pressure on Price, keep bugging him, probably. See which way he jumps—if he jumps at all." A pause. Then, burlesquing a bad imitation of a French soldier leaving for the front in earlier, more romantic times, he said, "It may involve long hours away from you, Mademoiselle—days, weeks, even. And there will be danger, too. So perhaps this may be our last night together." As he spoke, he took her head in his hands, kissing her fervently—until she sputtered, laughing.

"God, is this what it'll be like, involved with an actor?"

"Actors have feelings, Mademoiselle. You must never forget that."

"Well, then—" Suddenly, with surprising strength, she grasped his shoulder, turned him, pinned him with the full weight of her body and kissed him deeply, passionately. "Well, then, Gaston, let's do it. Take me. I'm yours."

"Aha!"

SATURDAY
August 19

10 A.M.

About to bang down the telephone, Price heard a click.

"Yes?" A cool, calculated monosyllable, one of Theo's little affectations.

"Where the—" He looked at the staircase, looked down the hallway, furiously lowered his voice. "Where've you been?"

"When?" Another cool, round monosyllable. The jet-setter, very with-it.

"Never mind. I want to see you."

"Well, I've got to—"

"I want to see you now. I want to see you in an hour and a half. At the—" Trying to think, he broke off. Someplace public, but not too public. Somewhere—

"You sound—" She, too, broke off. Momentarily her with-it persona, that cool, calm mask, had slipped. That, at least, was reassuring.

Reassuring?

He wasn't thinking clearly. Reassuring! Christ!

"You sound agitated." Cool, once more. Constantly, compulsively cool, first things first. Christ!

"That's right, I'm agitated. You're exactly right." But he couldn't say any more. Maria could be anywhere. And John, too, listening. When he was a kid, he'd listened to his parents constantly. Especially when they were on the phone, tethered by the cord, fair game.

"Ah—" Was this monosyllable meant to soothe him, steady him? Was that the game they were playing now?

"At the Sausalito yacht harbor," he said. "Near that dolphin. That bronze dolphin."

"Yes. All right. So—what—twelve-thirty?"

"Yes. Twelve-thirty. I'm leaving now." He broke the connection.

12:30 P.M.

About to lock the driver's door and turn away, Price glanced at the parking meter, expired. Even before he explored his pockets he knew he hadn't brought change.

A ten-dollar parking ticket was almost certain; the Sausalito police waged perpetual war against sightseers, clogging the streets on weekends.

Ten dollars . . . nothing, compared to the millions on the table, his for the taking—or the losing.

As he walked across the wide, tourist-littered lawn toward the statue of the dolphin, he looked for her car: the white Toyota Supra. A power car for a power lady. Theo Stark. Twenty-eight. Twice divorced. Theo's career was men; she made no secret of it. And it was that take-it-or-leave-it candor that held him. As long as he could afford her, she'd stay with him. But when the beat fell off, when the lights began to dim, she would move on. Her body was all she had, she'd once said. Someday, the flesh would begin to sag. When that time came, Theo wanted a fast car in the garage and money in the bank.

She was leaning against the hood of her car, parked on the road that bordered the yacht harbor's lawn. Even at rest, the line of her body was dramatic: shoulders back, breasts lifted, hips and thighs outthrust, buttocks resting against the hood of the white Supra. Her features were classic Californian: a golden girl's profile, crisp of feature, healthy of hue. Her hair, too, was golden and fell loose around her shoulders. Her jawline was wide and decisive, her mouth generously sculpted, her blue eyes bold. She was dressed in the mandatory stone-washed jeans, narrow at the waist and tight at the crotch. The Indian madras shirt was worn loose, yet hinted at the perfection of her breasts and torso. Because the morning fog still lingered over Sausalito, she'd thrown a white cable-knit sweater loose across her shoulders. With her chin lifted, eyes squinting slightly, she was gazing out across the yacht harbor, watching the endless lines of masts moving with the waves, eternally crisscrossing.

Had she seen him coming, and chosen to strike this aloof, arrogant pose? It was a possibility, he knew. Even making love, Theo could be aloof. Whatever the power was, Theo had it. She had it, and she knew it.

He knew it, too. And she knew he knew it.

As he drew closer to her he loosened his stride, squared his shoulders, lifted his chin. He must soothe the roiling surface of his thoughts. If he didn't—if he faltered—she would fix him with a single look of casual contempt.

When he could almost touch her, she turned. He came close, kissed her lightly. It could have been a cousin's kiss. San Francisco, Sausalito, Marin County—so many of the faces were the same, one face fitted all. The beautiful people. Watching. Remembering. Remarking.

He gestured to her car. The car was only a month old. Price tag: twenty thousand, everything in. He'd run it through the books at the winery as machinery repair.

"Let's get in the car."

She let a beat pass while she looked at him, a quizzical look, perhaps a worried look.

If not worried now, then soon. Very soon.

She got in the car on the driver's side, gesturing him to

the other door, which was unlocked. She seldom bothered to lock.

He slid into the car's bucket seat and closed the door. The seats were leather, a seven-hundred-dollar option.

She turned to face him. "So what is it?" Still cool. Still calm.

"There's a private investigator, asking questions. His name is Bernhardt."

"When?"

"Yesterday. I tried to call you, yesterday. And last night, too."

Friday night. A night they'd often spent together, if Connie was in the city, and he was ostensibly at the winery.

She chose not to reply, not to reveal where she'd been last night.

"Do you know who hired him?" she asked.

"No. But I think it's Janice. Who else?"

"Where was this, that you talked to him?"

"At the winery."

"Did he talk to John?"

"Yes. Th-that's what's got me worried."

In the silence that followed, staring at each other, he saw the muscles of her face and throat tighten. Theo had gotten the message.

"Did *you* talk to John?"

"Yes. But—" Helplessly, he shrugged. "But it didn't do any good."

"It's been two months," she said. "By now, I'd think you'd have some idea what he saw—and didn't see. Even if he didn't tell you in so many words, I'd think you'd know. Just by the way he treats you. Just by the way he acts."

"But I *don't* know. That's the thing. I simply don't know."

"If he didn't say anything right at first—when it first happened, and the sheriff questioned him—then the chances are he isn't going to say anything now."

"I was there, though, when Fowler questioned him. If

someone else were to talk to him—Janice, for instance, just the two of them—" Once more, he shook his head. "I don't know . . ."

"If he thinks you were—involved—he could be trying to protect you. He's already lost his mother. He wouldn't want to send his father to jail." She spoke quietly, in a neutral voice. Her eyes were expressionless.

"Christ—" With his right hand, he struck the padded dash. "Christ, don't talk like that." He let a long, tight moment of silence pass as he stared out through the windshield at the bucolic summer scene: sailboats bobbing on the calm waters of San Francisco Bay, triangular white sails on sparkling blue. Many years ago, Connie and her parents had gone out on a boat like these. And only Connie had come back. Ten years old—and rich.

And now it would be his—millions.

Hardly aware that he was talking, he heard himself say, "That's what was so terrible about the funeral—about staying with Janice, overnight. She kept trying to get John alone. It was—" He blinked, cleared his throat, shook his head. Suddenly he was aware of the constriction at his throat. It was a band of fear. His eyes, he knew, were moving erratically.

"So now she's hired a private detective."

"I'm not sure she has. That's just an assumption."

"Who else would do it?"

"Well, that's the point. Outside of an aunt, who's got Alzheimer's, Janice is the only family Connie had."

Now Theo, too, let her eyes wander out across the bay. He watched her touch her upper lip with the fingers of her left hand, as if to smooth a nonexistant mustache. Sometimes they played backgammon, and she touched her upper lip like this. Theo was thinking. Calculating. Carefully calculating. Finally she spoke: "So what now?"

"I—I don't know. Keep them apart, John and this Bernhardt, that's all I can think of."

"I wonder—" Thoughtfully, she frowned. "How old is John?"

"He's seven."

"I'm just speculating—" As if to offer reassurance, she turned to face him. "In court, for instance. Would they take the word of a seven-year-old? Would the judge even let him testify?"

"I don't know. I do know, though, that the judge would talk to him in chambers. I'm sure of that."

She nodded, reflectively bit her lip, returned her gaze to the boats. Then: "What about sending him away to school?"

"Sending him *away*?" Hotly incredulous, he let his voice rise. "Christ, what would happen if this Bernhardt found out where he was? And what about Janice? I couldn't keep it a secret from her where John was. And then all she'd have to do is spend a little time with him—a weekend, and—" He let it go unfinished.

"Don't get upset."

"I'm not upset. I'm just *telling* you, that's not the answer."

"Well, what *is* the answer?"

He was aware that his head was loosely, ineffectually bobbing from side to side. Why had he come? What if Alan Bernhardt had followed him?

Beside him, she was impatiently stirring, waiting for an answer. Theo didn't like to be ignored. Ever.

"There's no answer," he answered finally. Then, after a long silence, he said, "I've just got to assume that John didn't see anything. That's all I can do."

10:30 P.M.

Theo lifted the TV wand, pushed the buttons, ran through the channels. Nothing. On television, on Saturday night, nothing. She pressed the power button, watched the image of a long-dead matinee idol fade from the screen.

Saturday night . . .

There was an old song from the forties, about Saturday night, the loneliest night of the week. If you weren't with someone on Saturday night, the ache of loneliness was the worst of all.

But she wasn't alone, not technically.

Technically, she was waiting for Bruce.

It could be another forties song, another funky title. Something about a beautiful, desirable woman, a woman who could have her choice of a half-dozen men, but who chose to sit in the cramped living room of a cramped apartment, staring at the screen of a dead TV.

A half-dozen men?

Should she count?

The tally began with Dennis and Bruce, the two men she was sleeping with. One exciting, one limp. At the thought, she smiled. Yes, it had happened once, to Dennis. Twice, really. Limp.

Two men, one for pleasure, one for profit.

Following in the field, a handicapper's word, by Stephen, who was rich, and Jay, who was old, and also rich, followed by Chris, the options trader with the wonderfully lithe body and the Ferrari, followed—or preceded, more like it—by Jeff, who was only twenty-two. Jeff had been her fantasy come true. One incredible night. In the past tense.

Twenty-two . . . God, she'd never forget that night. He was in Harvard now, studying law. Someday, though, Jeff would be back.

She rose, went to the kitchen, poured a glass of wine. Cheap jug wine, the kind she'd outgrown years ago.

But rich or poor, every woman needed a man like Bruce. Someone who made the night light up. Someone who—

At the door, she heard the lock rattle. Carrying the wine, she walked into the living room to stand facing the door as it swung open. The August night was warm and airless. Barefooted, she wore jeans and a loose-fitting T-shirt, one of Bruce's that she'd taken from his bureau. It turned him on, she knew, to see her wearing something of his, to feel her flesh beneath his own clothing, oversize on her. When he kissed her she would move in close, send him the message. It had been that kind of a day—and that kind of a night, waiting for him in his small, littered apartment, feeling herself quickening whenever she thought of him.

A coincidence, they were dressed alike. Except that his white T-shirt was tight, displaying the muscles they both loved to touch. His T-shirt was smudged and stained. Bruce worked around the Sausalito yacht harbor, doing free-lance maintence work for boat owners. He was to sailing what ski instructors were to skiing. Junkies, all of them. He pushed the door closed behind him, and shot the bolt. Slowly, purposefully, he moved toward her: the Saturday night stud, advancing. The muscles of his arms and torso and thighs were tensed, bulging beneath his clothes. Within arm's length, he began pulling up his T-shirt, exposing a flat, tanned stomach. She would take it from here.

12:30 A.M.

Sated, finally sated, they lay on their backs, covered by a sheet. Bruce was finishing a cigarette, the glow illuminating his face. He'd never tried to quit; he smoked like he displayed his muscles, truculently self-indulgent. And he drank like he smoked. Coors. Two six-packs of Coors, every day. And when he drank, he could get ugly. He was a man attracted to violence. When he drank beyond a certain point, Bruce began looking for a fight, usually at the

Top'sl, a small neighborhood bar a block up the hill from Bridgeway, Sausalito's main thoroughfare.

Bruce was attracted to violence, and women were attracted to Bruce. There was, she knew, a connection, cause and effect. There was also the body and the face. A linebacker's body, and a face to match. The elemental man. Shallow, narcissistic, moody. But, God, so beautifully built.

In some ways—perverse ways, she suspected—their relationship was the perfect solution. He had other women, she had other men, no questions asked. Occasionally, money changed hands. From Dennis to her, then to Bruce, who accepted it without comment—just as he received the constant admiration of women, no questions asked.

Coincidentally, both Dennis and Bruce were drawn to Sausalito—for different reasons. Dennis craved the company of the beautiful people, at play in a beautiful place. Bruce craved the water and the boats—and lived on the checks he got from the beautiful people. What would have happened, that morning, if they should have met, the three of them? Would Dennis have—?

"You're quiet, tonight." As he spoke, Bruce rose on one elbow and dropped the butt of his cigarette into the bowl half filled with water that he kept beside the bed. It was a seaman's habit, he'd once explained.

She considered, then decided to say, "I had a hard day."

"A hard day?" A small, smug smirk touched the corners of his mouth, and his eyes. "Doing what? Clipping coupons?"

"No, not clipping coupons."

"What, then? Having your nails done?"

She made no response. In the silence, Dennis's face materialized in her thoughts, small spasms of fear distorting his features, like the beginning of palsy, their little secret.

So far, their little secret.

"I'm going to take a shower." In the half-light of the

bedroom he stripped back the sheet, rose, stretched, posed for a moment, back arched, pectorals bulging. Then he smiled down at her, a lazy, go-to-hell smile, the self-satisfied singles-bar stud. "You didn't even give me a chance to shower, before you started humping."

"Sweat turns me on." Her smile, too, was lazily self-satisfied. This pleasure, she deserved. After seeing Dennis today—after listening to him, watching him, then writhing in the cage of her own thoughts, trapped—she'd begun to think of Bruce, of raw, wild sex. Bruce's kind of sex.

"You want to take a shower too?"

"No. The stall's too small. My place, yes. Your place, no."

"Hmmm—" He ran an exploratory finger up her stomach, to her breast. Would he begin again? At the thought, she allowed the smile to languidly widen. If it got worse—if Dennis came apart, and she became his full-time keeper—this night might have to last. It might have to last a long time.

But instead of turning up the heat, Bruce withdrew his hand. Still standing, he looked down on her as the light from the window played across her body. Then he asked, "How long have we known each other, Theo?"

"Oh, God—" She flung out an arm. "Bruce. This isn't the time. Believe me, this isn't the time."

"Why d'you say that?" He was frowning now. Perplexed, perhaps, and therefore frowning. Yes, it was starting. Bruce—Dennis—all the others, past and present. The faces changed, but not the questions. And it always started with this same slightly perplexed frown. Her fate.

"No. Seriously. What's it been?" he asked. "Three months, maybe?"

Resigned now, she nodded. "Just about three months. Right."

"And we don't really know anything about each other. Not really."

"That's because we've both got hot pants, Bruce. Like tonight. Two, three minutes, and we're in bed." She smiled. "I'd've thought you'd've figured that out by now."

"Okay, hot pants is fine. I'm not complaining."

"Good." Slowly, she pulled the sheet up over herself. Why was it, whenever pillow talk turned serious, she always covered herself? Had she ever thought about it?

"But I'm not even sure how many times you've been married, for instance. I don't even know how old you are, how about that?" His smile was earnest, genuinely bemused. Was Bruce really very smart? It was a question that, so far, had never come up.

She sighed. Reciting: "I'm twenty-eight years old. I've been married twice. You know that, for God's sake. And you've been married once. *I* know *that*." Suddenly exasperated, she let her eyes sharpen, her voice flatten: "What're you getting at, Bruce? What's on your mind?"

Ignoring the question, he put an edge on his own voice as he said, "Oh, yeah. You married once for love and once for money. Wasn't that how it went?"

"I married once when I was nineteen and once when I was twenty-four. I learned a lot, in those five years. And I'm still learning."

"But now you're worried. And it's got something to do with this rich dude who buys you things like cars. Am I right?"

She turned sharply away from him. "I thought you were going to take a shower."

"If this guy's giving you trouble, Theo, all you've got to do is give me the word. You understand that, don't you? You understand what I'm telling you, don't you?"

Suddenly it seemed funny. Grotesquely funny. Here he was: Bruce Carter, muscle man. Cheerfully volunteering to come to her rescue, no questions asked. All for love.

Love?

That, too, was funny. A joke. A three-way joke. A sick joke.

She realized that she was smiling now: a small, resigned smile. She turned back to him. "You'd punch him out for me. Is that what you're saying? You'd punch him out, and solve my problems. Right?"

"Definitely, that's what I'm saying." In his voice, she could hear the elemental lust for violence. Nothing then, had changed. Same old Bruce. Good old Bruce. She felt the smile twisting sardonically as she said, "Well, I'll certainly keep that in mind." She reached forward, rested her hand on his thigh, counterfeiting a friendly thank-you pat. Then, watching him respond, she moved her hand up the inside of his thigh, stroking him. God, he was so easy.

SATURDAY
August 26

11 A.M.

"The truth is," Bernhardt admitted, "that I haven't found out a damn thing. Nothing. I could've knocked off after the first day, for all I've accomplished in a week or more. Fowler—the sheriff—won't talk to me, and Price won't allow me on the goddam property, much less let me talk to John. After the first interview, I've seen Al Martelli twice. Both times I was parked on the county road, a hundred yards from the entrance to the winery. When Martelli came out, in his pickup, I followed him into town, and talked to him, bought him a cup of coffee. He's a very nice guy. And he's obviously very fond of John. But—" Bernhardt shook his head, flung his arm out in a frustrated arc. "But that's it. Period. The end."

At the mention of the boy, Janice Hale's interest visibly quickened. "They see a lot of each other, John and Martelli. Is that your impression?"

Bernhardt nodded. "Definitely. John follows Martelli around—you know, the admiring puppy dog. I had some sense of that, when I saw the two of them together, that first time."

"Has Martelli ever talked to John about the night Connie died?"

Bernhardt shook his head. "I asked Martelli about that, at least twice. He says he and John never talk about it. And I believe him."

"Have you asked Martelli to talk with John? That could

103

be the key to everything. If John trusts Martelli, maybe he'll open up."

Bernhardt let a beat pass as he looked away from the woman seated across the small marble coffee table. They were in her hotel suite, where they'd first talked, ten days ago. Room service had brought coffee and sweet rolls. Bernhardt bit into a roll, sipped coffee, then looked her directly in the eye as he said, "You're assuming there's something to open up about, Janice. I have to tell you, it might be wishful thinking. I'd like you to think about that. Really." He paused again, holding eye contact. "I realize how tough it is, to be cut off from John. I—" He swallowed. "Except for a grandfather, my father's father, I'm alone. And there's really no contact between us, just like there isn't any between you and your aunt Florence. So—" Eloquently, he raised a hand. It was a gesture that suggested the ancient resignation of all the Jews, over all the centuries. "So I know what you're feeling. If I were in your position, I'd be doing everything I could do, to make contact with John. That, I applaud. But this other thing—investigating Connie's death, blaming Dennis—it could be actually working against you, if you want to reestablish your relationship with John." He searched her face. "See what I mean?"

She sighed, smiled wistfully, leaned across the table, and patted his hand. "You're a nice man, Alan. You care. I'd never say it with Paula in the room, for strategic reasons, but I hope the two of you get married. I really do." She patted his hand again, briskly this time, before she leaned back in her chair. With the businesslike gesture, Bernhardt saw the now-familiar transition begin as Janice's wistfulness faded, replaced by a quiet, ladylike determination that was actually an iron resolve. And the resolve was reinforced by the Hale family fortune.

"But I know John," she said. "And I know Dennis. And I'm sure—absolutely sure—something's wrong, I *know* it."

"Well, I—"

"What's Martelli say about Dennis—about his relationship with Connie?"

"He doesn't say much about their relationship. But it's pretty obvious that he doesn't like Price. It's also obvious that he liked your sister. It's as if—" He hesitated, chosing the words. "It's as if he felt sorry for Connie."

Decisively, Janice nodded. "If that's the way he saw her, then he knew her, liked her. Not everyone picked that up, about Connie. She was so beautiful, so rich, everyone assumed she couldn't have any problems. And she played the part, too. She internalized her problems. Connie punished herself, not other people."

"That's characteristic of someone with a guilt complex."

She nodded agreement, then asked, "What else did Martelli say? What's he say about Dennis?"

Bernhardt considered, then decided to say, "At one point, the third time we talked, Martelli said he thinks Dennis has a girlfriend. A blonde girlfriend who drives a white sports car."

Janice snorted. "That's nothing new. I think he always had girlfriends, all the time they were married."

"Did Connie know?"

"She chose not to know." Regretfully, Janice shook her head, remembering. "It was another way to punish herself, I guess—suffer through Dennis's extramarital affairs." She drank her coffee, refilled her cup, then asked, "So what now?"

"Well—" Bernhardt spread his hands again. "I can keep on doing what I'm doing. A couple of times I've seen John riding his mountain bike on the driveway that connects the house and the winery to the county road. He's not supposed to go on the road—and he doesn't. A couple of times, though, he's gone *to* the road. Once I got out of my car, and tried to talk to him. But, surprise, Dennis showed up."

Her eyes sharpened. "And?" She moved forward in her chair.

"And he gave me a lot of lip, and threatened to call the sheriff and swear out a complaint for harassing him. He even said he'd get me arrested for attempted kidnapping."

"When was that?"

"Two days ago. Thursday."

"But he didn't call the sheriff."

"I didn't really think he would," Bernhardt answered laconically.

"It's significant, though. Don't you see? If his conscience was clear, he'd've called the sheriff."

"Janice . . ." He shook his head. "That's not really—"

"I think I should get involved. We've got to increase the pressure. He's nervous. I *know* he's nervous. He's afraid. If we increase the pressure, he'll start making mistakes. I'm sure of it."

Bernhardt smiled. "If we increase the pressure, and he calls Sheriff Fowler, who doesn't appear to like me very much, I could end up in jail." He let the smile widen, gently ironic. "Would that convince you Price is innocent?"

"What'd convince me," she said, speaking in a calm, measured voice, "is if the police find Connie's killer. And from what you tell me about this Sheriff Fowler, I don't think that's about to happen."

Bernhardt grimaced. "On that point, we're in agreement."

In silence, they both drank their coffee and nibbled on their sweet rolls. Then Janice Hale returned her cup to its saucer with a decisive click of fine china.

"Tomorrow," she announced, "I'm going to drive up there. I'm going to demand to see John. I'm going to shake Dennis up, rattle his goddam cage. If I'm right, and he's frightened, he'll start making mistakes."

Bernhardt smiled, shrugged, once more spread his hands. "Maybe you're right, Janice. Maybe you're right."

SUNDAY
August 27

3 P.M.

Ahead, Janice saw the entrance to the winery. In the mirror, Bernhardt's car had disappeared. Aware of a sudden uncertainty, she slowed the car, signaled for a right turn. Ready or not, the game was about to begin.

The drive from San Francisco in Sunday sight-seeing traffic had taken more than two hours. She'd gone first; Bernhardt had followed. A careful man, Bernhardt had suggested that if they became separated on the freeway, they should meet in Saint Stephen, at the small, picturesque town square that she remembered from a previous visit. Bernhardt had given her the game plan. He would park a half mile from the winery entrance, on the county road. While she confronted Price, Bernhardt would do his best to find a gap in the wire fence surrounding both the house and the vineyards. Pine trees and scrub oak bordered the road. Concealed among the trees, Bernhardt would find a vantage point that would allow him to see the house. She'd asked him what he intended to discover, watching. As rueful as an awkward, amiable teenager, he'd smiled. He had no idea what he might discover. "You get him stirred up," Bernhardt said, "and I'll see which way he jumps. Hopefully." Hearing him say it, seeing the small, self-effacing smile, she could imagine him directing theater. His method would be diffident: a quiet, aw-shucks approach. Then, slowly, the cast would come to

109

realize that Bernhardt was a determined man. Quiet, but determined. Men like Bernhardt didn't give up.

She turned between the two stone pillars that marked the driveway. Just ahead, the graveled driveway forked. The left fork led to the circular driveway in front of the house. As she made the turn she saw Dennis's green Porsche 911, one of his many vanities. The Porsche was parked just beyond the flagstone walkway that led to the house's old-fashioned, full-width front porch.

She parked behind the Porsche, set the hand brake, and got out. The weather was almost perfect, no more than eighty-five degrees, a golden August afternoon in the wine country. In fog-bound San Francisco, she'd had difficulty buying the floppy straw hat she now put on as she began walking slowly toward the house. She'd only been here twice; she'd forgotten how wonderfully substantial the house was, how comforting. It was two generous stories, with a small third floor under the eaves. The construction was generous, too: hand-hewn redwood beams and cornices, shingles that were aged by the years, not chemicals. The massive chimneys and the broad front steps that led up to the verandah were fashioned of fieldstone.

A child's coaster lay on the grass beside the flagstone walkway. Other playthings lay closeby. Suddenly she remembered John's face as she'd seen him last, boarding the airplane at Santa Barbara. He'd waved to her, and smiled. The wave had been wistful; the smile had been sad.

Her foot had just touched the first step when the screen door swung open to reveal Dennis. With the wide brim of the straw hat concealing her face, she was a momentary stranger to him, and his lean, improbably handsome face reflected displeasure: the decadent aristocrat, confronting an unwelcome interloper. But two steps changed the angles, and surprise now overlay his displeasure as he recognized her. Surprise, quickly displaced by eye-darting caution.

"Janice. Wh—" He broke off, stepped clear of the door,

came toward her with hand outstretched. "What're you doing here?" As he spoke, his eyes left her face, obliquely straying somewhere beyond her, in the direction of the winery. Instantly, she knew why he'd looked away. John was out there somewhere.

During the entire time driving up from San Francisco, rehearsing this scene, she hadn't decided on an opening line. Not until now, this moment, catch-as-catch-can: "I came to talk to you, Dennis." As she withdrew her hand from his, she realized that she'd left her purse in the unlocked Celica. Already, she was making mistakes. Should she get the purse, before they went inside? It was an elemental conflict; from earliest childhood, a woman was conditioned to always be in possession of her purse.

So she briskly excused herself, walked to the Celica, retrieved the purse. Its bulk beneath her arm was reassuring; she'd been right to get it.

As she again climbed the stone steps, she saw him posing with his left arm crooked as he consulted his watch. She'd lost the initiative, then, given him time to concoct an evasive strategy, decide on a pose.

"Janice, I'm sorry, but I've got to be in the city by five-thirty. I was just going to get into the shower. If you'd called—" He lifted his shoulders: Dennis's imitation of an overbred aristocratic regretfully shrugging. Dennis's father was an actor: an unsuccessful Hollywood bit player who was constantly on stage, chronically posing. Like father, like son. It was plain in their faces: petty poseurs, otherwise unmoored.

But now, two months after Connie's death, Dennis's mask was slightly askew. Dennis was afraid. Behind his second-generation actor's face, Dennis was afraid.

"Is John here?" Inquiringly, she looked behind him, through the screen door and into the wood-paneled entry hall, even though she was sure John was somewhere nearby, outside.

As he widened his stance, using his male bulk to block

111

her entrance to the house, Price's answer came too quickly: "No, John's—out. He—he's out for the day."

"When'll he be back? I can wait."

As Price drew a deep, uneven breath, his aggrieved voice rose a ragged half-octave: "Listen, Janice, You—I can't have you just—just dropping in like this, driving up here, and just dropping in. You—you should've called."

"Given you fair warning . . ." She held his eyes until they slid away. "Is that what you're saying?"

"That's exactly what I'm saying." Pumped up by his own pompous displeasure, Price tried for a note of righteous indignation: "It's been hard enough these last two months, without this."

"Without what, Dennis?" She spoke quietly. "Why does it bother you so much, my being here?"

"Well, it—it's disruptive." He blinked. Then he nodded, as if the phrase satisfied him. "It's very disruptive."

"Disruptive to whom?"

"Me, that's who. I—I'm trying to put my life back together, and you—your phone calls—they bring it all back. And I—I can't have it."

"Actually, Dennis—" She waited until his skittish gaze finally met hers. Then, quietly: "Actually, it's not you I want to see. It's John. You know that."

"Well, that—that's what I *mean*. *John.* You—whenever he sees you, or talks to you on the phone, he gets upset. He gets very upset. And the doctor says—"

"That's bullshit, Dennis. That's nothing but bullshit. And you know it."

Blinking rapidly now, playing the part of an outraged Colonel Blimp, he began to bluster: "The doctor doesn't want John reliving Connie's death. It's unhealthy. Very unhealthy. And, in fact, the doctor's very concerned. He—"

"I'd like to talk to this doctor. Who is he? Is he a psychiatrist?"

"Listen, Janice, this—this is exactly what I'm talking about. You come up here, and you start—"

"I'm John's aunt, for Christ's sake. The three of us are Connie's beneficiaries. You and I are all John's got. I love him—and he loves me. We *need* each other. And if this doctor of yours doesn't recognize that, then—then—" The words wouldn't come. Whatever they were, they wouldn't come. Suddenly she was drained of the anger that had taken her this far. Her throat was burning; sudden tears stung her eyes. Was she going to cry? At the thought, she realized she was shaking her head, a mute protest to whatever fate was driving her.

Seeing her falter, he raised his arm again, consulted his watch. Now he spoke with more assurance, as if to patronize her: "Listen, Janice, this isn't getting us anywhere. You may be John's aunt, but I'm his father. It's my responsibility to protect him as I see fit. Any lawyer'll tell you that, legally, you don't have any rights where John's concerned. And right now, for the foreseeable future anyhow, I just don't think it would be wise for me to let you—"

"What's the 'foreseeable future,' Dennis?" As she said it, she felt the anger return, roughening her words. Once more, tears were stinging her eyes. "Until after Connie's will is probated, and you have the check in your hand? Is that the foreseeable future?"

The blow landed. Momentarily his mouth moved impotently; his eyes faltered. But he managed a pale, desperate anger: "So that's it. The money. That's what's really bothering you, isn't it?" As if he pitied her, he shook his head. It was a mediocre portrayal of contempt. "You're jealous because Connie left me as much as she left you."

"It's not jealousy, Dennis." She let a beat pass. Then: "It's suspicion."

He managed a short, harsh laugh. "Ah—now we get down to it. You think I had something to do with her death. Is that what you're saying?"

"You were here, in the house. You had the opportunity. And God knows, you had the motive."

"The money, you mean."

"The money. Yes."

As if the words triggered a fury he could hardly contain, fists clenched, face contorted, he half-turned away from her. He stood motionless for a moment, head lowered, his whole body rigid. When he spoke, still half-turned away, his voice was clotted: "I think you'd better leave, Janice. I think you'd better get off my property."

"*Your* property—" Her voice rose uncontrolled. "Who signed the check, Dennis? *Who?*"

"Get out. And don't come back."

"I'll get out, Dennis. But I'll be back. Count on it. I'll be back."

3:15 P.M.

As he drew back behind the trunk of a huge pine tree, Bernhardt could picture the incongruity: middle-class Jewish intellectual, New York born and bred, actor, director, a playwright with one off-Broadway play actually produced, billing his client at forty dollars an hour while he skulked behind a pine tree. What qualified him to be here? All those summers in the Berkshires, at Camp Chippewa? Making leather bookmarks for his mother?

Across the clearing, he had a clear view of the confrontation: Janice and Dennis Price, toe to toe, having it out. Now, in pantomime, Price was pointing a furious forefinger, plainly ordering his tormentor off the property.

So far, so good.

According to the script, Janice would confront Price, stir

him up, demand to see John—all of this while Bernhardt, hopefully, found a vantage point from which to watch, concealed. When Janice left, so the script went, Bernhardt would remain concealed, on stakeout. Janice, meanwhile, would return to her hotel, awaiting his call. While Price, hopefully, did something incriminating.

Even at this distance, he could see the anger in the pattern of Janice's movements and gestures as, now, she was descending the stairs from the porch, a furious Dennis Price behind her, glowering, gesticulating. "Pull out all the stops," Bernhardt had coached her, once more the director, exhorting his female lead. Then he'd smiled, adding, "Let's you fight him."

In her car again, Janice was starting the engine, leaving the scene. For once, the plan was playing out according to the script—at least in its first scene, first act.

3:25 P.M.

Still standing on the porch, right hand shading his eyes, Price watched Janice's bright red Celica stop at the county road, then turn left.

If she were going to San Francisco, directly to San Francisco, she would have turned right. Was she going to Saint Stephen? Was she staying in Saint Stephen, at a motel? Would she talk to Sheriff Fowler?

Behind him, the screen door squeaked on its hinges. Maria. He'd forgotten Maria. Standing in the open doorway, a big, solidly built Mexican woman with an impassive Inca face, she had her purse in one hand and a plastic shopping bag in the other, ready to leave. He'd promised her the evening off. And tomorrow, too.

But he couldn't do it, couldn't let her go. He had to find Theo, had to talk to her. But he couldn't leave John alone, not with Janice there, not with Bernhardt surely somewhere close by. Martelli? Could he send John to Martelli's house, as he sometimes did? No. Martelli was—what was the word? Disloyal?

"Maria, listen—" He smiled, reached for his wallet. "I know I promised you the night off. But something's come up. A problem. *Comprende?*" As he scanned the broad, brown peasant face, he took a twenty-dollar bill from his wallet. Yes, the black eyes glinted, following the money. "I need you to stay with John, until I take care of the problem—three, four hours, maybe. It's very important."

Still eyeing the bill, she said, "But *mi hermana*—my sister. I meet her in Saint Stephen. At the bus station. Al, he will drive me."

"When?"

She shrugged her wide, meaty shoulders. "Maybe in an hour. Whenever Al say, we'll go. My sister, she's already at the station, I think."

As she spoke, he looked in the direction of the winery, and the vineyards beyond. Earlier in the day, an irrigation pump had failed. Martelli was working on the pump. Of course, John had tagged along—to "help." Wherever Martelli went, John was close behind.

"Al and John are in the vineyard, working," he said. "They aren't back yet. But when they come back, either Al or I will meet your sister at the bus station. We'll tell her that you have to stay here, this evening. We'll explain that there's a problem."

Still eyeing the bill, she was working her lips, rolling them under. This, he knew, meant that Maria was thinking, laboriously forming a plan. Finally: "How about if Al bring my sister here? She stay with me, tonight. Watch TV."

Quickly, he shook his head. "No, I—I don't want to do that, Maria. We've talked about that, your sister staying with you. It wouldn't work. But here—" He extended the bill, waited for her to take it. Then: "You know that woman who was just here? Just now? With the red car?"

Maria lowered the shopping bag to the porch, carefully tucked the money in her purse before she nodded. "*Sí.* Red. Just left?"

"Yes." He nodded again. "She's a—she's no good—no good for John. You understand?"

"No good. *Sí.*" She nodded.

"If she ever comes back, don't let her in. Don't let her talk to John. It's important. It's very important."

"The *policía*? The sheriff? I call the sheriff, if she come?" As she said it, she frowned. Wetbacks avoided the law, it was an instinct.

Hastily, he raised a hand. "No—no, not the sheriff. I— just tell her to leave, that's all. Lock the door, if necessary. Then find me, tell me. But no police."

"Yes. *Sí.*"

"Okay, that's settled, then." He moved quickly around her, went to the small study off the living room, picked up the phone, punched out Theo's number. In San Francisco, the line was ringing. On the fifth ring, her answering machine began. He broke the connection, dialed the San Rafael number. Had she gotten a machine, at that number? They'd only rented the place a month ago. She was still buying furniture, still buying—

"Yes . . ." It was a lingering, languid monosyllable. Had she been drinking? Snorting? Was she alone?

"It's me."

"Ah—" She was smiling as she said it, he was sure of it. That slow, provocative smile.

"I'm coming over. There's something—" He broke off. Then: "We need to talk."

"I've got to shop, pick up a few things. If I'm not here, I'll be back soon. Let yourself in, have a drink. After all—" He could visualize her smile, twisting into a quirky challenge: the female, diddling the male. "After all, it's a love nest, isn't it?"

3:40 P.M.

Moving cautiously from one tree to another, carefully planting his feet on the uneven ground, crouched low, cowboys and Indians, Bernhardt moved slowly up the gentle rise. From inside the house, could Price see him? Yes. It was axiomatic. If he could see the house, then someone in the house, looking out, could see him, simple geometry. From where he now stood, crouched, Bernhardt could see two sides of the house and the garage, plus the graveled driveway that led through a fringe of trees to the county road. Bernhardt's car was parked on the county road, about a quarter mile to the north. The car, the house, and his position made a rough equilateral triangle. If Price should spot him, therefore, and get his shotgun and come running, Bernhardt could make it to his car in time, allowing enough margin to negotiate the barbed wire fence that bordered the road. But if he continued toward the crest of the rise for a better view, the geometry changed, working against him. Therefore, he—

A figure appeared from behind the angle of the house, walking toward the three-car garage. It was Price, head down, striding purposefully. Leaving.

Bernhardt turned in the direction of his car. Time and distance were the problems now, no longer concealment. The geometry was changing against him. Long before he could climb over the fence and get to his car, Price would be in his car, under way. If he turned left at the county road, Price would see Bernhardt's car, parked on the shoulder. If he turned right—south—he would be long gone before Bernhardt could reach his car.

Concealment forgotten, Bernhardt broke into a trot, dodging trees and fallen logs, crashing through brambles. Never had he felt more ineffectual: the city boy, the innocent abroad. Already, he'd torn his jacket. Would Janice offer to pay? Would he dare to ask?

5:15 P.M.

"First there was that private detective," Price said. "And now Janice. For all we know, Fowler'll be next, poking around." He shook his head, clenched his fist, lightly struck the arm of the sofa. The sofa had just been delivered yesterday, she'd said. The cost, fifteen hundred dollars. How long could he keep siphoning money from the winery's receipts, to keep all of it going? The cars, the airplane, payrolls, the servants, now the hideaway apartment. All of it negative cash flow, covered by borrowing against his inheritance. How long would the creditors go along? When would someone discover that rental on this apartment was buried in the winery's expense items as "rent on business property"? The winery had never made money. Without income from Connie's investments, all those dividends, all that accrued interest, it could all come apart. Soon. Very soon.

"What Janice really wants," he said, "is to see John. But the question is, why?"

Theo sat at the other end of the sofa, her back against the arm, her legs drawn up, facing him. At her crotch, skintight blue jeans revealed her cleft. Her expression was calm. As always, calm: the Nordic goddess of power, a Valkyrie. Never had she seemed more desirable—yet more remote. Theo was thinking. Calculating. Planning.

"From what you've been saying," she said finally, "it sounds like the conversation blew up too soon. You should've let her talk. Maybe she'd've told you whether she'd hired the detective—whether she intended to talk to the sheriff. We'd know where we stand. This way—" She shook her head, shrugged. As her head moved, her thick, tawny hair came sinuously alive. God, how he craved that hair lying across the bare flesh of his chest. He needed that feeling. It had only been three months since they'd first met. But the touch of her—the sensations she generated—were never far from the core of his thoughts. He was addicted.

"Christ, I *did* let her talk. I couldn't shut her up. And I'll tell you, she's not about to slink back to Santa Barbara. No way. The lady is out to get me."

Holding her pose, she made no response. In the silence, each sitting at opposite ends of the long sofa—the fifteen-hundred-dollar sofa—they stared silently at each other. He couldn't read her face. Had he ever been able to do it? Did he ever know what Theo was thinking? Was that part of the attraction—the obsession? In three months—three erotic months—they'd done it all, woman to man and man to woman. Everything. But the woman he faced now was a stranger. An inscrutable, desirable stranger.

Now, speaking slowly, her eyes shifting beyond him, plainly articulating the thoughts as they came to her, she said, "It sounds like she misses John. It sounds genuine. And it could be—" As the thoughts outdistanced the words, she broke off. Then: "It could be that you're worrying too much. You're assuming the worst, where John's concerned. You're assuming he was awake, and heard it all. Everything. But you never've talked to John about what he heard—or saw."

"But—"

"Wait." She raised an abrupt hand. Repeating: "Wait." It was a short, harsh monosyllable. Her eyes were hard, her mouth set. She let a beat pass before she began speaking crisply, decisively. Her eyes had come alive now, locked with his, compelling his close attention. "What we could be doing," she said, "is assuming the worst. Erroneously assuming the worst. We're assuming that John knows what happened—or suspects, anyhow. And we're assuming that Janice wants to talk to him because she's suspicious. But that could be wrong. It could be completely wrong. So why don't we assume the best, instead of the worst? Why don't we assume that John didn't hear or see a thing? And why don't we assume that all Janice wants to do is spend some time with John? Why don't we—"

"That could've been true, at first. But today, she sure as hell—"

"*Wait. Let me finish.*" Her voice rose, her eyes snapped. Was it anger? It was the first time he'd seen her eyes like this, the first time he'd heard this edge to her voice. In response, he shrugged, spread his hands, looked away. He'd let her have her way. Then he'd speak. Didn't she know that they *had* to assume the worst? Didn't she realize that—

"What about this—" Now she spoke calmly, earnestly. Her eyes, too, were earnest. Intense, but earnest. "What if you take John away for a few months? What if the two of you went to Europe, traveling around? No one would really know where you were—no one but me. Before you go, you call Janice. You apologize. You say she has to realize how disturbed you've been, these last couple of months. And John, too, of course. Emphasize that you've done it all for John. Then you tell her that when you get back from Europe she's welcome to have John for as long as she wants. In fact, you'll say, you like traveling so much that you've decided to live in Europe for a while. Spain, maybe in a small village. You'll say that . . ."

As she continued to speak, his thoughts turned inward, overlaying her voice. She was right. God, she was right. He would stay in Europe, traveling, out of touch. Then he'd come back to San Francisco. No, he'd go first to Los Angeles, then up to Santa Barbara. He'd give John to Janice—*give* him to her. Then he'd go to San Francisco, and pick up the inheritance check from his lawyer. The winery, he'd leave for the creditors. The townhouse, one-third his, one-third John's, he'd instruct his lawyer to sell, and send the check to him.

Then, back in Europe, he would send for Theo. Janice and John would live happily ever after.

Theo was no longer speaking. She was looking at him. Watching. Waiting.

"I wonder . . ." Suddenly he rose, walked to the view window, stood for a moment looking out at the Marin County vistas: Mount Tamalpias, shimmering in the afternoon heat. Because of the view, the rental was fifteen hundred, for a small three-room apartment. "I wonder, would it work?" Frowning, biting his lip, he turned to face her. Uncertainty clouded his eyes.

"Why wouldn't it work?" As she spoke, she lowered her feet to the floor, and turned on the couch to face him. The urgency was gone from her voice now, the tension had gone out of her body. The message: having expressed her opinion she would abide by his decision. There was another message, too: a suggestion of sexual quickening.

"There's the winery to run. And bills to pay," he said.

"Couldn't your lawyer handle that? What'll it be, another three months, before the will's probated?"

"Closer to four, I think. The whole process takes six months."

"You could keep in contact with your lawyer through me." As she spoke, she raised her arms over her head, stretched, then moved closer. Yes, her eyes were softening, the pattern of her movements invited his caress. Sud-

denly it suffused him: the aura of her, the promise of re-
lease, of abandon, of oblivion.

6:10 P.M.

From the bathroom she heard the sound of the shower.
Soon, she knew, he would begin to sing: big, booming,
masculine songs. A rooster crowed after screwing a hen.
Was that what Dennis thought he was doing: crowing
after he'd screwed her, thrust into her, left her gasping,
helpless, lying across the bed, her part of the barnyard?

How little he knew.

How little they all knew: men liked Dennis, more vanity
than cock. Pretty boys, posing. Thirty dollar hairstyling,
tight jeans, smooth talk, a knowing smile. Children. Vain,
spoiled children, smiling for the camera. All his life, Dennis's smile had been his fortune; he was a vain, indulged
pretty boy. Somehow his parents had scraped together
enough money to send him to UCLA—a business major,
so called. A fraternity boy, really, a party boy. Even
then—especially then—Dennis's face had been his fortune. He'd met Constance Hale at a frat party. On gradu-
ation day, they'd driven to Las Vegas, four of them, two
couples, and gotten married. Constance Hale, worth millions—and millions. Constance Hale, hooked. A meal
ticket for life.

Constance Hale. Dead.

More than two months, dead.

But, still, a meal ticket, a passport to a lifetime's riches.

Letting her eyes close, she allowed her thoughts to return
to the night of June sixteenth. Because it was necessary, she

knew, that she remember. Otherwise, in years to come, she'd be in trouble. Psychiatrists, she knew, "peeled the onion," removing the outer layers of time, working back to the cause of it all: the single incident, the poisonous seed that lodged in the psyche, and began to fester.

And murder was the most poisonous seed of all.

It had been only the second time they'd made love at the winery. Earlier in the day, they'd been flying. She'd driven up from the city, and met him at Buck Field. With Connie out of town, in Disneyland, they hadn't hesitated to spend the day together, flying. They'd first met at Buck Field, when she was taking flying lessons.

Had it only been three months, since they'd met?

In three months, a lifetime could change.

Three months . . . plus three seconds, on June sixteenth.

They'd flown up to Clear Lake, a beautiful flight through clear summer sky. They'd had lunch, rented bicycles, taken a swim. The weather had been perfect, not too hot, not too cold. They'd stayed at Clear Lake until just after six, leaving enough time to return to Buck before twilight. They'd intended to drive into San Francisco, to her place. But Dennis had an appointment the next morning with a lawyer representing a potential buyer for the winery, a possibility Dennis was secretly exploring. So they'd gone to the winery, the night of June sixteenth. They'd been careful not to—

Suddenly he was in the room. Showered, scented, smiling, hair carefully combed, his acceptably porportioned body posed for her approval. Pleased with himself. An hour ago, frightened, he was quaking. Now he was preening.

"You look very—" She hesitated. "Very self-satisfied."

The smile widened. "So do you." Appreciatively, he studied her. Beneath his eyes, also posing, she subtly moved her body, responding to his gaze as she might to his touch. Soon—very soon, perhaps—they would make love again. When the flesh was willing—and able.

But now she saw the shadow of fear return, clouding Dennis's remarkably clear gray eyes. What would those eyes be capitalized at? she wondered. Athletes insured their arms, their legs, the muscles that let them make millions. What part had those eyes played in winning the hand of Connie Hale?

As he came into bed, she pulled up the sheet, then decided to ask, "So what'd you think? Are you going to call your travel agent?"

"It's not that simple. I can't just buy tickets, and get on an airplane, and go to Europe." In his voice, she heard a peevish note, a petty whine. She drew slightly away from him, to see his face. Yes, his mouth was pursed, pouting.

"Christ," he protested, "there's the house in the city, and the housekeeper. And the winery—a buyer, maybe, for the winery. There's the bank, too. I've had to borrow money on the inheritance, to pay the bills. Everything's frozen, you know. Everything."

"There's your lawyer. Could he—?"

Sharply, he shook his head. "I've already *told* you, he'd be all right to handle the probate, get the money. But I can't let him deal with the creditors. It just wouldn't work."

"Why not?"

"Because I'm living on money borrowed against assets in probate. That's tricky. That's very tricky. Especially when I've used the money to buy you a car, and furniture."

"I told you, they could deal with you through me. As far as they're concerned, I could be your business manager. Your lawyer could handle some things, I could handle other things."

"Jesus, Theo, that's the last thing we want, for people to connect the two of us." He spoke irritably. "Don't you *see* that? Now, everything's cool. But the last thing we want is—"

"An hour ago, you didn't think everything was so cool."

"With the sheriff—Fowler—everything's cool. That's

what I mean. The other—Janice, and John, and Bern-hardt—that's something else."

"That could be everything else."

"Not necessarily. It's still Fowler's jurisdiction. I know that much about the law. Whatever happens, anything legal, it's got to go through Benedict County law enforcement. So Janice and Bernhardt have to go through Fowler."

"Are you sure?"

"Yes." Staring up at the ceiling, he lapsed into silence. As the silence lengthened, she saw the fear return to his face. Reacting, once more frightened by his own thoughts, he shook his head. It was a sharp, involuntary movement. Then, heavily, he said, "I've got to talk to him, to John. Now. Tonight, I've got to talk to him, when he goes to bed. I've got to *know*."

"*We've* got to know."

He nodded. "Yes, 'we.'"

She watched him for a moment. Then, speaking very distinctly, she said, "You aren't forgetting that it's 'we,' are you, Dennis?" Still watching his face, she saw the words register: tiny muscle spasms around the eyes and mouth, a tightening at the throat. She let a beat pass before she said, "I wouldn't want you to do that. Ever."

As she said it, she saw the spasms quicken. Yes, the threat had registered. If she didn't get hers, the message read, then he'd never get his. Ever.

6:30 P.M.

"A blonde lady who drives a fancy sports car," Al Martelli had said.

Satisfied with himself, Bernhardt smiled. The sports car—a white Toyota Supra—was in the carport, parked beside Price's dark green Porsche 911. And the lady herself—blonde and, yes, beautiful—had just stood in front of a picture window, looking off in the direction of Mount Tamalpias. Only a few minutes ago, bare chested, Dennis Price had stood in the same window, looking at the same view.

Whether or not Price was a gigolo, or a villain, or even a murderer, he was certainly a philanderer. Finally, after more than a week's surveillance, after accomplishing nothing beyond a few minutes' conversation with Al Martelli and John Price, Bernhardt had a wedge: Price, and a good-looking blonde, one of them bare chested, sharing a picture window in San Rafael, an hour's drive from the winery.

A sports car, an airplane, a boutique winery, a Pacific Heights townhouse—an heiress for a wife and a blonde girlfriend, Price had it all.

Plus a son. A towheaded boy. A quiet, sensitive boy. A sad boy, without a mother. With a father who probably wished he wasn't a father.

Bernhardt yawned, stretched, checked the time. Six-forty. How long would Price stay? Another hour? All night? Would they go out for dinner? Eat in? Snack? Drink? Fuck? All of the above? At what stage in the love cycle were they? If they'd just met—even, possibly, after Connie's death, thus negating the philandering rap—they'd probably make love again and again. If they'd known each other for a year, the fires might be burning low. A quickie, and Price could be back in the Porsche and driving to the winery, where he would resume his vigil, keeping John incommunicado. He would—

On the stairs leading down from the building's two upper apartments, a pair of legs materialized. Faded blue jeans. And now the torso: a striped rugby shirt. Price. Alone. Leaving. Almost certainly leaving. Surreptitiously, Bernhardt lowered himself in the front seat of his Corolla. Yes, Price was striding to his upscale Porsche, bending down to open the door. His movements were ragged, his mannerisms mismatched, as if he were trying to project a decisiveness he didn't feel, an actor at odds with his lines. On the stage of life, Price was a type: a pleasing face, with nothing behind the mask.

The plan, then, might be working, the script playing out as written. They'd stirred Price up, put him in motion, probably found his mistress.

Leaving Bernhardt with a choice: follow Price, or talk to the blonde.

8:20 P.M.

Maria stood beside his bed, looking down at him. "Your daddy's gonna be here pretty soon, John. You wanna read a book, till he come?"

"Okay—" Without enthusiasm, John nodded.

Irresolutely, Maria frowned. Should she try to tell him a story? It wasn't her job, to put him to bed, get him ready, see that he washed himself, brushed his teeth, peed, like she did tonight. It wasn't her job to tell him stories, try to read books to him. Sometimes he knew the words better than her, made her feel bad, like a fool. Jennifer, from down the road, always did all that. Jennifer stayed with John, nights when Price was away. Baby-sitter, Jennifer was, got good money. Better money than she got, figure it by the hour. But she had her place over the garage, free. Good place, one big room. Plenty of space for her sister. But Price, that bastard, say no. Then he ask her to baby-sit. All day long, she cook, do the washing, clean, work hard. But after dinner, that was her time. Watch TV. Go into town, if Ricardo or the other ones come by for her, grape pickers with cars, trucks. They drive her, she buy them beers. She let them touch her, fool around, sometimes, what the hell, get their rocks off.

Especially tonight, with her sister come to town, staying with the Ochoas for a week, maybe more, she wanted to be in town. Drinking beer, laughing, talking about Mexico, the old days. But Jennifer, she went swimming in the river, cut her leg bad, have stitches. Fever, too. Kids.

"Okay," she said, "you read. Okay? I'm gonna go downstairs, watch TV. Okay?"

"Yes—okay." He sat up in bed, reached for a book, the top book on the pile beside the bed.

"Okay," she said. "Your daddy come home soon. He already phoned, say he'll be here, say good night to you. Okay?"

"Okay." John nodded, watched her turn away, and leave. His third-floor room was small, with gabled eaves. Maria was so big she almost filled the doorway. He heard her going down the hall, heard her steps on the stairs. Maria walked so heavily he could almost tell where she was anywhere in the house. Sometimes she reminded him of a cow.

The book was about dinosaurs, one of his very favorite books. They'd bought the book in San Francisco, he and his mother. They'd gone downtown, and had lunch at a real restaurant, with waiters and white tablecloths. Then they'd gone shopping, first at a store that sold dresses, then at the bookstore. At the bookstore he'd seen Amy MacFarland, from his class. Amy was always very quiet, very shy. Even on the playground, at recess, Amy almost never yelled.

It was only two weeks, his father had said, until they went back to the city, and he started school. Second grade. In the second grade, they wrote longhand, and did arithmetic, and even worked on computers.

Who would take him to school, now?

Would his father take him? Every single day, like his mother?

Would they know, at school, that his mother had died? Would they ask him about her? Would Miss Case, the art teacher, talk to him about his mother?

They'd gone to Disneyland right after school was out, he and his mother. It was a celebration, she'd said. They'd go to Disneyland, and see his Aunt Janice in Santa Barbara. Then they'd come home.

His mother had been going to drive from Santa Barbara to the house in San Francisco. Then they'd go up to the winery later, in a day or two, she'd said. But she'd promised to buy him a mountain bike, to ride during the summer at the winery, a real twelve-speed bike like Al had. So he'd wanted to go to the winery rather than to San Francisco. That way, they could buy the bike in San Rafael the first day they got back from Santa Barbara, not the second day, or even the third, still in San Francisco, waiting.

He'd heard his father and Sheriff Fowler talking about it, about how it had happened that they'd come to the winery rather than to San Francisco from Santa Barbara. Had his father expected them to come to the winery? No, his father had answered, he hadn't. Had there been anyone else in the house, that night? No, his father had answered. There were just the three of them.

The three of them, and someone else.

Someone who—

From outside, below his window, he heard the sound of his father's Porsche, that special burbling sound that only the Porsche made. Maria had been right, then. His father was home.

He reached up over the bed, and turned off the light.

Whenever he thought of that night, he didn't want to see his father. And if the light was off, his father might not come into the room. Especially if he pretended to be asleep, eyes closed, breathing deep.

How long did it take, to go to heaven?

How long did it take to come back from heaven?

He'd asked his mother about it, once. She had smiled, and patted his hand, and then looked off, the way she did when she was trying to say something so it wouldn't hurt his feelings, or explain something he might not understand. Finally she'd said, "It's instantaneous."

Instantaneous . . .

He'd remembered the word, and sometimes said it to himself. He knew what it meant, because it meant the same as instantly.

So in a second, only a second, someone—his mother— could travel from her bedroom, where his father now slept, all the way up to heaven. It no time, really. That's what his mother had really said: no time.

And then she could have traveled back—in no time. Instantaneously. She could have come back, and she could have seen everything. And heard everything that his father said to the sheriff, and the sheriff said to his father. She could have heard him talking to the sheriff, too. Invisible, able to float through the air, probably able to see through walls, his mother would have—

From downstairs, he could hear the sounds of voices. His father's voice, and Maria's voice. Soon Maria would go to her room over the garage. And then his father might come up the stairs.

Eyes still closed, he settled himself, cleared his throat. Sleeping. Soon, sleeping. But pretending, now. Worried, and pretending.

Just as, that night, he'd had to pretend.

At first, he *had* been asleep. Until he woke up on the couch downstairs, the last thing he remembered was the sway of the station wagon and the headlights of passing cars on the freeway. But then he was lying on the couch, downstairs. He'd been lying on his right side, his face turned to the back of the sofa. So that, in the dim light, in the half-darkness, really, no one could see whether or not he was asleep, even if he'd opened his eyes. So when—

From the stairway, he heard the sound of footsteps. His father, coming up the stairs. Coming slowly, tiredly. Sadly, maybe.

As the sound of footsteps came closer, he seemed to hear the voices he'd heard that night: his father's voice, and the other voice. Footsteps, coming closer down the stairs. They'd been—

"John?" It was his father's voice, now. Just his father's voice. The other voice had—

"*John.*" His father's hand was on his shoulder, gently shaking him. "John, wake up."

He opened his eyes, blinked, dug his knuckles into his eyes. Had he been sleeping, after all? Dreaming? Was he still on the couch, in the living room? Or was he—

The light over his bed came on, shining harshly in his eyes. He blinked again, turned away.

"Awww—"

"John, come on. Wake up. Sit up, John." His father was tugging at his armpits. "Come on, wake up. It's only a quarter to nine."

Yawning, he sat up in the bed, leaned forward while his father pulled up the pillow against the headboard, then leaned back. It was like he was sick. Like he was in bed with a bad cold, and his father was taking care of him. Now his father was smiling, sitting on the foot of his bed. Just like he was sick.

"Did you and Al go fishing?"

He nodded.

"Catch anything?"

"Al caught one. Not me." He yawned again.

"Well, maybe tomorrow we'll go fishing. We could try the Petaluma River. How about it?"

"Sure." He shrugged. Then he thought he should say it again: "Sure."

His father nodded, then allowed the smile to fade. So it was serious, then. Whatever it was, it was serious. He could see it in his father's eyes, hear it in his voice:

"I—ah—wanted to talk to you, John. I—ah—I've got to do it, there isn't any choice. It's—ah—it's about when your—ah—when your mother died. It's—ah—" His father broke off, frowned, settled himself more firmly, still sitting at the foot of the bed, left leg drawn up, so they faced each other, right leg over the side of the bed, foot touching the floor. "It's about how much you—what you remember, about that—that night. I want you to tell me everything that you remember. Do you understand?"

As he heard his father say it, the images returned: strange cars arriving in the dead of night. Cars with flashing lights. Police cars. Strange men in the house. Heavy footsteps, hushed voices. Men going up the stairs. Men carrying guns, men carrying boxes, and cameras. Whenever the strangers looked at him, their eyes went soft, as if they were embarrassed. Footsteps overhead, in the big bedroom. After he'd talked to the sheriff, his father had taken him to Al's house. They'd whispered together, his father and Al. Then his father had walked back to the big house. Gone. So it had been Al—Al had been the one to tell him what happened. There'd been a burglar, Al had said. A murderer. There'd been a lady with Al, a stranger, wearing Al's bathrobe. She'd made hot chocolate while—

"John?" It was his father's voice. For a moment it was confusing, being here with his father and still thinking about Al and the lady and the mug of steaming chocolate, all of it so clear that it seemed real.

"John, tell me." A pause. Then, more firmly: "I want to know. Tell me what you remember, John."

"But I—" He shook his head. "I can't. I mean, it—it's all blurred."

"Do you remember getting from the car to the house?"

"Mommy—" He broke off, swallowed. *Mommy*. It was the first time he'd said the word, out loud, since that night. Summer would soon be over, and he'd never said the word.

"Yes. . . ?" Fingers tightening on the bed clothing, eyes bright, his father was leaning forward. "Yes?"

After the first word, the first time he said it, the word came easier now: "Mommy carried me, I think. She—" Suddenly his throat closed. He coughed, swallowed, blinked against sudden tears.

"Go ahead, John. Go ahead."

"She put me on the couch, I think."

"You think? Aren't you sure?" His father's voice had gone hard. His eyes had gone hard, too.

He tried to answer, but could only shake his head.

"It sounds like Mommy carried you inside, put you on the couch. Then you went back to sleep."

"I—I guess so."

"Mommy was bringing in the suitcases, while you were sleeping."

"I—I—" His eyes were filling. He began to shake his head.

"John . . ." His father came closer, reached out, touched his thigh. His voice was softer, now: "John, I know this is hard for you. But it—it's necessary. If you don't talk about it, then it'll fester inside you, like an infection. Do you understand?"

He snuffled, wiped his nose on the sleeve of his pajamas. If his mother were here, she'd tell him not to do it, wipe his nose like that.

"*Do* you understand?"

"An infection . . ." He nodded. "Like my foot, that time."

"That's right." On his thigh, his father's fingers were tightening. "That's exactly right. And an infection of the mind can be worse than any other kind. So that's why you've got to tell me. You've got to tell me everything you remember, from the time you came into the house to the time I woke you up."

"I—" He swallowed, dug his knuckles into his eyes. Then: "I remember there were voices. That's the first thing I remember. Voices, from upstairs. Loud voices."

"Wh—whose voices?"

"Mommy's was one, I think. But I'm not sure."

"Were there other voices? Someone else's voice, besides Mommy's?" As he asked the question, his father's voice wavered, as if his own question frightened him.

"I—" Sharply, he shook his head. "I don't know."

"All right, never mind about that, now." His father drew a deep, shaky breath. A long, silent moment passed, while they looked at each other. Then, speaking very slowly, very distinctly, his father asked, "What happened then? Did you get up, get off the couch?"

"N—no. Not until you told me."

"All right. Good. So—" His father licked his lips, leaned forward. On his thigh, the fingers tightened again, uncomfortable now, almost painful. "So then what'd you hear? After you first heard the voices, then what'd you hear?"

"I heard you, coming down the stairs. I—I think I went back to sleep, first. But then I think I heard you. I heard you talking."

The pressure on his leg momentarily tightened again, then abruptly ceased as his father suddenly drew back. Now his father's face had changed, as if a stranger was there, beneath the flesh. A frightened stranger—the same stranger he'd seen at the funeral, so very long ago.

He'd known it, known he shouldn't have said it. From the first, that very first moment, lying in the darkness, pretending to be asleep, fearful of a presence he couldn't escape, he'd known how dangerous it would be, to—

"Who was I talking to, John?" The question was asked very softly, very carefully.

"I—I don't know."

How much longer would it go on? Already, his father had drawn back, drawn away. First his mother, gone. And now his father, suddenly a stranger.

"Was it—" A pause. One final pause. Then, still very softly: "Was it a man's voice? Or—" Another pause. "Or was it a woman's?"

"It—it was a woman's voice."

"Did you recognize it, this voice?"

He shook his head.

"But it was a woman's voice. You're sure of that."

He nodded again. Why couldn't he speak? He wanted to speak, wanted to say something. But he couldn't.

"Did you see her, this woman?" His father's voice sounded discouraged, as if he knew what the answer would be, and didn't want to hear it.

"No."

"Why not? We—" Quickly, his father caught himself. Then, just as quickly: "You heard her, you said. Why didn't you see her?"

"Because I—because I wasn't looking."

"You were awake, you said."

"Y—yes."

"If you were awake, then your eyes were open. Isn't that right?"

"I—I don't—I can't—" How could he say it? How *should* he say it?

"Your eyes were open—you were awake—but you didn't see anything." Now his father's voice was hard. And his eyes, too. His eyes were very hard. "Your eyes were open the whole time?"

"Yes . . ."

"What about me? Do you remember seeing me?"

"I—" How could he answer? How could he say it?

But now his father was nodding. Meaning that no answer was necessary. Whatever it was, everything had been said. Now, slowly, the hardness was leaving his father's face. His father looked sad, now. Sad and discouraged.

Gently testing him, his father spoke quietly: "I don't understand. You were awake, you knew I was there. Why didn't you look at me?"

"I—" Suddenly he felt the anger, burning his throat. His voice rose. "I *don't know*. I was—maybe I was still asleep. Half-asleep, anyhow."

Gravely, his father was shaking his head. It had been the wrong answer, then. "That doesn't make sense, John. You said your eyes were open. So you—"

"It *does* make sense." Suddenly his body was twisting. He was turned away from his father, face buried in the pillow. His eyes were brimming, hot with tears. His voice was muffled by the pillow. "I was *too* asleep. And I was scared, too. *Scared.*"

And then the tears came. First the tears, then finally his father's hand on his shoulder, to comfort him. That touch, so long remembered.

So very long remembered.

8:30 P.M.

Dropping his eyes to the window of the apartment, Bernhardt used a penlight to consult a small notebook, lifted the cellular phone from its cradle and dialed Janice Hale's number: a small, discreet, very expensive residential hotel on Nob Hill. What would it be like, never to worry about money, about making ends meet? Janice had estimated Connie's wealth at twenty-five million, even though the winery was losing money. Janice, with no winery to support, must be richer than her sister had been.

But, for Janice, there was no husband, no children. And now no sister. She was—

"The Stratton." It was a cultivated voice, perfectly suited to the hotel's aura.

"Suite six-oh-one, please."

"Six-oh-one. Yes."

As Bernhardt waited while Janice's phone was ringing, he saw Price's blonde girlfriend move into the illuminated rectangle of the big picture window. Even at a distance, Bernhardt could see the supple line of her torso, the swell of her breasts. Now she raised her arms above her head, enhancing the spectacle. Even with darkness falling the night was hot, at least ninety. With both hands, she pulled her long, loose hair away from her neck. Was she wearing anything beneath her blue T-shirt? With luck, he might soon know. Or, at least, conjecture.

"Yes?"

"Janice, it's Alan."

"Ah—" Her voice shifted, lifted. Bernhardt recognized the inflection. It was the excitement of the chase. Rich or poor, amateur or professional, they all responded to the hunt. It was, Bernhardt had decided, bred in the bone, a throwback to life in the cave. "What happened?" she was asking. "I drove by your car, but I didn't want to stop."

"That wasn't the game plan."

"I know. How'd it go?"

"I think," Bernhardt said, "that we could be on to something. I'm not sure, but I think he might be spooked."

"How do you mean?"

"Just a few minutes after you left the winery he got in his car and drove to San Rafael. He visited a woman, here. He got here about five o'clock, and left a little after seven. When he left the winery, just picking up on his body language, I had the feeling that he was agitated."

"Are you in San Rafael now?"

"Yes. I had to make a choice, either follow him or stay here. I decided to stay here, and talk to her. She went out for a while, after Price left. But she's back now, and I'm going to see what she says. What about you? Just watching, it looked like the two of you were really going at it."

"We *were* going at it. That son of a bitch, I'm sure he's hiding something. I'm *sure* of it."

"You may be right, Janice. You just may be right."

"Will you call me, later?"

"Sure. Listen, one reason I'm phoning, I'd like to call in

someone else, to help me. I think it's about that time if we're going to get a handle on this. Right now, for instance, I'd like to be at the winery, assuming that's where Price went. I could hop over that fence again, when it gets dark, and use a listening device to find out what he's doing, who he's calling. But if I get into that kind of thing, I'd like someone to back me up, stand lookout—someone who's a professional. I'd also like to know more about Price's beautiful blonde girlfriend. And I can't be in two places at once."

"Do you have anyone in mind, to help?"

"Yes. His name's C. B. Tate. He's very large, and very black, and very, very tough. He's also very smart. He grew up in the projects, and got into trouble when he was young. But he's honest, and he's reliable. And he's very talented, a natural actor. Years ago, when I first came out here from New York, and started directing little theater, I did *The Emperor Jones*."

"And he played Emperor Jones?"

"He sure did. Brilliantly. He was on parole, at the time. Being rehabilitated."

She chuckled. "God, two actors, for private investigators."

"A lot of investigating is acting. Telling lies, in other words, that sound like the truth."

Once more she chuckled. "I thought that's what politicians did."

Appreciatively, he laughed. God, she was quick.

"Of course, get him. If you trust him, get him."

"He charges the same as I do, forty dollars an hour, while he's actually working. I add ten dollars to his time, for markup."

"Alan. I told you once, it's not the money. You *know* it's not the money."

"Okay. I'll call him. I'd better get off now. How late can I call you?"

"As late as you want."

"Good. Talk to you later, then." He broke the connection, checked the notebook again, then punched out the number for C. B. Tate. On the fifth ring, Tate's answering machine kicked in, and his rich baritone announced that he would return the call as soon as possible—and please wait for the beep.

"C.B., this is Alan Bernhardt. I've got a job for you. It's surveillance, good solid client. So call me at—"

"Hey, Alan. What's happening?"

"I've got a job for you."

"Surveillance . . . that's not my favorite sport, you realize that, don't you? I mean, I sometimes fall asleep, you know?"

"Suit yourself."

"This good, solid client. Tell me more."

"She's also rich. Very rich, C.B."

"So who pays?"

"She'll pay me, and I'll pay you. I'll guarantee your end—forty an hour. But I won't front the money."

"In my experience," Tate said, "rich folks don't pay any better than poor folks. Worse, sometimes."

"I told you, I'll guarantee your end. Thirty days after the job ends. Max."

"Yeah . . ." It was a dubious monosyllable.

"Well, what'd you say?"

A pause. Then: "You say I'll get my money, that's good enough. What're we talking about? A week?"

"Maybe more like three days. I'm not sure. Why? You got something else?"

"Nothing I can't move back a week. No more, though. I've got an insurance fraud case that looks good. Real good. Big bucks. I might be able to use you, come to think about it. How's that sound?"

"Sounds great."

"You still working out of your apartment?"

"Yeah. You still working off your houseboat?"

"It's the only way to go, man. The ladies, they're crazy about boats. It's—you know—that wave action, I guess."

"Are you on your boat now?"

"I am indeed."

"I'm up in San Rafael. This job is up in Benedict County, mostly. Saint Stephen. I've got a motel room at the Starlight Motel. Why don't you drive up there first thing tomorrow? Let's meet at the Starlight at ten. How's that sound?"

"Sounds fine. Is it portal-to-portal?"

Elaborately, Bernhardt sighed. "You're money mad, C.B. You know that?"

"It's the culture, man. I'm helpless."

"Ten o'clock. The meter starts running at ten. Why don't you bring a suitcase, figure on probably staying for a night or two? On the expense account, naturally."

"Naturally."

"Have you got another car except that red Camaro?"

"Sure. I got a plain-Jane Ford, what'd you think?"

"Well, bring the Ford."

"What about a gun?"

"Sure," Bernhardt answered. "I thought you always carried one."

"I do. I just thought I'd ask."

"Getting the feel of the job, is that it?"

"That's it."

9:10 P.M.

It was a standard commercially built Marin County apartment building: two stories, four units. The building had been planned for profit, built of glass and redwood and plywood to just satisfy the building codes, nothing more. Walking softly, Bernhardt ascended the outside steps to her apartment door. There was an illuminated slot for a name card, but the slot was empty. A few minutes before, cautiously using a shielded penlight, he'd checked out her car, an expensive looking Toyota Supra, in the building's carport. He'd hoped to find a door open, hoped to find something in the car with a name—just as he'd hoped to find a name card in the slot. No luck.

After a last look around the typical Marin County residential premises, everything in order, everything quiet, everything secure, he drew a deep breath, took his ID folder from his pocket and pressed the door buzzer. He would play it as it lay, taking his cue from her, the good-looking blonde in the blue T-shirt. He would—

Almost instantly, the door opened. Plainly, she was startled. She'd taken off the blue T-shirt, changed into a white blouse worn loose over jeans. A large saddle-leather handbag was slung over her shoulder. Inside, the hallway light was on, but the living room light had been switched off. She was leaving.

Five minutes earlier, leaving, she might have caught him at her car. To benign providence, thanks were due.

"Oh—" She frowned, took a quick backward step. The frown was deepening, darkening. In seconds, the questions would begin. These seconds were his; the next seconds would surely be hers.

"I was looking for Mr. Price. Dennis Price."

"You were looking for—?" Complex emotions were working at her face, some of them puzzled, some hostile. "You're looking for *who*?"

He'd done it wrong, fucked up. He should have waited until tomorrow, run her plates on the data base, gotten her name, gotten some background. Instead, half-cocked, he was about to lose the initiative. Without a name, going in, nothing went right. It was the first rule.

Only the ID move remained, buying time.

He flipped open the leather folder, extended the license. Yes, her eyes were widening. Reprieve. "My name is Alan Bernhardt. I'm a private investigator. I've been retained on behalf of the estate of Constance Price. I missed Mr. Price at the winery, this afternoon. So I thought I'd try here." As if he expected Price to materialize in the darkened living room, he looked behind her.

"You—*what*?"

This woman, he realized, was tough. And aggressive. And smart, probably. Her eyes were sharp-focused, her stance assertive. Most women, alone, surprised by a stranger on a dark porch, would shrink back. Not this one.

"May I have your name, please?" It was his best imitation of a brisk, census-taker's pose, nothing if not official.

"It's Stark. Theo Stark. But I don't see—"

"How long have you known Mr. Price, Miss Stark?"

"Why're you asking?" It was a sharp, shrewd, hostile question. She had her balance—but he had a name.

"I already told you, it's a legal matter, having to do with Constance Price's estate. It's in probate." He pointed to the empty card slot beside the door. "I was looking for your name. Have you just moved in?"

"About a month ago. This is just a—" She hesitated. "It's a summer place."

"Ah—" As if she'd answered a question that had perplexed him, he nodded. Then, gambling: "You live in the city, then. San Francisco."

"I—" She eyed him for a long, speculative moment. Then: "Yes, I live on Nob Hill, as a matter of fact."

"Ah." He nodded again. High-priced real estate for a high-styled lady. Certainly, this was the woman Al Martelli had described, Dennis Price's playmate. Bernhardt took out his notebook. "May I have your address?" The census taker again, innocuously smiling. Expectantly waiting.

She drew a deep, determined breath, took a fresh grip on the shoulder strap of her handbag, lifted her chin. The handbag was actually a small leather shoulder satchel, the kind policewomen used, to carry their guns. "I don't give out my address or phone number unless I know the reason, Mister—what was the name, again?"

"Bernhardt. Alan Bernhardt." The smile was still in place. Precariously, still in place.

"Mr. Bernhardt." The words were sharp-edged. Her eyes were hard. In this interrogation, the free rides were over.

"Names don't mean much without things like addresses, phone numbers, license numbers." As he said it, he saw her eyes shift almost imperceptibly downward. She was thinking of her car, in the carport below, and its license plate.

"You still haven't told me why you're here—what you want."

"I thought I explained that. I'm trying to locate Mr. Price. It's got to do with—"

"I know what it's got to do with. What I don't know is why you're here, looking for him."

"Miss Stark . . ." Pretending regret, he spread his hands. "I'm sorry, but I can't—" He broke off. On this merry-go-round, there was no brass ring. Indicating, therefore, another personality shift. First, a guileless smile: the small boy, caught with his hand in the cookie jar. Then the aw-shucks admission: "Okay, I followed him here, I just missed him at the winery, so I thought I'd follow him, wait until he stopped somewhere. This was the first stop."

"He left a couple of hours ago."

"I know."

"Did you talk to him when he left?"

"No, I didn't."

"Why not?"

"I—I decided I wanted to talk to you."

"About what?"

Aware that she had the initiative, he let a beat pass. Somehow, he had to knock her off balance. He let the smile fade, let his eyes flatten, let his voice drop.

"I'm checking Dennis Price out, Miss Stark. I've been

144

hired to do it, and that's what I'm doing. We have information—there's been an allegation—that he's—that there's a woman in his life. And I'm checking on it." Once more, he spread his hands. "It's what private investigators do, Miss Stark. I'm sure you know that."

"Yeah, well—" She took a step forward, then another, forcing him back. Now she stood in the doorway; he stood directly beneath the porch light's pale cone. She was the aggressor now, the dominant one. "Well, I'll tell you something, Mr. Bernhardt. If you're looking for smut, you aren't going to find it here. You want to find out about Dennis and me, you ask Dennis. Okay?"

Her face was in shadow, but he could sense her anger, her rage. Could she see his response—a cool, sardonic smile?

"Yes," he answered softly. "Yes, okay. I'll ask Dennis. I'll definitely ask Dennis." He stepped back, casually waved, left her where she stood.

The contest, he decided as he descended the stairs, was a draw. But, to mix a metaphor, there were drops of blood on the trail. Several drops of blood.

10:05 P.M.

Theo stopped the Supra on the gas station's broad concrete parking apron, snatched the keys from the ignition, slung her purse over her shoulder, and strode to the brightly lit phone booth. She jammed the big purse into the space between the booth's glass wall and the telephone, leaned against the purse to keep it from falling, and punched out the eleven-digit number, drumming on the booth's glass wall with meticulously polished fingernails as she listened to the phone ringing. How many telephones—extensions—did he have? Before that night in June, she'd only been in his house twice. Both times, they'd had a lot to drink. Both times, they'd gone directly up the broad oaken stairs to the huge master bedroom.

Both times, and one more time.

Friday night, June sixteenth.

Eight rings. Nine. Where could he—

"Hello?" His voice. Finally.

"Can you talk?"

"No. But I've been trying to get you. Where *are* you?"

"At a phone booth on the highway. The Paradise Drive turnoff."

"We've got to talk." His voice was low and tight.

"You talked to him, then. Asked him."

"Yes, I asked him."

"And?"

"We've got to talk," he repeated. His inflection, the ragged cadence of his speech, both told the story: yes, he'd finally talked to John. And, yes, John had been awake, that night.

"Why don't you go back to San Rafael?" he was asking. "I'll come there tomorrow morning, as early as possible."

"No, not San Rafael."

A pause. Then, plainly dreading the answer, he asked, "Is something wrong?"

"After you left, I had a visitor."

"Ah—" It was an exhausted exhalation: the spent fighter, taking the final blow. Now fear shadowed his voice as he asked, "Where're you going now? Home?"

Incredibly, until that moment, she hadn't thought about it. Was Alan Bernhardt out there somewhere in the dark, watching her? If he *was* out there, and he followed her home . . .

Would it matter? He knew her name, knew her car, doubtless had her license number. Could private detectives get addresses from license plate numbers?

Would it matter, really matter? The damage, certainly,

had been done. She and Dennis were connected, probably placed together that night in June. From the fear in his voice, probably placed together, by John.

Could she ask him, ask that one vital question? Had they tapped his phone?

Could she wait until she saw him, to learn the answer? How many hours would it be? How long did a day in purgatory last?

Murder. The charge would be murder.

"*Are* you going home?"

If she were being followed, under suspicion, it might be best to go home, might be best to do the expected.

She would go home. The hell with them.

If they wanted to follow, whoever they were, whoever hired Alan Bernhardt, they would eventually find their way to her apartment. So it was better to lead the way. Pretending innocence, complete innocence, it was better to lead the way.

"Yes, I'm going home."

"I'll drive into the city, tomorrow. Let's meet—where?"

"There's a place on Columbus, an espresso place, at the corner of Vallejo."

"Where we've gone before? That place?"

"Yes."

"All right. I should be there by ten-thirty."

"Yes . . ." A few feet from the phone booth, a fat, red-faced man wearing a planter's straw hat caught her eye. She nodded, smiled, raised one finger. Pleased by the smile, he nodded, made an obvious effort to suck in his ponderous gut. God, they were all the same. They never quit.

"I have to ask you . . ." It was a cowed, craven lead-in. She could imagine him, sitting hunched over the phone, involuntarily holding it close. His improbably handsome face, a genetic gift from his bit-playing father, would be in ruins. "The reason you called—does it have anything to do with Alan Bernhardt?"

"Yes, it does."

"Ah—" It was another soft, wounded exhalation.

MONDAY
August 28

10:10 A.M.

Appreciatively, Bernhardt watched C. B. Tate swing the Tempo deftly into a parking slot, lock the car, and stride toward the Starlight Motel's small office. Built like a fullback, as perceptive as a fortune-teller, and shrewd as a racetrack tout, Tate was a man who saw himself clearly—and liked what he saw.

Bernhardt left the office, met Tate halfway, and steered the big black man to the motel's coffee shop. Settled across from each other in a Formica-and-Naugahyde booth, Tate was the first to speak:

"So how you liking it, on your own?"

"Anything's better than working for Dancer."

"You getting enough business?"

Bernhardt shrugged. "Everyone wants more business. But it's coming along."

"How long's it been, since you flipped Dancer off?"

"About six months."

They ordered coffee; Tate ordered a sweet roll.

"What about acting? Directing? Writing plays?"

"Directing's a problem," Bernhardt admitted. "It's a commitment that goes on for a month or more. Three, sometimes four nights a week."

"You directed when you were a part-timer for Dancer, though."

"Then, I could pick my assignments. Now, I've got to take everything that comes along."

"So your art's suffering. Is that what you're saying?"

Bernhardt looked into the other man's eyes. Yes, it was a concerned comment, a serious question from a friend. Requiring that he answer in kind:

"Yes, I guess that's what I'm saying. For now, anyhow."

"Too bad. You got talent."

"So do you."

"Yeah, but you can write the words, not just act them out. Writing the words, the scenes, that's a big deal."

"So's earning enough money to buy a set of tires when the time comes. Besides, I can still write. And act, too."

"Didn't you tell me once that you got an inheritance?"

He nodded. "Fifty thousand dollars, a long time ago. I blew half of it backing a play that couldn't miss, the promoters said. After that, I decided I wouldn't touch the principal. Ever." As he sugared his coffee, experiencing the habitual discomfort he felt whenever the questions came too close, Bernhardt let a silence fall before he asked, "What about you, C.B.? How's business?"

"I been doing some bounty hunting, lately. I like that. Trouble with being a PI, a one-man show, it's feast or famine. You get a plum, steady work for a month, say, that's fine. Forty, maybe fifty dollars an hour, you're in good shape. But you gotta pass up other work, chances are. Bounty hunting's not like that. It's one job after the other, bring one jumper in, get a warrant for another one, everything neat and tidy. And no shit from the boss, either. It's just you and the jumper, one on one." Tate bit into his sweet roll, appreciatively swallowed, drank most of his coffee, signaled the waitress for a refill. Bernhardt had forgotten Tate's lusty appetite.

"Another problem with the PI business," Tate said, "it's all electronics, these days. And that's a drag. It's like auto mechanics, you know? I mean, you never get a chance to get your hands greasy, anymore. Everything's computers. You're a PI, you don't have microprocessors, modems, a fax machine, listening devices, all that shit, you're out of it."

"An answering machine is a hell of a lot cheaper than a secretary, though. And a data base is cheaper than an airline ticket, or legging it down to the courthouse, and spending all day trying to find a name and address."

"Answering machines, they're all right. And bugs, they're okay. I understand, about bugs. The rest of it, though—those goddam little green words on a black screen—" Tate shook his head. "No, thanks."

"Speaking of data bases—" He took an envelope from his pocket, withdrew a sheet of paper, slid the paper across the table. "There's your mark."

Tate read as he finished the sweet roll and signaled for a third cup of coffee. Approvingly, he nodded. "Nice address. Nob Hill, the upscale part, looks like to me. Nice car. Nice lady?"

"Not so nice lady, I'd say. Good looking, though. Tough, but good looking."

"Big tits and big balls, eh?"

"Something like that."

"So what's the plan?"

For almost an hour, they discussed the case. Finally Tate stretched his massive arms high overhead, rotated his neck, rotated his shoulders, stretched again. "So far," he said, "I don't think you got much. What you got, mainly, is a feeling this Janice Hale has, that the kid knows something. From what you tell me about Price, looks like he's just protecting his kid, doing what comes naturally. And it's no crime, you know, to be a gigolo. This Janice Hale lady, sounds like she should find a man, make herself her own kid, forget about falling all over her nephew."

Bernhardt smiled. "C.B., you're not being paid to think. You're being paid to follow Theo Stark around, ask questions, find out if she sees Price, maybe plant a bug in her apartment, maybe a homer, on her car. You know—" The smile widened. "Electronics."

Tate muttered a cheerful obscenity.

"Seriously," Bernhardt said, "you're dumb, if you don't

get plugged in. It's the age of the silicone chip. If you don't get on board now, you're going to be left at the station."

"Bugs, they're okay. I told you that. They don't talk back. But staring at that fucking screen, doing what it tells me, getting stressed when the screen goes blank—" Tate shook his head. "Sorry, I pass." As he spoke, he moved restlessly on the plastic seat. Sitting in one position for long worked against Tate's metabolism. "You got a picture of the lady in question?" he asked.

"No. You got a camera?"

Tate nodded.

"Okay, get a picture, then. Here—" Bernhardt handed over two photographs. "That's Price, and that's John."

Tate snorted. "Not very good camera work, Alan."

"Telephoto."

"Hmmm." Tate slipped the pictures in his pocket.

"Here's my car phone number." Bernhardt wrote on a business card. "It's new."

"Car phones." Tate snorted again.

"Are you acquainted with the word 'iconoclast'?" As he asked the question, Bernhardt rose, dropped money on the table.

"As a matter of fact," Tate answered, his voice heavy with sarcasm, "it so happens that I am."

"Well," Bernhardt said, "that's you. An iconoclast."

"And proud of it."

10:35 A.M.

He was wearing dark glasses and a cloth hat, like the tourists wore. But the light sweater, designer khakis, and running shoes were strictly San Francisco casual, compatible to the city's cold, chronic summer fog, just now beginning to lift.

Was he in disguise?

If he was disguised—thought he was disguised—it was an ineffectual attempt. Like his voice on the phone last night, ineffectual. Craven, and ineffectual.

Like Dennis in bed.

Even though she knew he'd seen her, he pretended differently as he strode so casually into the espresso house, still wearing his dark glasses. Finally, pretending to spot her, surprise, two acquaintances meeting by chance, he came over to the table and sat beside her.

She smiled. It was, she knew, a well-executed smile, precisely calculated to express an amusement that could turn to derision.

And later, perhaps, contempt. Perhaps, now, it was time for the contempt to show through.

"Who're you supposed to be?"

Not replying, he placed the hat on an empty chair. Then, in the approved manner, he hooked the sunglasses in the *V* of his sweater.

She'd chosen a table against the café's back wall, with empty tables on either side. It would be impossible for anyone to overhear them.

She sipped her espresso. Then, after a precautionary glance at the nearest patron, two tables away, she asked, "What'd John say?"

"He heard us. He might've seen us, too, coming down the stairs. I think he did see us, but won't admit it. But, definitely, he heard us."

"Are you sure? Absolutely positive?"

"Absolutely."

"Shit."

The waitress came, took their orders, smiled, left. They sat in silence now, staring hard into each other's eyes. Then she said, "That's not the worst of it. That's bad enough, but it's not the worst of it."

"Jesus—" He ran unsteady fingers over his lips. Fixed on hers, his eyes were widening. Plainly, Dennis was losing it. Whatever he had, he was losing it. Now, behind his hand, he muttered, "Bernhardt. You're talking about Bernhardt. He knows about us."

"He must've followed you from the winery. Didn't you check, to see if he was following you?"

"I—yes." Distractedly, he suddenly looked away, toward the street. Bernhardt could be out there now, watching them through the plate glass window. "Of course I checked. But how the hell do you know whether someone's following you?"

"There're things you can do, if you're followed."

"How do you know he didn't follow you, last night? He could've—"

The waitress was serving their coffee and croissants, making a small ceremony of arranging the dishes and silverware. When the waitress had left them, Theo spoke quietly, holding his eyes with hers. "We don't want to get rattled. That's what Bernhardt's trying to do, probably—get us rattled."

"It's not Bernhardt. He's just a hired hand. It's Janice. I suspected it, the first time Bernhardt came around."

"I still think you and John should get out of the country. If this thing—if the sheriff comes around again, if he questions John—" Ominously, she let it go unfinished. Then: "How old is John?"

"He's seven."

"I wonder how much weight they'd give his testimony," she mused.

"He was there, in the house. He was the only one, besides . . ." Helplessly, he shook his head.

"But if—if it ever came to a trial, I wonder whether they'd allow his testimony."

"Jesus—" As if her intent was hostile, he raised a quick, defensive hand. "Jesus, don't say that." His eyes had gone hollow, haunted by visions from within. "A trial . . . Do you have any idea what that'd mean? The money—the inheritance—it'd all be tied up, until the trial was over. And then, sure as hell, the will would be contested."

"Maybe you should hire a lawyer."

"I've already got a lawyer. You know that."

"Well, tell him what—" She frowned, broke off.

Infinitely weary now, he smiled: a grotesque counterfeit of wry amusement. "Tell him what happened? Is that what you were going to say?"

"What I meant was, you should be taking the initiative. They're harassing you. Now they're harassing *me*. Maybe, if we don't take the initiative, it'll look suspicious."

"Suspicious?" As if he dreaded the sound of the word, his voice was hardly more than a whisper.

"Think about it. If you had nothing to hide, and a private detective questioned you, started following you around, what would you do? You'd complain. You'd—" She broke off, momentarily awed. "You'd go to the police, probably."

"The police . . ." The word hung between them, a palpable presence.

The police . . .

The law . . .

On June sixteenth, in seconds, they'd crossed over the line. Forever. They were on one side, the two of them, and whoever they could hire. On the other side, legions were arrayed. Watching. Waiting. John, and Fowler, and Bernhardt, and Janice, and countless others. Watching. Waiting.

". . . If we hire a lawyer," he was saying, "that's practically an admission of guilt."

Vehemently, she shook her head. "*No*. You're *wrong*. You're—Christ—you're begging the question, don't you see that? You're thinking like a guilty man."

A long, defeated beat passed. Slowly, his head dejectedly fell, as if the muscles of his neck had suddenly gone slack. "I am a guilty man," he muttered. "And you're guilty, too."

"Goddammit, that's not true, Dennis." Her eyes were

hot; her voice throbbed with suppressed anger. "She came at us. She struck the first blow, don't you understand? She *started* it."

With great effort he raised his head, looked at her squarely. "But you picked up the tongs. She was backing off. She was leaving. And you went wild." As he spoke, the scene came alive: the darkened room, lit only by pale moonlight. The two women, one of them naked, in front of the massive stone fireplace. Connie, her first screams of fury now broken sobs of outrage, turning away. The fireplace tongs, flashing in the half-light . . .

The sad, soft sigh, as Connie sank to her knees, remained motionless for a moment, then toppled over. Dying. Theo, coked up, panting like an animal, a wild, manic stranger, standing over her victim.

Even in that first moment, he'd thought of the money: the millions that would go to him. If the truth came out, if the police discovered how she died, he would never inherit.

Once more, his eyes had lost focus. His head had fallen again, an impossible weight.

Why had Connie done it, thrown herself on them in a blind fury? Never had Connie reacted violently. Always before, if anything, she'd been too passive, too accepting. She'd never . . .

"What're we going to do, Dennis?" Theo was saying. "Christ, we can't just—just sit and wait, hope for the best. We've got to *do* something. Don't you understand that?"

"What would you suggest?" Once more, he raised his eyes to meet hers.

"You've got to do something about John. He's the only problem. He's the only one who can hurt us. Don't you *see* that? If you don't want to take him to Europe, then send him someplace. Anywhere that Janice won't be able to find him."

"I've heard of private investigators tracking people all over the world. If I send him away, that'll make Janice all the more determined to find him. She'd never rest until she found him. I know Janice. She's already stirred up trouble, and she won't stop. She's got plenty of money, and she's got the determination. She wouldn't rest until she found him. She'd hire a dozen private detectives."

"Then what'd you suggest? What're we going to do?"

He sat for a moment in silence: a dull, dead silence. Then, speaking in a flat, uninflected voice that could have been a stranger's, he said, "It's been more than two months. It takes six months to probate a will in California. All I have to do is keep Janice and John apart for three and a half more months."

"And what happens then?"

Still speaking without inflection, eyes unfocused, he said, "I cash the check, and put the money in a Swiss bank account. I call Janice, and tell her she can have John. That's all she really cares about—John. And then—" He was smiling. The smile, too was unfocused: a vague, wan twist of the mouth, quickly gone. "And then we're gone."

"We." Theo leaned forward, trying to reach him, trying to make hard contact with his vague, evasive eyes. She spoke very precisely: "I'm glad you said 'we,' Dennis. Because this is a partnership. Beginning on June sixteenth, this is a partnership." She let a beat pass. Then: "I wouldn't want you to forget that. Ever."

5:40 P.M.

Bernhardt waited for his answering machine to come on, and instructed the machine to play back his messages. The last message was from C. B. Tate: "I've got some stuff on your lady, Alan. Call me. I'm on the boat." Bernhardt instructed the machine to erase the messages, then touch-toned the number."

"That was quick," Tate said. "I just called you."

"I know. What've you got?"

"What I got, maybe, was lucky. Do you want the deep briefing, or the condensed version?"

"Deep briefing, please. All I know about the lady is that she's blonde and built."

"There's that," C.B. agreed. "Even when she's sitting down, her motor's running, one of those."

"Did you talk to her?"

"Naw. I didn't think you wanted that, get her all stirred up. Was I right?"

"To be honest," Bernhardt said, "I'm not sure what I want. I just want to get something happening."

"Yeah, well, there's nothing happening, exactly. I was going for—you know—background."

"Background's fine." Expectantly, Bernhardt opened his notebook to a fresh page.

"Well, first, I checked out where she lives, naturally. It's one of those very upscale Nob Hill view apartment buildings, like I figured when we talked. New building, five, ten years old. Six stories, great views, only two or three apartments per floor. Very expensive. She's lived there for about a year. Lives alone. No husband, but lots of action. Guys, all the time, in and out. An assortment of guys. Old guys, young guys. Stuffy guys, swingers. All kinds. And, yes, your guy was one of them, beginning maybe six months ago, maybe less. But when he showed up in his Porsche, model 911, British racing green, most of the other guys fell off. All except one, a guy who wears tight T-shirts with the cigarettes rolled in the sleeve, one of those. So she's got Price for the bucks, looks like, and she's got this other guy for the kicks."

"Jesus, C.B. You were up here in Saint Stephen at eleven, this morning. It's about six now. You drove down to San Francisco. That's, what, two hours, for the drive.

What'd you do, tie the lady across her bed and inject her with truth serum?"

"Better'n that. I got lucky. I don't have to tell you, this goddam surveillance, this PI business, you don't get lucky, you can spend days—weeks—and get shit. That's one reason I like bounty hunting, like I told you. Temperamentally, I'm not suited to surveillance. And, matter of fact, when you consider that people who hire PIs got to be rich, and when you consider that most folks are white, and when you figure that the people they're mad at are also usually white, then you got to figure that I'm the wrong color for the PI business. Bounty hunting, though, that's different. You connect with a bail bondsman's got a good stable of drug dealers, most of which are black, and you're in business. Then you—"

"Listen, I appreciate the civics lesson, but speaking of money, this is a car phone we're talking on. Kapish?"

"Yeah, well, there really isn't much else to report. You got questions?"

"Sure, I've got questions. Can she make you?"

"I doubt it."

"What's your source, for all this information?"

"I told you, I lucked out, pure and simple. I found this guy—black, naturally—about thirty, I guess, name of Howard Brown. Interesting guy. He came out of the projects, same as me. Did a little time, too, same as me. So we have something in common, Howard and me. We speak the same language. Howard's a handsome devil, lots of muscles, looks like he's really hung. You know, one of those bronze gods that women can't keep their hands off. But Howard, he marches to a different drummer, it turns out. Instead of being a professional stud, or a muscle man or whatever, it turns out he's crazy about plants."

"Plants?"

"You know—ficus, fiddleleaf fig. It also turns out Howard's got a pretty good business. He rents plants to places like offices and apartment buildings. He rents them, and he maintains them. So Howard, he's all set, got a nice wife, nice family, lives out in the Sunset, with the rest of the middle class. But, of course, there's always temptation. It figures, a build like Howard's, going in and out of people's apartments and houses and offices all the time."

"So you're saying Theo Stark made a move on Howard."

"That's my supposition. I don't know whether she succeeded, that's not my business, I figure. But whatever happens between him and Theo, Howard is definitely acquainted with her habits and her tastes. Both of which, I gather, are pretty lusty."

"I imagine she's been married," Bernhardt said.

"Twice, according to Howard. Once for love, once for money. Not now, though. Definitely, not now."

Thinking about it, Bernhardt let a beat pass. Then: "You do good work, C.B."

"Thanks. Incidentally, being that Howard and I came out of the projects, where nothing comes free, I laid fifty dollars on him. I presume your fat-cat client won't object."

"No problem."

"And I also figured that, since I accomplished all this in a phenomenal four hours billable, I'm entitled to a bonus—plus mileage, naturally."

"I agree. How about eight hours, billable?"

"Perfect. So what now?"

"Do you think you could put a couple of bugs in her apartment, and a homer on her car?"

"Breaking and entering. For that, we charge a premium. Right?"

Bernhardt sighed. "Understood."

"And the bugs. I only use the best."

"Like what?"

"Meyers three thousand series."

"Good. Give it a shot. Maybe Howard can stand lookout while you do the installation. Give him a hundred."

"I already asked him. You understand, old buddy, that

I'll need a hundred fifty from you, up front, plus the invoice price of the bugs. I'll wait on the hourly pay, like we said. But if I front this, I want it right back."

"The next time I see you."

"Fine. So what're you saying, I should bug her place and then watch her for a couple of days? Is that it?"

"Let's start with that. Keep in touch, though. Every two, three hours."

"Indeed."

"Good luck."

"Thanks. You, too."

Bernhardt broke the connection, cradled the car phone, locked the Corolla's doors and strode across the Starlight Motel's parking lot to his room. Over the weekend the motel had been crowded, but now the parking lot was only half-full, and only a few swimmers were using the pool. All day long, with the temperature in the mid-nineties, he'd been anticipating the moment when he could dive into the welcoming water.

But first he would call Paula. All day long, another day spent on the perimeter of the winery, sometimes on foot, looking over the fence, sometimes slouched in his car, he'd thought of Paula, the constant companion of his psychic self. Always, at some level of his consciousness, he was thinking of Paula.

He opened the door to his room, stepped out of line with the window, took off his clothes, and slipped into swimming trunks.

Paula . . .

It had only been six months since they'd met. It had been the first casting call for *The Buried Child*, a play he'd persuaded the board of the Howell Theater to undertake. From the first informal, catch-as-catch-can read-through it had been obvious that Paula had acting experience.

And, yes, from the very first, there'd been something about her. Something that resonated from other places, other times and from other dreams, too long forgotten.

All through the read-through, he'd been aware of her. At first, inevitably, there'd been the male's automatic sexual inventory. She'd worn scuffed running shoes, faded jeans, and a long, loose sweater, the mandatory dress for tryouts in little theater. Her dark hair had been pulled into a casual ponytail, another convention. The sweater and jeans had suggested an exuberant swell of the breasts, a supple waist, an exciting curve of buttocks and thighs. Yet, if the body was provocative, her manner was reserved. The eyes told the story: dark, somber eyes set in a small, serious face. It was a vulnerable face, he'd decided, a wistful face, the face of a woman who yearned for something she hadn't found.

After the read-through they'd gone out for sandwiches and beer. Directors, he'd learned, enjoyed a license to ask questions. Paula's answers had come readily. She was an only child. Both her parents taught sociology at UCLA. Her father was a gentle man, she'd said, separating the two words to make the point. He'd come from the East, an Ivy Leaguer. Her mother had worked her way through the California college system, a fiercely self-directed woman. Paula had grown up in Los Angeles, had gone to private schools, gone to Pomona College. And, yes, sometime in her junior year, she'd gotten hooked on acting. It was in her sophomore year, she'd told him later, that she lost her virginity during spring break.

After she'd graduated, she began making the rounds of the casting offices, Hollywood's tribal ritual. A year later, she met a writer named Paul Fagan. She'd been twenty-two; he'd been forty, twice married, with children. Her parents had begged her not to marry Fagan, but she'd been in love. For almost a year, she'd been in love. For the next nine years, hating it, she'd stayed with the marriage. After the divorce was final, she'd come to San Francisco, yet another refugee, another searcher of the soul.

Then it had been his turn. From the first, the very first,

he'd been aware of how natural it felt to tell his story. He'd—

Beside him, the telephone rang. Startled, he picked up the receiver.

"Alan . . ."

"God, I was just thinking about you. Just this very second."

"And?"

"And I was reflecting on how it's been days, since I've seen you." He pitched his voice to a rich, low note: himself imitating his sensuous self. "And then I was contemplating this queen-size bed I've got, here."

"And?" Playfully, she mocked his erotic contralto.

"And I was thinking, what if Paula came up for a couple of days? She could swim and read books and tour the tasting rooms while I plied my snooper's trade."

"I guess you haven't talked to Janice today." In her voice he could hear a trace of different humor, Paula's private joke. But what private joke?

"Why?"

"Well, Janice and I had lunch today—yet another lunch. Of course, we talked about John and Dennis—the whole thing. She said she was thinking about going up there, staying there for a few days. I thought I might go with her."

"Did she tell you what happened yesterday, when she talked to Dennis?"

"Yes."

"And she still wants to come up here?"

"Don't you think it would be a good idea?"

"I don't know," he answered, speaking slowly. Business, he perceived, was about to conflict with pleasure. "I haven't thought about it. Does she want to come? Badly?"

"Janice'll do whatever it takes to get this whole thing resolved. *Anything*." She spoke decisively, emphatically.

"And you'll come, too?"

"I'll come, too." Once more, the lilt was back in her voice—and the eroticism, too, a mischievous play on "come." "I'm all packed. And so is Janice."

It was only six o'clock. If they left by seven, they'd be there by nine. An hour or two spent with Janice, at a nearby restaurant and bar, and they'd be in bed together, by eleven. Less than a month ago, they'd driven up to Mendocino for the weekend. Motels, Paula had said, made sex seem deliciously forbidden.

"Janice might be used to more elaborate accommodations than the Starlight Motel. This is all going on her tab. I didn't want an expensive place." As he spoke, he saw a white police cruiser entering the motel's parking lot. Behind the wheel he recognized the overweight profile of Sheriff Fowler. The car came to a stop in front of the motel office. While Fowler levered himself and his equipment belt out of the car and spoke briefly to the motel manager, another man got out on the passenger side. The second man wore seersucker trousers that doubtless went with a seersucker summer suit, a wrinkled white shirt, a regimental tie, and a Panama hat.

"Don't worry about Janice. She's not the idle rich. Not temperamentally."

"What I'm trying to decide is whether she'll help me or hinder me." Now the sheriff and the other man were walking across the parking lot, directly toward him. "Listen, I think the sheriff's going to call on me. Why don't you come, for sure? And if Janice wants to come, that's all right. There's a vacancy here, according to the motel sign." Quickly, he gave her directions as, yes, Fowler began knocking on the door.

"Just a minute," he called out. He hung up the phone, slipped into the clothes he'd just taken off and dropped on the floor: khakis and a sweat-dampened sports shirt over his swimming trunks. He finger-combed his hair and opened the door.

"Mr. Bernhardt—" Fowler said it heavily, as if the words described something distasteful.

"Sheriff—" Instead of offering his hand, Bernhardt decided to nod, awaiting developments.

Fowler gestured to the man beside him. "This is Clifford Benson. He's our DA."

Benson was a tall, lean, middle-aged man. His face was long and deeply creased into an expression of chronic skepticism. His dark eyes were watchful. The mouth fitted the face, thin and noncommittal. Unsmiling, Benson extended a long-fingered hand. His grip was firm, his voice was dry, his words were measured:

"You're a private investigator, I understand."

In the cadence and the timbre of Benson's speech Bernhardt could hear the remnants of an Eastern accent, somewhat less juicy than New York, but richer than Boston. Could it be an ivy league education, diluted by life in the provinces?

"Alan Bernhardt. Glad to meet you." Bernhardt stepped back from the door. "Won't you come in? There're only two chairs, but—"

Benson turned, pointed to patio furniture arranged beneath one of the two giant oak trees the developers had spared when they'd constructed the Starlight Motel's swimming pool. "Let's go over there, get some breeze."

"Fine. I'll be right with you." As the sheriff and DA walked toward the pool, Bernhardt slipped on socks and shoes, scooped up his wallet and keys, and walked briskly across the parking lot. The three men sat around one of the round metal tables. Benson took off his Panama hat, revealing thinning brown hair combed straight back, defying baldness. Placing the Panama beside Fowler's uniform cap on the table, Benson shifted in his chair to face Bernhardt squarely.

"I'll come directly to the point, Mr. Bernhardt." Maintaining steady, measured eye contact, Benson allowed a single beat to pass. Then, without inflection, he said, "It's my understanding that, for the better part of a week, you've had Dennis Price under surveillance. Is that correct?"

Eyeing Benson, then looking deliberately away, his eyes focused on the nearby swimming pool, Bernhardt finally decided to nod. "That's correct."

"Have you actually talked to Mr. Price?"

Bernhardt decided to nod again. "Yessir, that's also correct." The inflection of the "yessir," he felt, set the right tone: respectful, but firm.

As if he had carefully considered Bernhardt's response, Benson inclined his head, a judicial nod of acknowledgment. Then he said, "Before we came over here, Mr. Bernhardt, I took the time to run you at Sacramento. You've been licensed for almost five years."

"Right."

"You're associated with Herbert Dancer, Limited. Correct?"

He hesitated. "That's not really correct. I was always free-lance. I worked for several agencies."

"But mostly for Dancer."

Grudgingly, Bernhardt nodded. "Yes. But then, about six months ago, I decided to open my own agency."

"Ah." As if he might approve, Benson nodded. "And how's business?"

"It's spotty, frankly. But it's okay."

"Do you have an office?"

"No. I have an answering machine."

"And a computer? Data base?"

"Of course."

"So how long do you plan to keep hanging around Brookside Winery?" It was a genial question, deftly asked: a trial lawyer's quick, deceptively smooth thrust.

Appreciatively, Bernhardt covertly smiled as he said: "The honest answer is that I'll probably hang around as long as my client is willing to pay for my time."

"Or until Price lodges a complaint," Fowler said, his voice thick with both phlegm and intimidation. His fat, round face registered casual contempt.

Bernhardt studied the sheriff for a moment before he said quietly, "I'd be surprised if he'd lodge a complaint, Sheriff. I'd be very surprised."

"Yeah? Well—"

Smoothly, Benson interrupted the sheriff to ask, "Why do you say that, Bernhardt?"

Once more, Bernhardt took time to consider his reply. Then, pointedly addressing Benson, he said, "Because if my client's right, then Dennis Price has guilty knowledge of his wife's death. If that's the case, then I doubt that he'd be complaining about me to you. He'd just draw attention to himself."

"It'd be a waste of time, doubtless, for me to ask you for the identity of your client," Benson said drily.

"Not at all. Her name is Janice Hale. Constance Price was her sister—her closest living relative. Janice, Dennis Price, and John Price share equally in Constance's estate." He gestured to Fowler. "I showed Sheriff Fowler Miss Hale's letter of authorization."

Reluctantly, Fowler nodded. Yes, he'd seen the letter. Benson's face registered mild surprise—and mild disapproval. They were, after all, on the same team, he and the sheriff.

"Do you have any estimate of the value of the estate?" Benson asked.

"I'd say between twenty-five and fifty million."

"So . . ." Reflectively, Benson nodded. Then: "This 'guilty knowledge' you mention . . ." Benson's long, saturnine face was impassive, his voice as dispassionate as a judge's. "What're we talking about, here?"

Bernhardt drew a long, measured breath, raised himself slightly in the hard metal lawn chair, and said, "There were at least four people in the Price house that night— the victim, her husband, her son, and the murderer. Then there was Al Martelli and a lady friend, at his place. There was a struggle, and a death by clubbing, both of which have got to be messy—and loud. Yet no one heard anything, or saw anything. John was asleep, apparently, on the ground floor. Price was in a guest bedroom on the second floor, just down the hall from the murder scene, also asleep, we're told." Bernhardt shrugged, lifted his hands, palms up. "I just think there's more to it than that. I think someone must've heard something, or seen something."

"Have you talked to Price?" Benson asked.

"Yes, I have."

"And John?"

"Yes."

"Who else?"

"Al Martelli, too. And—" Instead of saying "Theo Stark," he turned to Fowler, gesturing with an open hand. "And the sheriff, naturally."

Fowler's response was a muttered obscenity.

As if he were deciding a difficult point of law, another judicial evocation, Benson reflectively pressed a forefinger to pursed lips as, involuntarily, his eyes followed two teenage girls, both wearing string bikinis, bound for the pool. Then, once more the low-keyed inquisitor, Benson said, "Your answers have been pretty straightforward, Mr. Bernhardt. Even if I were inclined to try and chase you off, which, as of now, I'm not considering, I probably wouldn't have grounds. However—" The skinny forefinger was lifted between them now, signifying a solemn warning: "However, the important point to remember, Bernhardt, is that we're on the same side, here. We help each other, we don't hinder each other. Is that clear?"

"Very clear." Bernhardt was pleased with his calm, steady response. So far, so good.

"That's the first point—" Benson rose, took his Panama hat from the table. "The second point, equally important, is that we don't needlessly stir up the natives. By which I mean, the rich natives." Looking down from his full, slightly stoop-shouldered height, Benson spoke softly. "Is that also clear?"

Bernhardt permitted himself a small, knowing smile. "Oh, yes. That's clear. That's crystal clear."

11:50 P.M.

Holding her in his arms, Bernhardt felt her body twitch, then begin to relax completely. She was falling asleep. Soon, she would begin to snore: a soft, companionable, ladylike snore, their little secret.

After several months together, the pattern of the secrets they shared was still evolving. The evolution had been backward: the big things first, little things later. The first time they'd been together, after that first read-through at the Howell, over sandwiches and beer, neither one of them even sure of the other's full name, they'd talked of the things that mattered most: the death of his wife nine years ago, the dissolution of her ten-year marriage two years ago. They'd shared their aspirations, their ambitions. He'd told her about his marriage to Jennie, about their funky apartment in the Village, near his mother's loft. He'd told her about his career, about his fast start: *Victims*, the third play he'd written, produced off Broadway. Good parts in experimental theater, small parts in three Broadway plays. And, yes, two TV commercial gigs, for the money.

Paula, too, had gotten off to a fast start. A Hollywood start, not a New York start. There was a difference. In Hollywood, a pretty girl who knew how to move, and had learned the rudiments of acting, could usually find work: walk-ons at first, then parts with a few words.

But soon—too soon, much too soon—she met a successful, incredibly manipulative screenwriter, the practicing sadist, the man her parents begged her not to marry.

The first part of his life had ended when Jennie's head had struck a curbstone in the Village. He'd been thirty-five when the two policemen had knocked on his door. Now he was forty-four. His wind was short and he needed bifocals and he'd already lost two molars.

The first part of Paula's life had ended when she'd walked out of the divorce court with her parents, one on either side. She'd been thirty-two. Instead of helping her in "the business," her husband had kept her from acting. Having already fathered two children, one by each of his previous wives, her husband had forbade her to have children. Later—after they'd become lovers, after Paula had come to trust him—one night after they'd made love, with her face buried in the hollow of his shoulder, she'd told him that her husband had forced her to have an abortion. Yes, her gynecologist told her she could have children. But she was thirty-four now. The clock was ticking.

A week after that first read-through, he'd invited her out to dinner. Instead, she'd invited him to her apartment: a small, expensive apartment in a remodeled Pacific Heights mansion. Later, she'd told him she wanted him to see how she lived, what kind of art she liked, what kind of music, what kind of wine. That night, they'd kissed: a grave, measured kiss, followed by a long, searching, lover's look.

The next time he'd come to dinner, he'd stayed.

Gently, he took his arm from beneath her neck, stroked her hair, kissed her lightly on the forehead, then turned to lie on his back, staring up at the ceiling. When he was a boy, lying like this, he used to imagine he could feel the earth turning as it circled through space, carrying him far beyond himself. It was the unknown beckoning from the void, the eternal mystery. When he was young, the mystery promised everything. Then Jennie had died, and the promise had faded.

But now—just now, these last months with Paula—the promise was returning, along with the mystery.

TUESDAY
August 29

8:30 A.M.

As the waitress turned away, Bernhardt spoke to Janice: "So how'd you sleep?"

She shrugged, then smiled at Paula: two old friends exchanging girl talk. "I don't imagine I slept as well as you two. But I managed."

"As I told Paula," Bernhardt said, "I didn't want to hit the expense account for an expensive motel. Little realizing"—he smiled—"that the boss would be arriving."

"So what'd you think?" Janice asked.

Bernhardt shrugged. "The truth is, it's pretty much a matter of instinct—feelings. You feel that Price is afraid John'll tell you something that'll incriminate him. But feelings aren't proof. Unless something happens—breaks loose—there's no way we're going to get Fowler or Benson to go after Price. It simply won't happen."

"What about this woman, Theo Stark?"

Bernhardt shrugged again. "There's no doubt Dennis and Theo had something going, before Constance died. But that won't light a fire under Fowler either."

"It could be a motive for murder, though," Paula offered.

Bernhardt looked at her. Seated beside him, she wore a lightweight cotton blouse and shorts. If they'd been alone in the restaurant booth, he would have put his hand on her thigh. If they'd been in their room, he would have drawn her close, caressed her, pulled her down on the

175

bed. It had been that kind of a night. "Motel madness," Paula's mischievous phrase, pronounced broadly, with a lascivious leer.

He smiled, teasing her: "You mean a motive as in the lovers' scheme to rid the man of the wife who'll never let him go? That kind of a motive?"

"No," she answered promptly, firing back. "No, I mean a motive as in money. Millions. They get each other, plus a fortune. All they have to do is kill her—or have her killed."

"C.B.'s watching her," he answered. "Let's see what he says."

"Is he really a bounty hunter?" Janice asked.

"Among other things. I guess—" Bernhardt paused, searched for the thought. "I guess C.B.'s really a Samurai. That's the way he operates—out on the edge where there aren't many rules. I hope you get to meet him. He's a fascinating guy. The longer I know him, the more I like him."

"Do you trust him?" Janice asked.

"Completely."

Satisfied, she nodded. "That's all that matters." Then: "This woman. Theo. She has a luxury apartment in the city, and another apartment in San Rafael?"

Bernhardt nodded. "Right."

"Is the place in San Rafael a love nest?"

The archaic phrase amused Bernhardt, but his reply was straight-faced: "It could be. C.B. found out she moved in about a month ago."

"Meaning, maybe, that they didn't want people to know they were meeting, after Connie was killed." As she spoke, Janice's eyes kindled. Paula was nodding encouragement. Affirming: "If they had her killed, they wouldn't want to be seen together. That makes sense."

They made room for the waitress to serve their juice and coffee, then Janice asked, "Well, what's the plan?"

Bernhardt smiled ruefully. "The truth is, I don't really have a plan, at least nothing dramatic. But we've got Price agitated, I don't think there's any question about that. And he hasn't gone to the authorities, which could be significant. So for now, I'd say we should continue doing what we're doing, keeping the pressure on."

"Alan—" Across the table, Janice leaned toward him. In the single word, in the sudden intensity of her eyes, in the timbre of her voice, Bernhardt sensed the sum-totaled focus of an entire life, of all hope. "You talk about my intuitions, my suspicions. I'll admit, they aren't evidence. But I'll tell you—" For emphasis, she let a beat pass. "I'll tell you, when I saw Dennis on Sunday—when I heard him talk, watched him, I saw fear in his eyes. Mortal fear. He's absolutely terrified that I'll talk to John."

"It seems to me," Paula said, "that what you should be trying to figure out is how to get John alone for a few hours with Janice, uninterrupted. Just the two of them, relaxed. A trip for an ice-cream cone, a long ride in the car."

"Easier said than done," Bernhardt answered ruefully.

"But Paula's right, Alan." Avidly, Janice nodded. "If we can get him away—if I had time enough to get his confidence, one on one, I think he'd open up. I'm *sure* he'd open up."

The waitress brought their breakfast, refilled their coffee cups, smiled, retired.

"I don't think Price is going to let him leave the winery, though," Bernhardt answered. "I've been watching for a week and it hasn't happened yet. John spends all his time on the property. That's the rule. Martelli told me so."

"Dennis leaves, though. He left yesterday."

"Sure. But he leaves someone with John. Al Martelli, or the cook, or a baby-sitter. If John leaves the property, he's always with his father, or Al Martelli. They . . ." As the first hint of a solution began to emerge, unformed, Bernhardt's voice trailed off, his eyes lost focus. Then, tentatively, he said, "That winery—the whole layout—is forty acres. There's the house, within a few hundred feet of the road. Then there're the winery buildings, in a hollow behind the house. Al Martelli's house is there, too. The rest of it's vineyard, except for an old, abandoned barn. There's a small stream that runs along the western corner of the property, close to the barn. I've walked around the whole property, I've got a pretty good picture of it, in my head . . ." Once more, his voice thoughtfully died; his eyes wandered away. Then, coming back, he said, "The whole property's fenced. There're only two entrances, one off the county road, the main entrance, and a gate on the western perimeter, not far from the barn. That gate's always locked—chained. The whole property is fenced. The fence that runs along the county road is split rail, for the rustic appearance. It's reinforced, though, and there's barbed wire concealed in it. The rest of the fence is wire. It's six feet with barbed wire on top. Now—" He ate some of his omelette, bit off a corner of toast, sipped coffee. "Now, as long as Dennis is in his house, able to see whoever comes in through the main entrance, and as long as he knows John's on the property, riding his mountain bike with Martelli, or playing close by, Dennis wouldn't think he had to keep an eye on John. Even if John and Al were fishing in the creek, or exploring that old barn, for instance, out of sight from the house, he'd still feel secure."

"So what you're saying is that—" As if she were a small girl, Janice touched her upper lip with the tip of a small pink tongue. Her eyes shone with barely supressed excitement. "What you're saying is that we should—"

Bernhardt nodded. "All it would take is a pair of bolt cutters. Which, as it happens, I have in the trunk of my car. It's part of the PI's standard bag of tricks."

"Wow!" Paula's eyes were shining, too. "We're getting down to basics, here."

"We'd need an edge, though," Bernhardt warned. "Some insurance."

"Insurance?" Paula was amused. "You mean like liability? That kind of insurance?"

"I mean insurance like Al Martelli. Or, anyhow, someone to deliver John to the right place at the right time. We might need a lookout, too." With his eyes on Janice Hale, he let a beat pass. Then, quietly: "So what'd you think, Janice?" he asked quietly. "Feel like doing a little fieldwork?"

Slowly, decisively, she nodded. Saying simply, "Yes, I do." Her eyes were rock-steady, her mouth was thin and firm.

"What about me?" Paula asked. "I could be the lookout." Her voice was pitched a full note above its normal timbre, another evocation of the past: the little girl who wouldn't be left behind.

10:15 A.M.

The cold morning fog was still thick, blurring the endless rows of masts that defined the yacht harbor. Even the Golden Gate Bridge, less than a mile to the south, had disappeared behind a solid mass of white.

Midway along the wharf Theo saw a figure crouched over a pile of multicolored sail bags. The figure was generically familiar: like Bruce, the stranger was someone who made his living maintaining other people's boats. As her footsteps came closer the figure half-straightened, looking at her over his shoulder.

"I'm looking for Bruce Carter. Someone said he was on this jetty."

The young man turned half-away, pointed. "He's on the next jetty. Working on that gaff-rigged sloop, there."

"Which one's that?" Theo smiled. It was the first time she'd smiled today. Would it be the last time? "I'm a landlubber."

His answering smile twisted meaningfully: the randy male's automatic response. "It's the white one trimmed in maroon. Almost at the end, there, on the right side. God, this fog's so thick, you can hardly see her."

"Thanks." She stepped around him and his sail bags and walked down the wharf to the next jetty, turned toward the maroon-trimmed sailboat. There was no gangplank; the rail of the boat was almost three feet from the wharfside, and two feet higher. On the teak deck, one of the hatch covers was off.

"Hey! Bruce!"

As she waited, overhead, she heard the sound of an airplane engine. Automatically, Theo tracked the sound: a light plane, flying above the overcast. By now, if she'd kept working at it, she could have had her student's license. A few more hours of dual—no more than ten hours—and it could be her, up there.

In Dennis's airplane, the Skylane, they could fly as far as San Diego without refueling. Escape, then, was always possible. If something went wrong, anything went wrong, the Skylane was their passport to freedom. The airplane was based at Buck Field, an airport with no control tower. Therefore no controllers; therefore no tape recordings. Therefore, with the transponder turned off, they could disappear in the sky, an anonymous, untraceable blip on the radar screens. They could land at a small uncontrolled airport in the desert below Palm Springs. Refueled, they could fly undetected into Mexico—while the feds struggled to trace every single blip flying in the opposite direction. They could—

In the open hatchway, Bruce's head appeared. He smiled his slow, musky smile.

"Hi—" Wiping his hands on an oil-stained rag, he slowly climbed up on deck. "Want to come aboard?" The smile widened meaningfully, his eyes turned lazily indolent. "The bunks are narrow, but they're comfortable."

"Give me a hand."

"I'll do better than that." He lifted a boarding ladder, lowered it down to the dock, and extended his hand. As she stepped onto the deck, he drew her roughly close, one of his muscle-man moves. Quickly, she twisted away from him, at the same time involuntarily looking back over her shoulder.

"What's wrong?"

"Let's go downstairs." She moved toward the open hatch.

Now the smile was patronizing. "That's 'below deck,' sweetie."

Not replying, she climbed down to the luxuriously appointed cabin.

"Want some coffee?" He gestured to a coffeepot steaming on a small two-burner stove.

"Fine." Theo stepped over to an open porthole. Her view of the dock was limited by the brass-bound circle of the porthole. Was Bernhardt out there somewhere, watching? Had he followed her from San Rafael into San Francisco, then here to Sausalito? Was there another detective, besides Bernhardt? More than one other?

"Sugar, no cream. Right?"

"Right." After a last searching look through the porthole she turned away, sat on a soft leather sofa. It was almost impossible, she knew, to discover whether someone was watching. Since Sunday night, when she'd opened her door to see the strange figure on the dimly lit landing, she'd felt the constant scrutiny of hostile eyes. Even in her apartment in the city, with the door double-locked, she'd felt pursued, spied on.

He handed her a steaming mug, then sat across from her. "You look jumpy. Something wrong?"

She smiled: a wry, rueful twisting of the mouth. "Yeah, something's wrong. Something's definitely wrong."

"Well—" He rolled his shoulders, flexed his muscles, smugly smiled. "Well, tell Bruce."

Theo sat silently for a moment, simply looking at him. How had it happened that they'd ever gotten together?

Except for back-street bars and second-run movies they never went anywhere, never did anything, never really talked about anything but what they would do in bed—and what they'd done.

But Bruce was tough. More than once she'd seen him fight—and win. Watching, she'd felt a deep, elemental excitement: the primitive woman, physically aroused. Sex was never better than after he'd had a fight—and won. Some men watched sports on TV, some played golf. Bruce fought.

"What's wrong," she said, "is that there's a private detective who's following me."

She'd known what to expect from him: that slow, indolent, knowing smile. "An irate wife, eh? Yet another irate wife. Theo—" Mockingly, he shook his head. "This is the second time, baby, just since we've been seeing each other. I'd think you'd be used to it, by now."

"It's not an irate wife. And it's not funny, either."

"Sorry." But the mockery of a smile remained. Of course, he wasn't sorry. He was amused.

"I didn't come here to play word games," she said. "And I can't stay long. If you want to listen, fine. Otherwise—" She let it go truculently unfinished.

"So go ahead—" He spread his hands. "Tell me. Tell Bruce."

Driving across the Golden Gate Bridge she'd decided how she would put it to him: "Constance Price," she said. "That San Francisco socialite, who was murdered two months ago, in Saint Stephen. Remember?"

She had the pleasure of seeing the supercilious, shit-eating smile slip, then fade. "Yeah—" Tentatively, he nodded. As, yes, his pale-blue eyes began to search her face. *Was this a trick?* he was transparently wondering. A put-on?

"Yeah, I remember," he said cautiously.

"Well—" She broke off, drew a deep breath, and stepped over the edge: "Well, I've been going out with her husband. Dennis Price. It's been about four months, now, maybe a little longer."

"Yeah—" With the smile fading, curiosity was narrowing his eyes, tugging at his scarred, fighter's face. Curiosity, and caution, too.

"And—" Another pause, this one for courage. "And he and I were alone in the house, when she showed up."

"Was this that guy with the winery? Is that the one?" She nodded. "That's the one."

He frowned. "It was a prowler. A burglar. That one?"

"That's the one. Except that it wasn't a prowler. It was Dennis. She—his wife—she caught us together. She went wild. Really wild. They fought like—like animals. He picked up a pair of fireplace tongs, and hit her."

His Adam's apple bobbed. Once. Twice. "He killed her? Him?"

She nodded.

"And you were there? In the same room?"

"Yes."

"Jesus, Theo. You'd better get a lawyer."

"A lawyer . . ." She spoke as if he'd suggested some strange ritual, some alien rite.

"Sure, a lawyer. Christ, this isn't something you want to fuck around with. You're smart. You should know that."

"Right now," she said, "it's this private detective that's worrying me."

"What's he doing?"

"He's putting pressure on Dennis. A lot of pressure. And Dennis isn't built for pressure. To say the least."

"All the more reason you should get a lawyer. Protect yourself."

"What I'm afraid of," she said, "is that, if the detective suspects what happened—really happened—and if he ever went to the police, and the police started questioning Dennis, then Dennis would fold up. First he'd fold up. And then he'd lie."

"Lie?"

"He'd tell the police I did it. I know that's what he'd do. I can see it coming."

"Except that the police think it's a prowler."

"I'm saying *if* the detective goes to the police. I'm trying to look ahead. Anticipate."

"How come you waited until now to tell me this? How come you didn't say something when it happened?"

"Because I promised I wouldn't say anything. That shouldn't be hard to figure out."

He sat silently for a moment, thoughtfully staring at her. Then: "So what now? Why're you telling me now? What'd you want me to do?" He rolled his shoulders again, flexed his muscles again. "This Price—he sounds like someone I'd enjoy teaching some manners, give him something to think about."

As she listened to his barroom-brawler's blandishments, she held his eyes for a long, searching moment. Could she count on him? Trust him? How far? At what cost?

"It's not Price that worries me," she answered. "I can handle him."

"Oh?"

She nodded, repeating: "I can handle Price. It's Bernhardt."

"Bernhardt?"

"The private eye—" She looked toward the dockside porthole, gestured. "He could be out there right now, on my trail, watching. He's already—" About to describe Bernhardt's appearance at the San Rafael apartment, she broke off. Then, recovering: "He's already been at my apartment, already given me a hard time."

"You want me to talk to him, tell him to lay off? Beat on him a little?"

There it was again: his elemental lust for combat.

"Could you?"

"Sure—" He shrugged. "You find him for me, I'll bounce him around, straighten him out." He stepped forward, put out his hands, to touch her. The message: for services to be rendered, payment was due in advance. She put up her hands, palms outward. "Honey, I can't. I—I just don't—"

Eloquently, she moved her head toward the porthole. The meaning: with alien eyes watching, she couldn't.

Following her gaze, his eyes came alive with the prospect more compelling than sex: the promise of violence. "Is he really out there, do you think? Now?"

"I don't know . . ." She made it sound wan: little girl lost.

But now she saw his eyes shift, drawn from the view through the porthole to the sailboat itself, to the floor beneath their feet. "I can't do anything about it now, though. Not now. This engine, I've got to get it running. The owner wants to leave for San Diego, day after tomorrow. But you find him, this Bernhardt—give me a name and an address—and I'll have a little talk with him."

"I'll give you a call. Thanks, honey."

"No problem."

She rose to her feet. "I'd better go. Listen—that gun I loaned you. Have you still got it?"

He frowned. "Theo . . ."

"I think I'd better take it."

"Now? Today?"

"Now. Right now. Where is it?"

"It's at my place. But—"

"Please."

11:15 P.M.

At the fifth ring, Bernhardt heard the click of an answering machine. The message was short and laconic: "This is Al Martelli. Sorry I missed you. Leave your name and number and the time you—" The machine clicked again. "Hello?"

Should he use Martelli's first name? They'd talked three times, amiably, once at the winery, twice in Saint Stephen, briefly. Which way should he gamble: too familiar, or too formal?

"Al—this is Alan Bernhardt."

He waited while the other man matched the name to the face.

"Yeah—how are you?" There was caution in the greeting, a distancing. But there was encouragement, too, a tentative warmth. Contradictions.

"Listen, I—this matter we've talked about—I wonder whether I could meet you somewhere, today? In town, maybe. It's important."

"Important?"

"Yes. I want to try and bring this thing to a head. And you could help."

"Is it about John? That?"

"Yes, it's about John—and Dennis, too." He hesitated, then decided to say, "Janice Hale—Constance Price's sister—is here, in Saint Stephen. And we need your help."

"My help . . ." Martelli let the two words linger in doubtful silence.

"Please. Let me buy you a drink this evening. Any time you say. Any place."

A silence fell—and lengthened. This, Bernhardt knew, could be the pivot point, the fulcrum. And if he read Martelli right, there was nothing to do but wait. Martelli was a man who couldn't be prodded.

Finally: "Okay. Do you know the Briar Patch? It's just south of Saint Stephen, on Route Twenty-nine."

"I'll find it."

"Five-thirty?"

"Five-thirty. Thanks."

Seated in his car, parked on a gravel road that commanded a view of the fenced western border of the Brookside vineyard, Bernhardt thoughtfully returned the cellular phone to its cradle. Should he include Janice in the meeting with Martelli? Or would it be better to—

Suddenly the phone's shrill buzzer came alive.

"Yes?"

"Alan—" Unmistakably, it was C.B.'s voice, a rich, deep, neo-Afro base.

"Yes—how's it going?"

"She left her luxury Nob Hill apartment this morning about nine-thirty, drove to Sausalito. She met a guy on the docks, there, at the yacht harbor. I'd say the guy was a workman. Middle thirties, lots of muscles. I got some pictures of them. They went inside the cabin of a big sloop, there. Belongs to some hot-shot clothing manufacturer. Or, at least, it did. She and this guy she met were in there for about forty minutes. Then she drove this guy to a nothing stucco building up the hill in Sausalito, six studio apartments, no view, like that. You know—housing for the peasants on the American Riviera. He went in, she stayed in the car. He came out with a paper sack of something. She drove him back to the yacht harbor, and then she drove up the highway to San Rafael. She's got an apartment, there. You know about that one, I guess."

"That's where I picked her up. Are you there now?"

"Right."

"No sign of Price?"

"None."

Thoughtfully, Bernhardt looked at his watch. "How are you for time, C.B.?"

"Couple a days from now—Friday, at the latest—I got something I got to do. It's an insurance job, big-ticket liability claim. It involves one of the black brothers, so I've got a lock. Other than that, I'm yours. Incidentally, speaking of skin color, this is pretty lily-white, as you know, up here in marvelous Marin. So I'm—you know—pretty visible. I just thought I'd mention it."

"I know . . ." Considering the possibilities, the combinations, he let a beat pass. Then: "Why don't you stay on her until about six, tonight. Then find yourself a motel room in San Rafael. Check with me, when you're settled."

"You don't want me to talk to her, put a little pressure on her?"

"Not now. I've got an appointment with Al Martelli, at five-thirty. Let's not get her stirred up until I've talked to him. I want to talk to the client, too."

"Gotcha."

12:10 P.M.

As she slowed the Supra, Theo saw them: two phone booths on the wide concrete apron of the Exxon station. She flipped on the turn signal, moved into the inside lane, checked the traffic, made a gentle left turn. Since it had happened—since June sixteenth—her driving had become more conservative, more cautious. There'd been other changes, too. Many other changes.

Visible changes?

Visible to whom? Under what circumstances?

Meaningless thoughts. Self-destructive and meaningless.

Gangsters, she knew, always used pay phones. It was more than an Eliot Ness convention; in the electronics age, it was a necessity. She'd once heard of a "spike mike": drill a small hole in an outside wall, insert the microphone, hear everything that's said inside the room—inside the house. Olives in martinis, tie clips, earrings, they all could conceal tiny microphones powered by microscopic batteries.

And if Bernhardt could bug the apartment in San Rafael, then he could bug the house at the winery.

But they had to talk, had to communicate—to plan, to

decide. Every day that passed—every hour—brought danger closer.

Theo braked to a stop beside the booth and swung the driver's door open. As if to stretch after a long drive, she placed two hands against the car's low roof and moved her head from side to side, back and forth, pretending to work out the kinks as she covertly looked for Bernhardt.

If Bernhardt had followed her, what would he have done? Would he have pretended to get gas? Air for the tires? Or would he turn into a side street, make a U-turn, park, watch?

It was, she knew, a fruitless speculation. In this congestion—Marin County at midday—he could be anywhere. He could even be a she: a lady private eye, hired by the day.

As if to protest, she suddenly pushed away from the Supra, turned toward the phone booth. Leaving the glass door open in the midday heat she punched out the number, waited, deposited the quarters, heard the phone at the winery begin to ring.

"Hello?"

"It's me."

"Where are you?"

"San Rafael."

"At the—" His voice dropped. "At the apartment?"

"No. I'm in a pay phone. A gas station."

"Ah—" The soft exhalation, she was discovering, was Dennis's reaction to stress. One of his reactions. One of many, since June sixteenth.

"What is it?"

"Our friend has turned up at a motel, here," Dennis was saying.

"Bernhardt."

"Yes."

"That's all? Nothing else? Nothing—" How to say it? "Nothing legal, nothing from the law?"

"No. Nothing."

"Have you been thinking about—" Once more, Theo broke off. Then: "Have you been thinking about a solution?"

"A solution?"

"Jesus, Dennis. You know what I mean."

John, she should say. *What about John, Goddammit?*

"I want to talk to you—to see you. We've got to—" He broke off. He was foundering, losing it. She could imagine his face, torn by torment, coming apart.

Bernhardt—all because of Bernhardt.

"What's the name of the motel?"

"It's the Starlight. It's the only motel in Saint Stephen."

She looked at her watch. Almost always, Bruce went home for lunch. "I'll call you back." Abruptly, she broke the connection. Her address book was in the apartment. Could she remember Bruce's number?

5:40 P.M.

"Ah!" Appreciatively, Martelli returned his half-drained glass of beer to the table and wiped foam from his upper lip. "That first sip of beer. In this weather, it makes the whole day."

"When does the heat break, up here?"

"A week or two, and it'll start to cool down."

"How long've you been at Brookside?"

"Four years. I was there before Price came."

Bernhardt nodded, drank his own glass down to equal Martelli's. It was an axiom of the investigator's trade: never drink more than the subject drinks—or less.

"So what's it all about?" Martelli asked. As he spoke, he exchanged nods and smiles with a man seated across the small barroom. It was, Bernhardt reflected, a cue worth remembering: in towns the size of Saint Stephen, in sparsely populated counties like Benedict, eyes were always watching.

"Janice Hale is here," Bernhardt answered. "I told you that. Have you ever met her?"

Martelli smiled cheerfully. "I'm the hired help. I get to swim in the pool, but I'm not invited inside the master's house."

"I doubt that."

"Okay—" Now the smile twisted ironically, an expression of indifference to the master's whims. "I've been inside, but not to drink or eat or hobnob."

"Well," Bernhardt said, "Janice Hale is a considerable person. I guarantee that you'll like her."

"Actually," Martelli said, "I've met her. And I agree, she's okay. A successful artist, I understand."

Bernhardt nodded. Then, lowering his voice as he leaned forward across the table, he said, "What I want—what Janice wants—is for her to talk with John, one on one, for an hour or so, without Dennis Price knowing about it."

Doubtfully, Martelli drew a brown hand across a stubble-darkened jaw. His eyes were narrowed, shrewdly appraising. "That sounds like it could be a pretty tall order. Dennis keeps close track of John, these days."

"I think I know how it can be done—if you'll help."

"Oh?" It was a noncommittal monosyllable.

"Almost every day you and John do something together—fish, go mountain-bike riding, whatever. Right?"

"Right." Martelli smiled. "Call me a paid baby-sitter. That's what it is, really."

"Well, let's say that, tomorrow, you and John go fishing. Janice and I would drive around to the gate on the western edge of the property, near the stream. I'd cut the chain on the gate. Janice and John could drive somewhere—have an ice-cream cone, whatever. Basically, that's what this is all about, you know. Dennis is keeping Janice and John apart, won't let her talk to John alone, even for a few minutes. Janice wants to know why."

"She thinks Dennis murdered his wife. And she thinks John can help make the case against him." Martelli spoke slowly, gravely. "That's it, isn't it?"

This moment, Bernhardt knew, was the moment that counted. This moment and the moment to come. Holding the other man's gaze, he nodded. "That's it."

"She's asking John to send his own father to jail."

"She's trying to find out who murdered her sister," Bernhardt countered. "She wants justice."

Martelli nodded in return, lifted his glass, drained it. His dark eyes had lost focus, blurred by recollection and recall. Then, speaking softly, eyes still far-focused, he said, "I like John. I like him a lot. I'm divorced. My kids are teenagers. Girls. I wasn't really a very good father, when they were younger. I wasn't a very good husband either. In this business—Benedict County boutique wineries, so-called—there're a lot of bored wives, looking for action while their husbands are off making money. I couldn't keep my hands to myself, and my wife took the kids and left. So John, he's—he's sort of a second chance for me, I guess. I—" He broke off, shook his head. It was an admission of defeat, a mute confession of failure, the wound that would never heal. Then: "Connie's gone. She's out of it. The question is, What's best for John? Dennis sure as hell isn't father of the year. But he *is* John's father."

"All Janice wants is some time with him. She wants to find out the truth. That's what this is all about, Al. The truth. It's as simple as that."

As Bernhardt signaled for two more beers, Martelli said, "Nothing like this is simple. If you don't know that, you're in the wrong business."

"I'm not saying this is simple. What I *am* saying, though—" For emphasis, Bernhardt let a long, sharp-focused beat pass, making hard eye contact. "What I *am* saying is that it all comes down to the truth. Bottom line, when the truth comes out, the bad guys get what's coming to them—and so do the good guys. Justice, in other words. That's what this is all about. Two words. Truth, and justice." He waited while the waitress put two bottles of beer on the table. Then: "Do you think Dennis is telling the truth about that night? You were *there*. What'd you think?"

Meeting his eyes squarely, the other man said, "I don't know. I honest to God don't know. I know Dennis was terribly upset, and wasn't really making a lot of sense. But that's got nothing to do with the truth. That's got to do with having your wife lying in a puddle of blood."

Bernhardt decided to make no response, decided to let the tension between them work for him. Then, shifting his ground, gently cajoling, he said, "Give them that time together, Al. That's all I'm asking. One, two hours. That's all."

Quietly, decisively, Martelli shook his head. "I can't help you, Alan. I'm sorry, but I can't."

"Why, for God's sake?" Feeling it all begin to slip away, he let the frustration show, let his voice rise: *"Why?"*

"When we're together, John's my responsibility. When I said I was a baby-sitter, I wasn't kidding. And sending him out through that gate with the chain cut—" Martelli spread his hands, shook his head. "No way."

"Well, then, how about if Janice comes *in*?" Urgently, he accented the last word, salesman-shrill. "What's wrong with that?"

Deliberately, Martelli reached for his beer, drank while he eyed Bernhardt over the rim of the glass. Then he smiled. "You're a funny guy, Alan. You come on real low-keyed. But you're stubborn, aren't you?"

Bernhardt made no reply. He'd come to the time for silence. Everything had been said; all the tricks had been tried. Only silence was left.

"Okay—" Amused at himself, Martelli drained his glass, signifying good-humored capitulation. "You got a deal. I gather you're familiar with the layout, the terrain."

Conscious of a rising swell of excitement he knew he must contain, Bernhardt ruefully smiled. "I've spent a lot of time the past week, hanging around that goddam winery."

"There's a dirt road that leads up to that gate you're talking about. It's hard to find, but it's there."

Bernhardt nodded. "I know it."

"The stream cuts across the northwest corner of the property, about a hundred yards from the gate. Right?"

"Right."

"There's a barn, just north of the stream."

"Yes."

"Okay—I'll see that John gets to that barn. Let's say about—" Calculating a time, he paused. "Let's say about four-thirty, I think that'd be good. Often as not, Dennis goes out, goes into Saint Stephen, between four and six. That's the time I usually reserve for John, work my schedule so that I can look after him, if Dennis decides to take off. Which, as I said, he does about half the time."

"So Janice and I'll meet you and John at the barn by four-thirty tomorrow. Is that what you're saying?"

"Or maybe I'll just send John, on his bike. I'll see how it goes. If Dennis is around, maybe I'll have to play that part by ear." As he spoke, Martelli looked at his watch. "I'd better go. I've got a couple of new field hands coming. I've got to pick them up at the bus station." He rose. "Thanks for the beer."

"Al—" Bernhardt rose with him, offered his hand. "Jesus, thank *you*. Whatever comes of this—whatever the truth turns out to be—it'll be thanks to you, believe me."

Shaking hands, Martelli's expression turned mischievous as he confided: "From the minute I met Dennis—two years ago, now—I figured him for a prick. And I've never seen anything to change my mind. I've got no idea

194

whether he murdered Connie, who I liked. But if he did do it, and if he goes to jail, well—I guess it could be worse, for John."

"Let's take it one thing at a time. Let's start with tomorrow, at four-thirty."

"Four-thirty. Deal."

6:30 P.M.

Bernhardt dropped his keys on the bureau and picked up Paula's note:

> *We're out wine tasting, should be back around 7 P.M. Janice wants to take us out to dinner. Fancy place. Smooches.*
>
> P.

He smiled, dropped the note on the bureau, began emptying his pockets. *Fancy place* meant a change from jeans to khakis, the best he could do.

As he turned toward the big picture window, about to draw the drapes before undressing and getting into the shower, he saw the driver's door of a white pickup truck swing open. The truck was parked three cars away from Bernhardt's Corolla; when he'd gotten out of the Corolla, Bernhardt had been aware of the driver's eyes on him. The unspoken message: between the two of them there was a connection, a secret yet to be revealed. The driver was about thirty-five. His face had been expressionless: flat, opaque eyes, a tight, hard mouth. There was a kind of fixed, frozen hostility in the face, as if the man might be standing for a police line-up.

Now the man was stepping out of the white pickup. He was about six feet, heavily muscled. Like Al Martelli, the stranger wore a tight T-shirt and jeans. Head slightly lowered, shoulders bunched, hands carried muscle-man-wide, the stranger was advancing purposefully, his flat eyes fixed on Bernhardt's door.

". . . *a guy who wears tight T-shirts with the cigarettes rolled in the sleeve, one of those,*" C.B. had said.

In seconds, the stranger would be at the door. Decision time. Fight or run.

Or talk, try to talk. Or don't answer the door: run, really.

Quickly, Bernhardt moved to the door, shot the bolt. Just as quickly, eyes on the window, he stepped back to stand beside the bed. Through the window he saw the stranger approaching. If he could see the stranger outside, could the stranger see him inside? Answer: perhaps not. The window was hung with white gauzy curtains. If he remained motionless, waited for the stranger's knock on the door, he probably wouldn't be seen.

Waiting—remaining motionless—it was the most difficult exercise of all.

Now, briefly, the stranger was framed in the window—and now gone, out of the frame.

Then, at the door, knocking: three sharp, hard knuckle-raps.

Yes, there was a connection, something between them. In the sound of the knocking, he could hear the connection. One word. Violence.

"Just a minute."

With his eyes on the window, Bernhardt knelt on the floor behind the bed, away from the window. Groping, he found the handles to the canvas satchel, his bag of tricks. He unzipped the bag, groped, finally found it: the sixteen-inch length of iron pipe wrapped in tape. He withdrew the pipe, shoved the satchel back under the bed.

Another series of knuckle-raps.

"Coming."

He put the pipe on the low bureau, took a folded newspaper from the wastebasket, covered the pipe with the newspaper. He adjusted the paper so that a few inches of the pipe projected. Then, sans the flee-or-fight adrenaline rush he needed, he stepped to the door, drew back the bolt, and swung the door open.

"Is your name Bernhardt?"

"That's right." He decided to smile. "Who're you?"

"My name is Carter. Bruce Carter."

"Okay." Bernhardt nodded. "What can I do for you?"

"You can lay off Theo Stark, for openers. Now. Right now, asshole."

Without looking, Bernhardt knew Carter's fists were clenched. For Carter, the adrenaline rush was working. For men like Carter, the rush was always working.

Bernhardt decided not to reply. Instead, he waited. How often, in forty-four years, had he been frightened? How badly?

Without the iron pipe hidden beneath the newspaper, how badly frightened?

"Well," Carter demanded, "aren't you going to say anything, asshole?"

"What I'm going to say," Bernhardt answered, "what I'm going to suggest, is that you leave. I don't know who you are, what your problem is, but I'd advise you to—"

"Hey. *Wait.*" Carter struck his shoulder with the heel of his hand, hard. It was a practiced bully-boy's blow, the ancient invitation to combat. Off balance, Bernhardt stumbled, caught himself, stepped back. As, yes, Carter came through the open doorway. Committed.

Bernhardt feinted a dodge to his left, away from the bureau. Carter's fist caught him high on the forehead, a glancing blow. He let himself fall away from the punch—toward the bureau. Following the feint, Carter dodged, crouched, recovered, swung his left hand, a practiced prizefighter's jab that struck Bernhardt's chest. Off balance, Bernhardt kicked for the kneecap, struck the thigh, a solid thud of shoe on flesh, sending Carter's next blow wide, too short. Bernhardt pivoted, brushed the newspaper aside, grasped the pipe. He crouched low, swung the pipe, a scythe.

Another sound: the crack of metal meeting bone. A sharp exhalation, an outraged obscenity as Carter's fury faded to round-eyed outrage, the injured innocent.

"Ah—*ah. Shit.*"

One arm, the left, dropped, grasped by the right hand now, supported. Furiously, Bernhardt drove his left fist into Carter's chest, sending him crashing into the wall beside the door.

"My arm—you broke my fucking arm."

"You're lucky it was your arm, you son of a bitch. How would you like it here, right across the face? Is that what you want? *Huh?*" He laid the pipe against Carter's face, threw his weight against the pipe, saw the pressure distort the nose, twist the lips, close one eye. He heard himself panting now: an animal, gasping for breath. Carter had done it, reduced him to this, a stranger to himself, panting into his victim's face.

"Fuck you." But it was a protest, not a challenge.

Bernhardt transferred the pipe to his left hand, grasped the T-shirt with his right hand. With his shoulder jammed into Carter's midsection, he felt the small convulsion, heard the sigh of pain. His victim, beaten. With the weapon, beaten. Tools separated men from animals, the wisdom of freshman anthropology.

"I want you to get in your fucking truck," Bernhardt breathed, "and I want you to get out of here. Take your broken arm, and go. And don't come back. Because if you do, you son of a bitch—*if you do*—I won't have this pipe in my hand. I'll have a gun." He brought up the pipe, jammed it under Carter's chin, hard. "Got it?"

No reply. No shadow of fear in Carter's eyes, only a dogged, street-fighter's defiance, an elemental hatred.

Not enough. No, not good enough.

"*Got it?*" With the adrenaline draining away, he gritted his own teeth against the other man's pain as he drove his shoulder against Carter's torso, saw the flash of agony in Carter's eyes.

Requiring that it continue, the barbarian's brutality, until Carter finally muttered, "Got it."

10:15 P.M.

"Give it to me, Alan." Sternly, Janice held out her hand, for the dinner check. "I absolutely insist."

Having moved to pick up the check in good faith, Bernhardt conceded. "Okay, thanks."

"Thanks, Janice." Paula reached across the table to pat her friend's arm. "This is a wonderful place." Appreciatively, Paula looked again at the restaurant's country-French decor, with its antiques and its continental-style staff, neither too servile nor too surly.

"Benedict County has a lot to recommend it," Janice said, sipping her coffee. "But it's pretty ingrown with beautiful people, I suspect."

"The beautiful people . . ." Bernhardt spoke thoughtfully. "Does Dennis qualify, I wonder?"

"I suppose he does." Janice spoke grimly. "The bastard." Then, unpredictably, she asked, "Are you in *Who's Who*, Alan?"

He guffawed. "Where the hell did that question come from?"

"*Are* you?"

"Not anymore," he answered. His face, he knew, would reveal too much, if he continued. But there was no choice, now. He must contrive a smile, and go on: "I was twenty-six when my play was produced off Broadway. *Who's Who* put me in their book right away, no sweat. They send you questionnaires, though, every year. So by the time I turned thirty—" He shrugged.

"*Alan*." Seated beside him in a booth, Paula moved closer, a spontaneous expression of pleasure, a teenager's wriggle. This was the Paula he loved most—the whimsical Paula. The girl, burbling up through the woman's persona. "Alan—*Who's Who*? At twenty-*six*?"

"The problem being," he answered, "that I'm forty-four now."

"You've written other plays, though," Janice said.

"Oh, yeah. But none've been produced. Writing for the stage—" He shook his head, sipped his tea. "The odds are very, very long that you'll get your play produced."

"What about screenwriting?" Janice asked.

"I tried a couple of screenplays, years ago. One of them was optioned, but that was the end of it."

Janice nodded, an expression of empathy. "Writing—painting—acting, they're all the same. You gamble your whole life—put all your chips in the pot, and hope to draw the right card. I painted for ten years before I sold anything."

"But now you're selling," Paula said. "You're a success."

"The past couple of years, yes. I just hope it continues."

Ruefully, Paula smiled. "We're in the same boat, all three of us. One way or the other, suffering for our art."

"Sometimes I think acting is the worst," Bernhardt said. "You get up on that stage, and you take off all your clothes. And half the time—more than half the time—they don't like what they see. If you paint—write—you've got the canvas or the typewriter to hide behind. But acting—" He shook his head.

The waitress returned with the credit card voucher. Janice signed the voucher, returned her wallet and pen to her purse, then spoke to Bernhardt: "So what about tomorrow? Do you think we can trust Al Martelli?"

"I don't think we have a choice. It's either that or try to get a court order for you to see John. And I've never heard of that happening. Fathers and mothers, yes. But aunts—" He shook his head.

"You'll be trespassing," Paula said. "What'll happen if Dennis finds you? You're going to cut his fence, for God's sake. And—" As a new thought took shape, her eyes clouded, her voice dropped. "He could even make a case for kidnapping, it seems to me."

"Trespassing, yes," Bernhardt said. "Not kidnapping, though. We won't be taking John off the property. Besides, kidnapping means you take someone against his will."

"Trespassing, then. Dennis could shoot you."

"Come on, Paula, don't dramatize. After dark, maybe, he could get away with shooting us, claiming he thought we were threatening him. But not in broad daylight. And not if we have John with us, he's not going to shoot us."

Considering the point, Paula looked thoughtfully away.

"Anyhow," Bernhardt said, "I'm going to be the lookout." He moved his cup and saucer away, took his table knife, and began drawing lines on the thick, white linen tablecloth. "That's the property, the vineyard. Forty acres. That's the county road, running along the east side. There's the entrance, and there's the driveway. It forks. The left-hand fork goes to the house—here, and the right fork goes to Al Martelli's house and the winery buildings—here. Those buildings are in a hollow. They can't be seen when you first drive into the entrance."

"They can be seen from the house, though," Janice offered. "At least, from the second floor."

"Thanks," Bernhardt said. "That's good to know." He continued drawing. "This is a small stream that cuts across the northwest corner of the property. And this—" He made a square. "This is the old barn. And this is a little dirt road that more or less parallels the property along the western perimeter. Here's the gate, here. So what'll happen—" He used the knife as a pointer. "At four o'clock tomorrow, Janice and I will drive to this point." He indicated the dirt road. "We'll conceal the car as best we can, and walk to the gate, here. It's secured by a padlock and chain. I'll cut the chain. Then we'll walk to the barn. It's about a hundred yards, I'd say. Maybe a little more. There're plenty of trees, so we can't be seen. If everything goes right, Martelli and John will meet us at the barn at four-thirty. Martelli'll go back to the winery. I'll walk to about here." He pointed. "There's a knoll there, with a few oaks. I'll be the lookout. If Price comes from his house, looking for John, I'll be able to warn you in time"— he looked at Janice—"so that we can get out through the gate, get to the car in plenty of time to get away."

"Will we take John?"

Bernhardt shook his head. "No. That'd look like kidnapping."

"Do you—" Janice hesitated, frowning. "Do you think there's any chance he'd shoot us for trespassing?"

"No," Bernhardt answered, "I don't. People don't get shot for cutting other people's fences. It just doesn't happen." He spoke sharply, emphatically. "He could certainly make a scene, no question. He probably *would* make a scene. He might take a swing at me. That's all, though. Believe me, that's all."

"But Dennis—" Framing the question, she broke off. Then: "There was something about him, on Sunday. He frightened me. He's—he's just holding on, it seems to me.

202

And that kind of a person, if he's scared, he can be dangerous, I think. Very dangerous."

Bernhardt reached across the table, touched her hand. "I agree, Janice," he said. "And I'm planning accordingly. Believe me."

"Do you—" Janice hesitated. Then, hesitantly, as if she dreaded the answer, she asked, "Do you have a gun—carry a gun?"

"Tomorrow," Bernhardt answered quietly, "I'll carry a gun."

11:15 P.M.

Bernhardt dropped his keys and change and billfold on the bureau beside the note Paula had left him, then stooped to pick up the newspaper. When he'd thrown the newspaper aside and grabbed the iron pipe, the newspaper had slipped behind a chair, forgotten when he'd straightened the furniture and put the bed back on its frame after the fight. He had been just about to examine the sagging drapery that hung askew between the door and the window when Paula had arrived, ready to wash up before they went to dinner. Pressed for time, she hadn't noticed the skewed drape. Now, though, as she sat on the bed and slipped off her shoes she asked, "What happened to the drape?" As she spoke, she circled the room with speculative eyes. Something, she knew, was wrong.

"While you were gone," Bernhardt answered, "some guy named Carter came by. He's a friend of Theo's, I gather. A real asshole."

"And?"

"We—ah—had a little shoving match."

Eyes quickening, she turned to face him fully. "A shoving match?" Her attention was sharp-focused now. "Alan—a *shoving* match?"

"I—ah—reasoned with him." He turned away, switched on the TV. "Let's see if there's any news."

WEDNESDAY
August 30

9:40 A.M.

Grunting, Fowler put the newspaper aside, levered himself forward in his chair, and pushed the button that connected the intercom to the speaker phone.

"Sheriff, DA Benson is on three."

"Okay." He pressed another button. "Hello?" He frowned, pressed a third button, to put the call on his handset. Then, remembering that Benson once remarked that speaker phones bothered him, Fowler switched back to the speaker phone.

"Hello?"

"Yeah, Howard. This is Cliff."

"Morning, Cliff. What's up?"

"You know, I'm sure, that Janice Hale and a friend, a woman, checked into the Starlight."

"The Hale woman is staying by herself. The other woman's staying with Bernhardt."

"With Bernhardt? In the same room?"

Fowler took a moment to savor the surprise in the other man's voice. Then: "That's right." He spoke laconically, allowing his satisfaction to come through. Benson, after all, was his natural antagonist: an aging college boy, a played-out, washed-out refugee from eastern big-city politics, one of life's losers. Without his law books and his seersucker suit, Benson would be taking orders, not giving them.

"So what's the story on this woman?" Benson was asking.

"Her name is Paula Brett. She's registered as staying with Hale. But she isn't. She comes from San Francisco."

"Bernhardt's girlfriend . . ."

Fowler made no reply. In the forties, he was reflecting, it would have been possible to charge Bernhardt and the Brett woman with cohabitating for immoral purposes. No more, though. Regrettably, no more.

"Have you talked to Janice Hale?" Benson asked.

"No."

There was a pause, then Benson said, "Howard, would you mind switching off that speaker phone?"

"No problem." He touched the switch. "Better?"

"Yes. Thanks."

"No problem."

"Do you—ah—intend to talk to Janice Hale?"

Fowler let his voice go flat as he said, "I don't see any need. Not now, at least. Seems to me, that'd get things stirred up, muddy the waters. Seems like our first priority should be to get Bernhardt and his lady friends back where they belong, so we can get on with everything."

In the silence that followed, Fowler could sense the other man's disagreement. Meaning that Benson was about to pull rank. It would begin, Fowler knew, with fake good humor, a slap on the back. Two good old boys just chewing the fat:

"Well, you know, Howard, I've been thinking about all this. I was able to check on Janice Hale, through the lawyer who's handling her sister's will, in San Francisco. And the thing is, this Hale family's got some pretty high-powered connections, down south. I guess you probably knew that, didn't you, Howard?"

"I knew that Constance Price was loaded, if that's what you mean."

Another long, uncomfortable silence. Then, no longer the good old boy, Benson said, "Listen, Howard, I think the time's come when we've got to take a new look at the Price homicide. We've been proceeding on the theory that it was a prowler, a transient, someone who's long gone. But, to my knowledge, at least, we don't have much in the way of proof—physical proof, or eye witnesses—that do much to back up that theory. In fact, when you come right down to it, we're really proceeding on the assumption that everything Dennis Price said is true. We've taken his account of events, and we've gone from there. We've done the same as concerns his kid. John. However—" For emphasis, Benson let a long, significant beat pass. "However, as I said, I think we've got to talk to Price again. And the boy, too. I think we've got to question them again. One reason I say this is that I happened to run into Al Martelli yesterday, in town. And just for the hell of it—we were having coffee, in fact—I asked him, right out, whether he believed it was a prowler that killed Constance Price. And he told me—right out—that he didn't think so. Now, I didn't want to take it any farther than that, with Al. I mean, it wasn't an official interrogation, and Al understood that. He also understood that I appreciated his leveling with me. So, just as we were leaving the coffee shop, he asked me if I'd talked to Bernhardt. And when I said that I had, then Al nodded, and he said that was good, because he thought Bernhardt was on the right track."

"I talked to Martelli about five days ago. He didn't seem to think so much of Bernhardt then."

"Only a fool won't change his mind once in a while, Howard. And Al's no fool."

Fowler made no response. Instead, he began to drum his fingers on the desk. From the tone of Benson's voice, and the cadence of his words, it was obvious that the fuss-budget DA was finally coming to the point: "So what I think we should do," Benson said, "is talk to Price again. And I also think we should talk to his boy. John." A short silence. Then: "I'll leave it up to you, Howard, how we handle it. Shall we both go out to the Price place, separate them, see what they say?"

Fowler drew a long, reluctant breath—followed by a short, rattling cough. He cleared his throat, coughed again, cleared his throat again. Finally: "I'll go first, see what they say. Then I'll get back to you."

"Will you do it today, Howard?" Unmistakably, it was a command, not a question.

"Why not?"

10 A.M.

In the bedroom, Paula heard Bernhardt talking on the telephone. She ran a comb through thick, dark hair, stepped back from the bathroom mirror, surveyed the effect. Was the gauzy blouse too sheer to wear without a sweater? She turned so that the sunlight from the frosted-glass window backlit her torso. Yes, the curve of her breast was clearly outlined, something she was unwilling to offer casual eyes. She would change to the cotton blouse she'd left hanging in the closet, the conservative alternative.

She dropped comb, lipstick, and eyebrow pencil into her toilet kit and put the kit beside Alan's on the bathroom counter. Was this a hint of domesticity to come: two toilet kits, side by side, along with Alan's electric shaver plugged into a wall socket, and her shower cap drying on the shower head? They'd both been through it before: the domestic experience, she with a husband she'd come to hate, Alan with his beloved Jennie, the young wife whose radiant memory would live forever in Alan's thoughts.

While she, Jennie's flesh-and-blood successor, grew older every day.

As she opened the bathroom door she saw Alan sitting on the bed, telephone to his ear, listening. Fulsomely aware of his eyes following her, she took off the sheer nylon blouse, put on the cotton one. As she worked at the buttons, she sat in the room's only armchair, propping her bare feet on the bed. Smiling, mischievously erotic, she began burrowing her toes beneath his thigh. Shifting the phone to his left hand, he began stroking her calf. Last night, this morning, and now—whenever they touched each other—the bells began to ring. Two months ago, weekending in Mendocino, their first time together in a motel, it had been the same: a feast of the senses. Motel madness, she'd called it.

He put down the telephone, began caressing her thigh as he leaned forward to kiss her.

Just as the telephone warbled.

Sighing, he lifted the phone with his left hand, shrugged broadly, withdrew his right hand from her thigh, reached for a notepad and pen—while he ruefully smiled.

"Hello?"

She watched his face as he listened. The first time she'd seen him, he'd introduced himself to the dozen-odd hopefuls who were trying out for *The Buried Child*, the play he would be directing. "Lincolnesque" was the phrase that had immediately come to mind. Alan's long, lean, gangling body, his deeply etched face with its hint of sadness, the somber dark eyes that saw so much and sometimes revealed so little—they were all part of his persona.

"So where're you now?" he was asking. Then, after a brief pause: "Do you think she made you, and was trying to lose you?" A short silence. "Well, let's decide on San Rafael. No, call my machine in the city, don't bother with this number." A final pause. "Okay. Good luck." He cradled the phone, shook his head, saying to her, "That was C.B. He lost Theo in Corte Madera."

"Hmmm . . ." She began to run one bare foot up his thigh.

"Behave, will you?" Suddenly he tickled the sole of her foot. Laughing, convulsed, she drew back her legs, twisting away. *"Don't."*

"Ticklish, eh?" He leered at her. "I'll remember that, when all else fails."

"What 'all else' did you have in mind?" She matched his leer.

"Right now, nothing. After all—" He glanced at his watch. "It's barely been two hours."

"Hmmm . . ."

"Besides, the meter's running. Would you feel right about it, billing your childhood friend for time we spent making love at ten o'clock in the morning?"

She laughed: almost a girlish giggle, pure, uncomplicated pleasure. "I guess that'd depend on whether you itemized the bill. Besides, you could always—"

The telephone came alive. Resigned, she suddenly rose, spoke quickly: "I'm going to find Janice, see if she wants coffee."

He nodded, lifted the phone. "Hello?"

"Alan, this is Frank."

"Frank—" He'd forgotten that, more than an hour ago, he'd called Frank Hastings to ask for a quick police check, up or down, on Theo Stark. Years ago, Bernhardt had worked with Ann Haywood, in little theater. Newly divorced from a venal society psychiatrist, keeping herself in circulation, Ann had volunteered to paint sets at the Howell. Later, she'd met Frank Hastings, who co-commanded the SFPD's Homicide Squad, along with the irascible Peter Friedman. Frequently, Bernhardt and Hastings exchanged favors, usually information from the police computers in exchange for small, not-quite-legal jobs the police needed done.

"No news," Hastings said. "As far as California is concerned, the lady's clean."

"I thought so."

"I know the building she lives in. Pretty fancy."

"Yeah . . ."

"Listen," Hastings said, "I've got to get off. How's Paula?"

"Fine. Ann?"

"She's great. We're going to take her two kids river rafting next week. My daughter—Claudia—is coming out from Detroit. She's going with us."

"Sounds wonderful."

"If you and Paula are interested, you could probably come along. There're several rafts, you know—eight-passenger rafts, I think. I can give you the name of the outfit that puts the trips together."

"I doubt that I can do it. Free-lancing, I'm discovering, doesn't let you plan very far ahead. Not if you're interested in cash flow."

"My father used to say that the only thing worse than working for yourself is working for someone else."

"Your father must've been a very wise man." As he said it, he heard Hastings cover the mouthpiece of his phone, and talk behind his hand.

Then: "Gotta go, Alan. See you soon. Come by for some of the city's coffee."

"Right. And thanks again." He cradled the telephone, rose, went to the window, adjusted the curtain so that he could look out across the parking lot to the pool. Three small children were playing in the wading pool. Two women, both in bathing suits, one slim, the other chunky, sat beside the pool, watching their children.

While, a few miles to the south, John might also be at play in the water of Price's swimming pool.

But John would be playing alone, watched over by a paid employee—or an indifferent father.

Was the tension building? Were the principals drawing together, entering the lists, ready for the final combat? Mixing the metaphor, was the third act about to begin?

Yes, ready or not, the curtain could be going up. Janice was about to commit herself. Price, at bay, could be turning dangerous. Al Martelli, the pivot character, was onstage, ready. Theo Stark, the mystery woman, was somewhere in the wings. All of it centering on John.

If he could write the play, could make fact follow fiction, how would he construct the plot? It would be rooted of course, in conflict, the essence of drama. A scene at the graveyard could be the opening, trite but serviceable. Janice and Dennis Price, the antagonists. John, the pint-size protagonist. Paula had been at the graveyard, too, a member of the chorus. The mourners—the shades, from Greek tragedy—defined the mood, silent messengers from beyond.

Enter the hero: Alan Bernhardt, the avenger. More conflict, more revelation. Enter Theo Stark, the mysterious presence. Fowler, a surly Rosencranz. Benson, lean and saturine, a stoop-shouldered Guildenstern. Martelli, the wayfarer—and, finally, C. B. Tate, the ghetto Falstaff.

Heighten the tension, draw the circle tighter—watch them begin to squirm, lash out at each other. While John, the innocent, held the key.

Yes, it was a workable plot, with a serviceable roster of characters, a good mix.

But how would it end?

What were the possibilities, the combinations? Would the ending be revelatory: finally the truth, dashing the evil-doers' nefarious designs?

Would the ending be upbeat: Dennis, the errant father, redeeming himself, embracing his son, with a fade-out to a swelling musical score?

A surprise ending, perhaps—a twist: Enter Fowler, with the murderer in chains, a stranger, glowering as he confessed?

Or another, more complicated twist: Martelli as Connie's lover, perhaps, the good guy unmasked as the murderer?

Or. . . ?

3:40 P.M.

Bernhardt drew the curtain, bolted the door, swung the canvas bag up on the luggage rack. Seated on the bed, Paula watched him as he stripped off his shirt and bent over the bag. Soon, she knew, Alan and Janice would leave for the winery. The contents of the bag, then, were essential to their mission, to their safety. Guns or communication equipment. Or both.

Conscious of a dull, nameless dread that translated into a constriction of the throat and chest, she watched him unzip the bag. The second time they'd made love, in the afterglow, lying side by side in her bed, pillow-talking, he'd told her how the black hit man had died. It had happened in the desert below Palm Springs. When he'd told her about it—how the black man had died, and why—it had been a confession, something he'd had to tell her.

He was remembering that night now, the night he'd told her what happened. She could see it in his face, read it in his eyes as, yes, he withdrew the revolver from the canvas bag. The revolver was holstered; only the walnut butt showed. Turning his attention to the pistol, he drew it from the holster and swung out the cylinder. She saw them clearly: the five brass cartridges, and the one empty chamber. Now he returned the cylinder to its locked position, careful to put the empty cylinder under the hammer. He returned the pistol to its leather holster, and slipped it down against the small of her back, above the butt. A large leather fob held the holster in position, an ingenious design.

Often, making love, she'd caressed him in the hollow of the spine above the buttocks, where the pistol now rested.

As he slipped on his shirt and began buttoning it, she saw him watching her. His face—the dark, Semitic face, the face that so often expressed so much—was now without expression. Watching her. Waiting.

"I—I hope you won't need that," she ventured.

"I won't need it. But it's nice to feel it there." Now, gravely, he was smiling. He turned back to the bag, took out a small cardboard box. He put the box on the corner of the bureau, and rezipped the bag. The box, she knew, contained cartridges for the revolver.

"It's time to go." He spoke quietly, seriously.

She rose, went to him, put her arms around his waist, careful not to touch the gun. "Be careful. Come back safe."

"I'm not going to war, you know. I'm just going to stand lookout for Janice."

"With a gun."

"Price can get pretty excited. People seem to calm down, I've noticed, when they see a gun." He slipped his arms around her waist, drew her close, felt her body's intimacy, his special privilege, arousing him. But now, smiling, he resolutely stepped back. "Got to go. We should be back in two, three hours. If C.B. shows up, tell him to try me on the car phone. If he doesn't get me—" He hesitated, deciding. Then: "Tell him to come here, to Saint Stephen, to the motel." As he spoke, he dropped his eyes to the canvas bag. Then he lifted the bag, shoved it under the bed, saying, "There's a sawed-off shotgun in that bag. It's very effective, but illegal as hell. If C.B. asks, tell him where it is, okay?" As he spoke, he took the box of cartridges from the corner of the bureau.

She swallowed. "Yes, I'll tell him."

"Okay—here I go." He stepped close, touched her cheek, smiled into her eyes. "Love you lots."

"Me too you."

It was a whimsical exchange that had evolved between them, one of their special secrets.

4:15 P.M.

As Fowler closed his office door and locked it, he heard the radio come to life: Andy Strauss, bored, was reporting from the field: "Base, this is Unit One."

Equally bored, Grace Perkins slid the microphone across the desk, keyed the microphone, pressed the "record" switch.

"Unit One, base. Go ahead."

"I'm on Route Sixteen at Baldwin's Lane, where some-one on the Crawford place reported there was a dead deer in the road."

"Roger." As she said it, Grace swiveled in her chair to face Fowler who stood before her desk. Reading Fowler's expression, she decided that the last call from Benson had cut it: beneath the glowing pink fat of his cherub's cheeks and jowls, Fowler was pissed. This time, really pissed. God, how she loved it, seeing Fowler pissed, and trying so hard not to show it.

"Well," Strauss was saying, "there's no deer here, dead or otherwise. And no blood, either."

"Roger." With a forefinger she lightly traced the line of her left eyebrow. On her next break, she would redo both eyebrows, and touch up the eyeshadow, too.

"Shall I ask around, see if someone carted it off and cut it up? Those Fisher twins, for instance?"

Grace looked at Fowler, who shrugged, then indiffer-ently nodded, what the hell.

"Give it an hour, maybe." Inquiringly, she looked at Fowler, who nodded again. "Yeah, Andy, an hour."

"Roger. Then I'll come in."

"Roger." She switched off the microphone, switched off the tape recorder, looked expectantly at Fowler.

"I'm going over to the city hall," Fowler said. "Then I'm going out to Brookside. I'm going to talk to Price. Then I'll go on home."

Pleasantly surprised, her little secret, she nodded. She might not have to wait for her break, then, to work on her eyes.

4:20 P.M.

"Goddammit." Bernhardt braced his legs wide, took a fresh grip on the bolt cutters, and strained. Nothing. The jaws of the bolt cutters had hardly marked the chain. Like the padlock's shank, the chain was hardened steel. The bolt cutters weren't powerful enough to do the job. He straightened, took a deep breath, looked at his watch. In minutes they were due at the barn. If he'd spent an extra fifty dollars, gotten a better pair of cutters . . .

Furiously shaking his head, Bernhardt moved to his right, began angrily snipping at the wire of the fence. Standing beside him, Janice said nothing.

"Can't be helped," he muttered. "Goddammit."

"I know . . ."

"I'm going to cut a flap, just big enough to squeeze through." As he spoke, he cut the final wire.

"Yes . . ."

"Here—" Bernhardt thrust the bolt cutters into a man-

218

zanita bush, concealed, then gripped the wire fencing with both hands and bent it back. "Get down. Way down."

As she crouched, then lowered herself until she was crawling on hands and knees, Janice chuckled. How many years had it been since she'd crawled in the dirt, conscious of the soil's warmth, aware of the earth's rich, loamy smell?

"Okay," Bernhardt said. "You're through."

She straightened, brushed off her hands and knees. Turning, she saw Bernhardt struggling with the wire. "Wait—" She stepped close to the fence, took hold of the wire. "Wait, you're caught." Carefully, she worked at his shirt. As the shirt came free, she saw the bare flesh of his back—and the revolver, tucked inside his jeans at the small of his back. Had this quiet, thoughtful man ever used his gun—ever shot anyone? Killed anyone? Would Paula know?

"All right—there." She watched him straighten, and look quickly around. They stood in a lightly forested grove of oak and fir trees bisected by a dirt road that led to the gate. Just ahead, through the trees, she saw the vineyard: row upon row of grapevines, following the rolling contours of the land. Beyond the low ridge of the vineyard to the left, she saw the cluster of winery buildings, only the roofs visible, metal and shingle. To the right she saw the roof of the main house, with its massive stone chimneys.

"The barn's this way." Bernhardt gestured to the left. "Let's stay close to the fence, in the trees." He spoke softly, cautiously. His eyes were in constant motion, traversing the terrain.

As she followed him over the hot, dry earth, she thought of the Hale family ranch in the San Ysidro Valley, behind Santa Barbara. The flora of San Ysidro was similar to Benedict County: scattered trees dotting the dry brown grass of the low, rolling hills. She could still hear her father's voice warning his two small daughters: "You must be careful of rattlesnakes in hot, dry country like this. You must always watch where you step."

Ahead, Bernhardt had stopped, and was standing in a half-crouch. Beyond him, through the trees, she saw the shape of a large barn, standing decrepit in the blaze of afternoon.

4:25 P.M.

"I'll tell you what—" Martelli reached for the fishing rod. "Why don't I take your stuff back to my house, and you can pick them up after you've talked to your Aunt Janice?"

"But we've only been fishing for a little while. And I almost had one," John protested. "I think they're biting."

"Yeah, well—" Firmly, Martelli took the rod, then began tying both rods to his mountain bike, and hanging the bait bag from his handlebars. "Well, we got a late start, because of that busted conveyor belt. We'll make it up, I promise. But for now—" He pointed to the path that led to the barn, just visible through the trees. "For now, you shouldn't keep your aunt waiting."

"But—" Lifting his own bike, just like Al's, only smaller, John looked toward the barn. How could he say it? How could he tell Al how he felt, when he'd learned that his Aunt Janice was here, and wanted to see him?

"She wants to talk to you," Al had said. "It's very important."

Very important . . .

At the funeral, he'd stood between his father and Aunt Janice. His Aunt Janice had held his hand. The touch of her hand and the shape of the coffin, one of them real, flesh on flesh, one of them a mystery from far beyond, together they had caused the whole world to shift around him. It was a lost, sudden ache, an emptiness that would never end.

And now, in this golden afternoon, with the sunlight slanting through these tall trees as he stood leaning against the bike, the world was about to shift again. He'd seen it in Al's eyes, heard it in Al's voice. Coming secretly, not to the house but here, to the barn, his aunt was connecting them.

He, his aunt, the image of his mother in his thoughts, they were all drawing together—all connecting, centering on him, on the memory of that night, and the terror at the top of the stairs.

4:35 P.M.

Standing with Martelli beside the dusty road that led past the barn and down to the winery, Bernhardt watched John push his mountain bike behind a screen of manzanita that grew close beside the barn. Janice stood in front of the big barn door that sagged decrepitly on its rusted hinges. Now the boy turned to the woman and gestured. Together, they tugged at the door, dragging it open enough to let them slip through. As Bernhardt watched, they pulled the door closed behind them.

"He likes her," Martelli said. "Otherwise, he wouldn't invite her inside. He's got some, you know, secret stuff in there. His fort, like that."

"Has he ever invited you inside?"

Martelli smiled. "Not really."

Remembering the forts of his childhood, most of them constructed of blankets and ropes stretched in the far corner of his mother's loft, Bernhardt returned the smile. Then: "Does John have many playmates?"

"As far as I know," Martelli answered, "he doesn't have any playmates, up here. Not—" He hesitated. "Not now, anyhow—not since his mother died. Before that, before she died, Connie would gather up some kids from down the road, to swim and roast hot dogs, things like that. And sometimes she invited kids from the city, on weekends."

"Does he go to school here?"

Martelli shook his head. "No. He goes to school in the city. It's a fancy private school."

"Well," Bernhardt said, "he probably has friends there, in the city."

"Yeah . . ."

Bernhardt thrust his hands in the pockets of his jeans, rose on his toes, took a deep breath and surrendered to the radiance of the late summer afternoon: the sound of the birds, the smell of the sun-baked earth, the oaks and the pines, the narrow dirt road that bordered the vineyards. It was a road made for a boy walking barefoot, whistling in the sunshine. Huckleberry Finn, Tom Sawyer—this was their kind of road, their kind of day.

"Do you think it'll work?" Martelli asked.

"John and Janice, you mean?"

"That—and everything." Martelli hesitated, then decided to say, "Price. The murder. Everything."

"Do you think Price did it?" Bernhardt asked.

"I doubt it. At least, I don't think he planned to do it. He just doesn't have the stones. But I think he knows more than he's telling. Maybe a lot more."

Still staring at the barn, Bernhardt spoke quietly, as a confidant might speak: "What about you, Al? What'd you know?"

Also staring at the barn, Martelli responded in kind: "I don't *know* anything. I'm just going on configuration, as the horse breeders say. And Price's configuration is the shits. He was a shitty husband, and he's a shitty father. And, what's more, he's scared. Very scared."

"Scared of what?"

Martelli shrugged, then shook his head, signifying that he couldn't—or wouldn't—answer the question.

Thoughtfully, Bernhardt stepped to the side of the road, picked a long stem of wild grass, put the stalk between his teeth. How long had it been, since he'd sucked at a stalk of green grass? For years—decades—his life had been shaped by the concrete slabs of Manhattan and the cityscape of San Francisco, two compelling urban imperatives. But where had the flowers gone, and the smell of the dirt?

"I think Price is seeing a tall blonde named Theo Stark," Bernhardt said. "She drives a white Toyota Supra."

Martelli nodded. "I told you about her."

"You didn't mention the Supra. Or her name, either."

"A white sports car, I said."

"That's right," Bernhardt said, remembering. "You did. Sorry."

"No problem." Martelli began checking the tension on the bungee cords that secured the two fishing rods to the mountain bike.

"Have you ever talked to John about what he saw the night his mother was killed?" Bernhardt asked.

"No," Martelli answered, "I haven't. Not directly, in so many words. But that's because he was so upset, at least at first. No way would I have asked him about that night. Then, later, it became—" He broke off, searching for the phrase. "It became habit, not to ask him what happened."

"You were present when Fowler interrogated him, that night."

Martelli shook his head. "I wasn't present during the interrogation. I was in the house. But they split us up, to question us. Fowler took John into the kitchen, with his father. Afterward, they asked me to take John down to my place, while they carried Connie out."

"I didn't know that."

His dark eyes clouded by painful memory, Martelli nodded heavily. "Yeah, that's what happened."

"He must've said something, then."

Martelli shook his head. "He said nothing. He was frozen. Absolutely frozen."

"How long was he there—at your house?"

"All night. He went to sleep on the couch, almost immediately. Price came down about three o'clock, I guess it was, after everyone had left. If John had still been awake, he would've taken him back to the house. But we decided to let John sleep."

Bernhardt nodded. "That was wise, probably." He looked at his watch. They'd been together for fifteen minutes, John and Janice. Almost certainly, more time would be required. "Listen—why don't you go back to the winery and wait for John? When they're finished talking, I'll send him down to you."

"You think that's best?" Martelli spoke speculatively, dubiously.

"If Price should be looking for John—if he's suspicious—you could head him off."

"How'd you get here? Into the vineyard?"

"I cut the fence," Bernhardt admitted. "I tried to cut the chain on the gate, but I couldn't do it. I'll try to wire the fence back together."

"Yeah . . ." Martelli frowned. Then, playing the part of the foreman: "I'll take care of it, later."

"Thanks. I'm sorry about the fence."

"No problem." Martelli nodded, swung one leg over his mountain bike, pushed off. "Good luck. And be careful."

"Thanks. I will."

4:40 P.M.

Before the telephone's first ring had ended, Price lifted the receiver. "Yes?"

"It's me."

"Jesus—" He lowered his voice, looked down the hallway to the kitchen, where Maria was cooking dinner. "Jesus, I've been trying to get you."

"There's another one, following me."

"*Another* one? Besides—" Instinctively, he lowered his voice. "Besides Bernhardt?"

"Yes. He's black. Very big, very black."

"Where are you?" As he spoke, he heard the sound of an engine, of tires on gravel. As the sounds registered, he felt his stomach contract. Someone was coming. Who? *Who?*

"I'm in Calistoga."

Calistoga—the next town up the valley, barely ten miles away. Why had she come so close? Was it wise for her to be so close? If she was followed, was it wise?

"Is he still following you?"

"I don't think so."

Outside, the engine-sound died. A car door slammed.

"Someone's here. Hold on, a minute." He laid the phone aside, went to a front window. A Benedict County Sheriff's white Ford sedan was parked behind his Porsche. Waddling as he walked, wearing a broad-brimmed felt hat with a gold insignia, Sheriff Fowler was rounding the rear of the white car. The car, too, had a gold insignia, painted on the door.

Quickly, Price stepped away from the window, crossed to the phone.

"Theo?"

"Yes."

"The sheriff's here. Fowler."

On the wooden steps, Fowler's steps began to thud: a slow, heavy cadence. Was this the sound of doom? Destiny, in a broad-brimmed hat?

"What's he want?"

"I don't know. Listen—" He looked at his watch. Now the sound of his footsteps placed Fowler on the porch. In moments the doorbell would chime. Price took the telephone's cradle from the hallway table and stepped around the corner, out of sight from the screened front door.

But was it wise, to hide?

Shouldn't he pretend to be casual, just talking to a friend, when the chimes began?

"Listen, you—you'd better call me in—" Once more, he looked at his watch. Quarter to five. "You'd better—why don't you call me in—"

The chimes sounded.

"Call me in a half hour, forty minutes. After Fowler's gone." Why was he whispering? *Why?*

"Okay." A moment's pause. Then: "Are you all right, Dennis?"

In the intersecting hallway, Maria was clumping toward the front door. She was displeased that her preparations for dinner were interrupted. He could hear it in the way she walked.

"I—call me back. Drive this way. Not here. Not to Saint Stephen. Near, though. Then call again." He broke the connection, cradled the telephone, drew a deep, unsteady breath. Should he step across the hall to the dining room, take a quick drink before he—

Voices. Fowler's voice. Maria's voice.

Too late.

He stepped quickly around the corner, replaced the phone on the table—feigned surprise: "Hello, Sheriff."

"Mr. Price—" Fowler nodded his boar's head, his multiple chins disappearing in rings of fat. Without being told, Maria turned away, clumped back to the kitchen. Extending his hand, Price met the sheriff at the archway to the living room. Fowler's grip was soft and flabby, disinterested.

"Come in." Price gestured to the living room. Grunting something unintelligible, Fowler entered the living room. Without hesitation, without being invited, he sat on the same leather couch John had been lying on the night Connie died.

Was it intentional, that Fowler chose the leather couch? Part of a carefully calculated plan, the opening shot in the law's campaign of harassment?

In minutes, he would know. Somehow it had all come down to minutes now.

Choosing a chair that faced the sheriff, he knew he must wait for the other man to speak first. It was essential, that he wait. The lord of the manor was his role. Fowler's role was the serf, tugging at his forelock.

"How's your harvest looking, Mr. Price? Up to last year's?"

Ah—first the pleasantries, of course, the disarming little questions. Fowler was a devious man, a shrewd man. A man easy to underestimate. Dangerously easy to underestimate.

"The chardonnay's looking good. It's too early to tell about the others."

"Everyone seems to be saying that. It's a chardonnay year by the looks of it."

Price nodded. "I'd say so. Yes."

Gravely, Fowler nodded. The gesture signaled the end of the pleasantries.

"I've just had a talk with Cliff Benson today, Mr. Price. He's the county attorney, you know."

Price nodded.

"And Cliff, Mr. Benson, seems to feel that we should be taking a fresh look at the circumstances surrounding your wife's death."

"A—" Suddenly his throat closed. Then: "A fresh look?"

"Right. Benson feels that maybe we missed something."

"I—I don't understand."

"Well—" Fowler waved a pudgy hand in a short, thick-armed arc. "Well, maybe 'missed something' isn't exactly the right wording. What I mean is—what Benson means— is that, with so much happening so fast, that night, we might've cut a few corners. Especially—" The sheriff

227

paused, for emphasis. "Especially, we're thinking of John. I mean, naturally, no one wanted to press the boy, under the circumstances. But when you think about it, with the exception of yourself, John was the only other person present in the house when the crime was committed—outside of the murderer, that is. So it's possible he might've seen something—heard something, whatever—that could open a few doors for us. Wouldn't you say so?"

"Well, I—I—" Helplessly, he shook his head. Then: "No, I wouldn't say so, as a matter of fact. I mean, John's already told you everything he knows. He told you that night, when Connie was—" He broke off, shook his head, lapsed into sudden silence.

"Well, that's true. Everything I asked him, he answered, no question." Fowler spoke equably. Fat-man-relaxed, hands folded across the tooled-leather equipment belt that girdled his enormous stomach, Fowler nodded genially, as if to encourage his victim. "But the thing is, you see, maybe there were some questions I didn't ask. See what I mean?"

"Well, that's—yes, I see what you mean. But the thing is—the problem is—I don't want John going back over that night. It's been two months now—more than two months. And John's just starting to come out of it, act like himself. So if you were to start questioning him again, well—" He spread his hands. "Well, it would be dangerous. Very dangerous, for John."

"Hmmm . . ." As if he were considering the point, Fowler frowned, nodded, squinted thoughtfully. Then: "Well, I certainly agree that it *could* be dangerous. So, of course, I'll be careful when I talk to him. But the thing is—the bottom line—I've got to talk to John. See, investigations like this—capital crimes, like this—it's pretty much required that we interrogate a witness at least twice. Like I said, at the crime scene, everyone's groping in the dark, you might say, trying to figure out what happened. But then, later, you've got to go back, pick up the pieces, sort things out. In fact—" Fowler raised one hand from his stomach, gesturing. "In fact, I'll be wanting to talk to you, too." The pursed lips curved in a fatuous smile. "You won't object, will you?"

"Well—well, no. Certainly not. It's just John, that I'm concerned about."

As if he sympathized, Fowler nodded. Then he shrugged, regretfully shaking his head. When he spoke, his eyes were cold, his voice was flat: "Sorry, Mr. Price, but it's got to be done. Orders." Fowler levered himself forward on the couch, ready to rise to his feet. "So if you'll just find John for me, and give us fifteen or twenty minutes together, we'll get it over and done with. That's the best way, you know. Just do it. And they're never as bad as you think they'll be, these things. After all, I'm not going to browbeat John, nothing like that. We'll just talk."

Just talk . . .

In court, the lawyers just talked.

The judge just talked, handing down the sentence.

Would the executioner just talk, as he dropped the cyanide capsules in the acid beneath the chair?

With great effort, he looked away from the other man's eyes: pig eyes, sunk deep in a pig's face.

Should he refuse permission?

The innocent talked willingly to the police. Only the guilty refused. The fifth amendment, refuge of scoundrels.

His eyes, he realized, were fixed on the window that looked out on the broad green lawn, circled by the white gravel driveway.

Less than an hour ago, John and Al had ridden down the driveway on their mountain bikes. Their fishing poles had been lashed to Martelli's bike. He stole a glance at his wristwatch. Almost five. At six o'clock, promptly, Maria served dinner. If Martelli took John for an outing, on the acreage or off, Martelli never failed to have John home by six. It was a house rule.

"I—" He began to shake his head. "I don't think John's here, right now. He—I haven't seen him for hours."

"Where'd he go?" It was an innocent question—elaborately, fatuously innocent. "You must know where he is—don't you?" The implication was clear: a "no" answer would admit to child neglect.

"Well, I—yes, of course, I know. I mean, I know he's on the property—the acreage. But I don't know where, exactly."

"Is someone with him?"

There it was: the make-or-break question, asked so softly, so guilelessly.

"I—yes, of course someone's with him. Al's with him, I think. Al Martelli. But they could be anywhere. They might even've gone into town."

"I thought you said John stayed on the property." The other man pretended elaborate puzzlement.

"Well, not if he's with Al. Then, of course, they go anywhere. But when he's not with Al, then he has to stay on the—" Suddenly his voice died. Had he made a mistake, contradicted himself? Fowler's face offered no clue, and a sharp, taut silence fell between them.

Finally Fowler spoke: "Seems like we should be looking for Al, then. Wouldn't you say?" Suddenly Fowler heaved himself to his feet. "I believe I'll have a look around, see if I can find them. That all right?" Moving forward, Fowler stood over him, a mountainous presence, implacable, a menace in wrinkled, sweat-stained khaki.

"Well, I—" Aware that his movements were uneven, out of phase, Price rose. They stood chest to chest, too close. "I'd better go with you."

"No need. I can find my way."

"No."

Fowler's brow furrowed. "No?" He said it gently, regretfully. "No?"

"I—I don't want you to talk to John unless I'm there. I'm sorry, but that—that's just the way it is."

"Ah—" Fowler nodded. Then he smiled. It was a strangely complacent smile. Cat-and-mouse content. "So that's the way it is . . ." He nodded. Then, very softly: "I see."

"It—it's just that—"

Fowler raised a hand. "I can see how it is, Mr. Price. No need to explain."

He made no reply. Should he order Fowler off the property, pretend to outraged innocence? Experimentally, he cleared his throat, lifted his chin, stiffened his back. "It's not a question of—"

"Tell you what," Fowler interrupted bruskly. "Why don't the two of you—you and John—come in to the office tomorrow morning. Say, ten o'clock. I'll talk to Benson in the meantime. How's that sound?"

"Ten o'clock—" He licked his lips. Then, anything to get rid of Fowler before Theo called again, he nodded. "Yes. Ten o'clock. That'll be fine. Just fine."

4:50 P.M.

"That's the haymow, up there—" John pointed. "The only way you can get up is that ladder—" He pointed again. "There used to be stairs, but they got rotten." As he spoke, he was aware that his aunt was turning to follow his gesture. For as long as he could remember, his Aunt Janice had always listened when he talked to her, and looked where he pointed. Once he'd heard his parents talking about his Aunt Janice. "It's a shame she hasn't married," his mother had said. "She was meant to have children."

Whenever he'd been with his mother and Aunt Janice,

he always felt the friendship, how much they liked each other, his mother and his aunt. "She raised me," his mother had said once. It had been a long time ago, maybe more than a year. They'd been on the beach at Santa Barbara, the three of them. Always, the beach at Santa Barbara had been one of his favorite places. His mother and his aunt had been talking about the things they'd done when they were his age. When she'd been seven, his mother had said, his Aunt Janice had been thirteen. And when his mother was ten, his aunt had been sixteen. That, they'd agreed, had been a big difference. Why, he'd asked, was the difference between ten and sixteen bigger than the difference between seven and thirteen? His aunt and his mother had smiled at each other, one of those special smiles between grown-ups, for special secrets.

"Boys," his mother had said. "Boys were the difference." And they'd laughed, the two of them, their eyes sparkling. Then his aunt had suddenly reached for him, and mussed up his hair. So he'd laughed too—the three of them, laughing.

"You want to go up in the hay?" he asked.

His aunt's eyes came alive: the same sparkle she'd shared with his mother so very long ago, the same grown-up twinkle. But then her eyes changed—and her smile, too.

"Sure," she said. "Great." But then, as she eyed the ladder, she said, "Do you think it'll hold me?"

He, too, turned toward the ladder. "I guesso."

"You guess so, eh?" The smile widened. "Well, let's see. You go first. In case I fall."

"Don't you want to?" he asked.

"Yes . . ." Now she was chuckling. "*Yes,* I *want* to. You know how girls are. We weren't trained to climb."

Aware that this was another grown-up joke, he strode to the ladder and began climbing. Moments later he stood on the platform, looking down.

What if the ladder broke? How would he get down, if it broke?

He was looking down at the top of his aunt's head. She was coming up the ladder slowly, cautiously, testing every step.

What if it *did* break?

What if his aunt fell, and hit her head, and was knocked out? What if she was bleeding, and would die, if he couldn't get help? Minutes would count. Seconds, even. So he would lower himself over the edge of the platform, and hang by his fingers. He would drop to the ground beside his aunt. Her eyelids would be fluttering, her lips quivering. "Get help," she would whisper. "It's a matter of life and death."

He would hug her, and tell her not to worry, leave everything to him. Then he would run outside, get on his bike, ride as fast as he could to Al's house. Al would be gone, but he'd know what to do. He'd dial 911, the way his mother had taught him. And pretty soon he'd hear the siren coming. There'd be a white ambulance, with red lights flashing, and two men wearing uniforms, with badges. They'd—

Her head was even with the platform, then her shoulders. He backed away, giving her room to climb up on the platform.

"Wow—" She sat up, breathing deeply. She was still smiling, this smile especially for him, their secret. "*Wow.* I think I'll start working out." Now she looked behind him, at the hay. As she did, her smile changed, this time to something private. She spoke softly, her eyes far away. "My God, real hay." A pause, also something very private. Then, quietly: "When I was a little girl—ten years old, maybe—we had a farm in the Santa Ynez valley. It was wonderful, that farm. I showed it to you, once. Do you remember? It was two years ago, maybe, that I showed it to you."

"Yes," he answered. "I remember. You told me you had horses, when your folks had the farm."

Slowly, she nodded. "That we did. Four horses. I was always a little afraid of them, to tell the truth."

"We've got two horses, here. Sometimes we go riding, me and Al—"

"You and Al—" She said it as if it meant something special. As she spoke, she turned to look at him. Like the smile, this look was just for him.

He decided to say, "Sometimes I'm a little afraid of horses, too."

She nodded. Now her smile changed again, as if she was sad. Slowly, she stretched out her hand, touched his hair. Then she gently mussed his hair, just like she'd done at the beach, so long ago. Then, still sitting, legs propped up, arms circling her knees, she turned to face him squarely. She spoke gently. Serious now, but still gently:

"Speaking of being afraid, John—" She drew a deep, final breath. "I have to ask you about the—the night your mother died." A pause, while her eyes held him. Then: "Do you understand?"

"I—" He swallowed. What could he say? What was there, to say?

"It—it's necessary, that I ask you about that night. That's why I arranged this—why I wanted to see you, today. That's why I *had* to see you, alone. Because—well—because I have to know what happened, that night. Do you understand?"

He realized that he was nodding. But what could he say? If he told her—and if she told the police, the sheriff—then what would happen to him? His mother was in heaven, and would never come back to him. If they came and took his father away, then he would be all alone.

"I know it's hard," Aunt Janice was saying. They were sitting close together now, and their voices were low. He couldn't look at her, not now.

"It's hard to tell the truth, sometimes. But—" Now she

was frowning, trying to find the right words. "But there's the law, you see. Someone murdered your mother. And if they don't find the person—the murderer—if the police don't find out who did it, then . . ." She was no longer speaking. Venturing to look at her face, he saw the sadness. It was the same sadness he felt.

"Then we'll never know," she said. "Now, when you're only seven, it might not seem so terrible, that we don't know. But—" Once more, searching for the words, she broke off. Then: "It's justice, you see. I know it's just a word to you, John. But it—it means everything. It really does."

Justice . . .

Had he ever heard the word before? He couldn't remember.

5 P.M.

Waiting for someone to answer, Price drummed the table: sharp, rhythmic finger-taps, a tattoo of ragged anger.

"Brookside Winery."

"Fernando. Where's Al?"

"Don' know, Mr. Price. He and John, they left on their bikes."

"How long ago?"

"Half hour, maybe, like that. I don' know, for sure."

"Which way did they go, on their bikes?"

"Up the hill, I think."

"A half hour ago, you say?"

"Som'th'n' like that, yeah. 'Bout that."

"Up the hill, you say?"

"Yeah. Toward the creek, maybe."

"Why do you say that?"

"'Cause they got their fishing poles."

The creek . . .

If Fowler found out—if Fowler somehow got to them, drove to the west fence, called to them, blew his horn— then it was all over. The inheritance—everything—gone.

"Has Fowler—the sheriff—have you seen him today?"

"The sheriff? Here?"

Fighting a sudden surge of rage, he nodded. "Yes. Here. Sheriff Fowler. Just a little while ago, he was here. Did you see him?"

"No—no sheriff."

They'd left a half hour ago, John and Al. Four-thirty. They would return by six, for dinner. It was Maria's one inflexible rule.

"All right. When you see Al, tell him to call me, or come up here. And John, too. If you see John, tell him to come right home. Understand?"

"Yeah, I un'erstan'."

"It's important. You understand?"

"Yeah. Right."

As he cradled the phone it came instantly alive: a nerve-shattering electronic shriek. Was it Theo?

"Yes—hello."

"It's me."

Yes—Theo. *Theo.*

"Where are you?"

"I'm just outside of Saint Stephen. In a phone booth."

"Is he—are you being followed?"

"I don't think so."

"I've got to talk to you. It's important. It's very important."

"Now?"

"As soon as we can do it."

"What's happened?"

"We've got to decide where to meet. I'll tell you about it then." He broke off, considered the possibilities, the risks.

He couldn't leave the winery, not with John missing, and Fowler on the prowl. But he had to leave, to see Theo. If she came to the winery, they would be seen together.

But he must see her. Whatever happened, he must see her.

"Drive toward the winery. Park on the county road. Make it a mile from here, toward Saint Stephen. Stay in the car. Wait for me. Understand?"

"Sure. But I don't—"

"Do it," he broke in. "Just *do* it, goddammit."

The outburst amused her; he could hear it in her voice, the casual contempt. "Sure. See you soon." The line clicked dead.

5:10 P.M.

As she began to pull the swimsuit up over her breasts, the phone warbled. She tugged harder, squirmed, succeeded—covering herself on the phone's third ring.

"Yes?"

"Yeah, I'm—ah—looking for Alan Bernhardt. Is he there?"

"No, not at the moment. I can take a message, though."

"Ah—" It was a knowing monosyllable. Then: "When do you expect him back?"

"Who is this, please?"

"It's C. B. Tate. Are you Paula?"

"Yes. Hi. Alan talks about you."

"Well, I can certainly return the compliment. We're both of us Bernhardt alumni, did he tell you that?"

"Bernhardt alumni?"

"He directed both of us."

"Yes, *The Emperor Jones*. Right?"

"Right." The single word said it all, confessing to the particular addiction they both shared: the sound of applause from the darkness beyond the footlights.

"Alan said you're very good. Very convincing."

"He says the same about you, Paula—and more."

"I'm glad to hear it."

They shared a moment of companionable silence before Tate changed the mood: "So what's happening there? Anything?"

"Alan told me to ask you—have you still got Theo Stark under surveillance?"

"Sadly, the answer is 'no.'"

"Well, Alan says for you to come here, to the motel. The winery is only a few miles from here. That's where Alan is now."

"Is he trying to wind this thing up, today? Is that the way it's looking?"

"I don't know . . ." She hesitated. Then: "He was carrying a gun, though, when he left."

"A gun, eh?"

"Yes."

A short, meaningful pause. "Okay. I'll see you in maybe a half hour, something like that."

"Good."

5:20 P.M.

As he climbed into the pickup Price saw a figure on a bicycle just topping the ridge to the west and pedaling down the slope to the winery buildings. A man. Martelli.

Price started the truck's engine, put the transmission in

gear, drove around the house's circular driveway and headed down to the winery. He stopped in the shade of a giant oak tree that grew beside the fermenting shed and stepped out of the truck. As Martelli came closer, coasting down the gentle incline, Price could easily read the uneasiness in the other man's dark Italian face.

"Where's John?"

"He'll be along in a few minutes. We were fishing. He wanted to stay and catch some crawdads."

"Why'd you leave him?"

"I—ah—" Martelli gestured to the nearby building: "There's a couple of calls I have to make."

"Business calls?"

Martelli shrugged. "One business, one personal."

He drew a deep, ragged breath. Self-control was important now. Mastery. He was, after all, the employer, the superior. "They must be very important calls, Al. You've never left John before."

Standing with his bike resting against his thigh, wearing his habitual blue jeans and white T-shirt, Martelli made no reply. His face revealed nothing—and everything. His body language, as always, suggested an independence that bordered on insolence. Between them, the silence lengthened—and tightened.

It was necessary, therefore, to assert himself, necessary to dominate: "I think there's more to it than that."

"I don't know what you mean." Arms defiantly folded across a muscular chest, thighs bulging beneath tight jeans, dark eyes smoldering, Martelli was the instant's reincarnation of the sullen peasant, silently confronting his angry master.

Speaking slowly, deliberately provocative, Price said, "I mean that I don't think John is in the woods by himself. I don't think you left him alone."

"I don't remember ever promising that I wouldn't leave him alone."

"*Did* you leave him alone?"

"Look—don't sweat it. He'll show up. Give it a half hour or so."

"I asked you whether John is alone."

Holding his pose, arms still crossed, eyes still flat, Martelli made no response.

"Goddammit—" Back bowed, chin outthrust, Price took a half step forward. "Goddammit, I asked you a question. *Tell* me."

Sardonic amusement twitched at the corners of Martelli's mouth. He let a long, defiant beat pass. Then, very quietly: "You'd get further, you know, if you'd say 'please.'"

"You—you—" Price half-raised his hand. "You'll be sorry, if you don't tell me." But his voice had suddenly cracked, an ineffectual falsetto now. In the dark peasant eyes, he saw a glint of derision. If he had a gun—a weapon—he would make Martelli falter, give ground.

A gun—yes.

The thought changed the balance, let him step back, lower his voice, make a fresh start: "It's Bernhardt, isn't it? That fucking private eye. *Isn't it?*"

Half-smiling, enjoying himself now, Martelli shrugged. Taunting him. Daring him to act, do something decisive.

"You're fired, Martelli. I want you out of here. Now. Right now."

The reaction was a sharper twist of the mouth, a more contemptuous quirk around the eyes. "You're really worried, aren't you, Dennis? This Bernhardt, he really jangles your bells. Doesn't he?"

"Don't—don't call me 'Dennis.'"

"Oh—Jeez—sorry."

"I—want—you—to—tell—me, has Bernhardt got John? Or Janice? Has Janice got him?"

"No comment."

But the answer was there: that dark, Italian face, peasant-cunning. Taunting him. Telling him that, yes, Bernhardt had John.

"All right—" Hardly aware that he was doing it, he swung his arm toward the driveway's two stone pillars and the county road beyond. "Then get out of here. Now. Right now. This—this is kidnapping. *Kidnapping*, do you understand? And you—you're a part of it. You're an—an accessory." The arm swung toward the house. His fingers, he saw, were shaking. *Shaking*. "I'm going to go up to the house, and I'm going to get my rifle. And if I were you, goddam you, I'd be gone before I get back here. Because if you're not gone—" His voice choked by sudden fury, uncontrolled, he was forced to break off.

Now Martelli's grin turned ugly. Imitating his antagonist's gesture, Martelli half-turned away as he pointed toward his own house. "I'm not leaving, Dennis. At least, not now. Not this minute—and not this hour, either. But I *will* go down and start packing. Gladly. And I'll leave. I'll pack up my truck, and I'll leave. But between now and then, if you really do get that rifle, I wouldn't advise you to point it in my direction. Not unless you're ready to pull the trigger. Do you understand, you sad-ass bastard?"

As if his body was in control, no longer his will, Price realized that he had turned away. He was running toward his house. In his thoughts, only the gun was real—the rifle, and the power it held for him.

5:30 P.M.

He jerked the bolt open, checked the chamber. Yes, it was empty. He threw the rifle on the bed, went to the closet, reached high on the shelf for the box of cartridges. Connie had always insisted that the cartridges were kept high, out of John's reach.

He picked up the rifle, closed the bolt, released the clip, began loading it.

Big game . . .

He jammed the clip home, automatically set the safety, even though the chamber was empty. As he turned away from the bed he caught a glimpse of himself in the mirror above the bureau: the hunter, the avenger.

But where was the anger, the rage?

"Unless you're ready to pull the trigger," Martelli had said.

It would be a mistake, to challenge Martelli. Italians were hot-tempered, heedless of consequences. And Bernhardt was the real enemy, therefore the real target. If Bernhardt had John, and was asking questions . . .

He opened the bureau drawer, thrust the half-full box of cartridges inside, slid the drawer shut. Then, reconsidering, he opened the drawer, shook a handful of cartridges into his hand, thrust the cartridges in his pocket.

Bernhardt was a trespasser.

A trespasser—and a kidnapper.

Fair game. Fair, legal game. Big game, for a big game rifle.

He slammed the drawer shut again, took the rifle, strode down the second-floor hallway toward the front staircase. Arms laden with folded linens, Maria was below him on the staircase. Lifting her face, she saw his face— saw the rifle.

"Mr. Price—what?" Her broad, Inca face registered slow, phlegmatic alarm. Another brown face, another enemy. Savages, all of them. Peasants, and savages.

"Somebody's got John," he said, brushing past her. "A kidnapper. He's got John."

"Aiiie!" She blinked, then began speaking wild, anguished Spanish. As he reached the front door, he heard "Sheriff," spoken in broken English. He whirled. "No. No sheriff. Comprende? *No sheriff.*"

She frowned, shrugged, nodded.

"No sheriff," he repeated, his voice rising. *"Sí?"*

*"Sí—*yes." She nodded again.

He banged open the screen door, walked to the waiting pickup. From here, he could only see the roof of Martelli's cottage.

Would Martelli call the sheriff, report being threatened? No, not Martelli. Not the stud, the macho ladies' man. Martelli would—

Ladies' man

Theo, waiting for him on the county road. By now, certainly, waiting for him. How could he have forgotten?

5:35 P.M.

It had been a mistake, this meeting—a grotesque miscalculation. Wishful thinking, feeding on itself. Loneliness and loss, compounded. A woman alone, that terrible phrase—a childless woman, even worse. Yet both described her, defined her. And in her desperation, counting out the hours and the days and the years that were left in her life without Connie, she'd fixed on John, her one last hope. If she had John, the one person left in all the world that connected her to Connie, and therefore to her parents, then she would be whole again. She and John, they would heal each other.

It had seemed so simple.

Once she'd convinced herself of Dennis's guilt, it had all seemed so simple—so checkbook-simple. She would hire a private detective; expense was no object. She would talk to John, reason with John, get the truth from John. With Bernhardt, she would go to Dennis, dictate terms. If Dennis would leave—just leave—and if he would let John come to her, then she wouldn't tell the authorities what she'd learned from John, wouldn't demand that they prosecute Dennis. He could have the money. Give her John, and he could have the inheritance.

That had been the plan.

But they'd been talking for more than an hour, now, she and John. Whenever they talked about times past, the good memories shared, he'd opened up, offered her warmth, and need. But when she mentioned Connie, his face began to cloud.

And when she asked him about Dennis, about the night of June sixteenth, his face closed, the words stopped, the trust turned to wariness.

If only she'd been more careful. If only she'd first gained his confidence, before she'd plunged into the death of his mother. If only she'd been gentler.

Finally, when she'd realized that her questions were causing him pain, she'd broken it off. She'd pretended interest in the old barn, asked him to show her around. Instantly, he'd risen to his feet, asked her if she'd like to see a room he'd discovered, his special secret. Then, gingerly, she'd followed him down the ladder. He'd shown her "the truck," the rusted-out hulk where they now sat side by side behind a windshield with no glass, she on the passenger side, John at the big wood-rimmed steering wheel. The truck, she calculated, must have been built soon after the turn of the century. Its cracked floorboards were wood, its pedals were of ancient design, the faces of its instruments were beveled glass, large and round, with cursive numerals. Its—

"—dinner with us?" John was asking.

"Wh—" She blinked, focused on him. "What'd you say?"

"I said are you going to have dinner with us tonight?"

Momentarily nonplussed, she could only stare at him. Then, as realization dawned, she could only shake her head. God help him, he didn't know. He simply didn't know.

Or maybe God *was* helping him. Shielding him. Protecting him from the madness of the adult world that would give him no peace.

5:40 P.M.

"For Christ's sake—" Theo banged her hand on the steering wheel. "Slow down, will you? Tell me what you know, not what you think. Tell me—"

Heedless of the contempt he saw so clearly in her face, he broke in: "What I know is that Martelli's fucking us over, that's what I know. And I know—I'm absolutely certain—that Bernhardt's behind it. Bernhardt and Janice."

"But what about John? Are you sure they've got him? Absolutely sure?"

"Al never leaves John alone. *Never.* So that means John's with someone. If it were a friend—if it were innocent—Al would tell me. So it's got to be Bernhardt. They've gotten to Al, probably bribed him, the bastard."

"If they've taken John somewhere—anywhere—then it's kidnapping. You could have them arrested."

"Arrested—" Sharply, he shook his head. "Who would arrest them? Fowler? Is that what you want, for Fowler to find John? Jesus, Theo, use your head."

"We've got to find John. Then you've got to take him away. Now. Right now." As she spoke, she gripped his forearm, hard. Her eyes were on fire. The softness was gone from her face. It was a stranger's face—a stranger's voice. And a stranger's grip on his arm. Suddenly a hostile stranger.

"But I—if I do that, take John, run, they'll know I've got something to hide. They'll *know* it." His voice, he knew, was rising, thinning.

"Listen, Dennis—" The grip tightened, compelling him to meet her gaze. Ominously, her voice lowered: "You keep talking about what'll happen to you. And I keep telling you that it's us—you and me. Both of us."

"It's you, really." His voice was hardly more than a whisper. His eyes fell away as he heard himself say, "You were coked out. You picked up the tongs. You hit her."

She waited until he'd forced himself to raise his eyes to hers. Then, very softly, she said, "But only we know that, Dennis." She let a beat pass before she said, "That makes this a partnership. What happened that night—the risk, the money—it's all fifty-fifty. Especially—" She released his arm, measured her last words with great deliberation: "Especially the money. Whatever you get, we split. And then—" She smiled. It was a complex smile, an inscrutable signal. Now she raised her hand, touched his cheek. It was a grim evocation of other gestures, other places, other times, together. "And then we live happily ever after." She said it as if she might be telling a joke. An intricate, obscene joke.

She let another beat pass, once more waiting for him to meet her eyes. Then she pointed to his pickup, parked in front of them on the shoulder of the road. The rifle was visible in the rack behind the driver's seat. "Can you shoot that?"

"Yes—sure."

"Okay—" She nodded, reached beneath the driver's seat, withdrew a revolver.

"Jesus—careful, Theo."

The casual contempt came back in her voice as she said, "I shot skeet with my second husband. He never won any trophies—but I did." She thrust the revolver in her saddle-leather shoulder bag, took the keys from the Supra's ignition, and swung open the door. "Come on. Let's find John."

5:45 P.M.

"Is it six o'clock yet?" John asked. "I have to be home for dinner at six."

Shifting to avoid the broken springs in the derelict truck's cracked leather seat, Janice looked at her watch. "It's a quarter to six." She spoke quietly, regretfully. According to her brave plan, John would have come to the motel with them. She and Bernhardt and Paula would protect him—the three of them and the man called C.B. The sheriff would come, and the DA, Benson. There would be a confrontation, revelations, a resolution. The law would call Dennis to account. Home free.

She pushed at the rusted door, which swung out with a squeal of protest. Using the high, old-fashioned running boards, they climbed down on opposite sides of the truck, met in front.

"Will you come visit me, John? Will you ask your father to let you come for a weekend. Soon?"

"Maybe you should ask him. You know—" The boy shrugged. The gesture evoked the helplessness of the very young, faced with the mysteries of the adult world.

"You *want* to come, though, don't you?"

Gravely, he nodded. "Yes." He nodded again, for emphasis. *"Oh, yes."*

5:47 P.M.

As the pickup drew even with the house and dipped down the incline to the winery, Theo pointed ahead. "Look."

Cradling a rifle in the crook of his right arm, Martelli stood beside the driveway. As they closed the distance, Martelli stepped into the driveway, raised his right hand, signaled them to stop.

"Goddammit." Price depressed the brake pedal, brought the truck to a stop, let the engine idle.

"What's he want?" Theo spoke softly.

"I don't know."

"Is he trouble?"

"He can be trouble. He's a hothead."

Still cradling the rifle, Martelli was walking to the truck on the driver's side. With his eyes fixed on the foreman, Price was aware of movement beside him. Glancing down, he saw a manicured hand slipping the revolver from the saddle-leather shoulder bag.

"Jesus, put that away."

"Shut up." With her eyes on Martelli, she put the shoulder bag on the seat between them, then tucked the revolver behind her right thigh, concealed.

Turning to Martelli, now at the open driver's window, rifle still cradled, muzzle down, Price spoke curtly: "Well?"

"You forgot to mention my pay," Martelli said. "There's two weeks. Plus, I figure, a month's severance pay. That's fair, I'd say, considering the circumstances." He smiled that slow, insolent smile.

"Leave an address. I'll send it to you. I'm in a hurry."

"Oh, yeah? In a hurry to do what? Find John, and Bernhardt? Is that why you're so uptight—why you've got the rifle? What're you hunting, Dennis? People? Private detectives? Me, maybe?" As he spoke, Martelli came closer, put one hand on the windowsill, looked inside the truck's cab, at Theo. "Hello, there—" Now the taunting, troublemaker's smile twisted into a mocking leer. "I've seen you, a couple of times. But we've never met. It's always dark, whenever I've seen you. I'm Al Martelli. I'm being fired."

"Take your hand away. Stand back." Price jammed the transmission in gear, revved the engine. Quickly, deftly, Martelli reached behind the steering wheel, switched off the engine, took the keys.

"*Hey*." Futilely, he grabbed for the keys, which Martelli held out of reach. "*Give* me those, you bastard."

"First the check, Dennis. Then the keys." Quickly, Martelli stepped back, pocketed the keys, used both hands to half raise the rifle. It was a lever-action 30-30 Winchester, the traditional Western saddle gun. The hammer, Price saw, was lowered, uncocked. He put his shoulder to the door, swung it open. Enraged, he threw himself blindly out of the truck as Martelli fell back, raised the rifle higher.

"Hold it, asshole." Martelli brought the rifle's muzzle up, swung it toward Price. "Don't—"

The crash of the shot was shattering: a numbing cataclysm of sound and fury, the world rocked on its hinges, total terror. Physically staggered, ears ringing, Price turned toward Theo. She held the revolver steady, still aimed at Martelli.

"Ah—Jesus—" Still gripping the rifle, Martelli was on his knees. The rifle was pointed at the truck. Not aimed, but pointed. The white T-shirt, Martelli's macho trademark, was stained with bright red blood. "Jesus—" Blinking, diligently frowning, Martelli began drawing back the hammer of the 30-30, using both hands. Price grabbed for

249

the rifle barrel, jerked it savagely, felt it come free. The rifle was at half cock. Carefully, he lowered the hammer.

"Ah—" Shaking his head now, eyes unfocused, Martelli was toppling slowly to his left. He lay in the dusty road, in the fetal position. The bloodstain on the T-shirt was spreading: larger than a small bouquet of red roses.

"My God—" Price turned to face the woman with the gun. Theo, turned savage. "You—you shot him."

"If I hadn't shot him, he'd've shot you. Come on—" With the revolver, she beckoned. "Get in. Bring his rifle."

"But we—we can't leave him. We can't—" From the direction of the house, he heard a shout. Maria's voice, wailing. Spanish words. Meaningless.

"She can take care of him. Tell her to call a doctor. Not the sheriff. A doctor."

"But we can't—but you—" Helplessly, he shook his head. "But he could die."

"If he'd pulled the trigger, you would've died. You, not him." Her voice was very low, very steady. Her eyes were stone cold.

5:55 P.M.

Frowning, Bernhardt checked his watch. Martelli had told him that John must be on his bike, headed home, by ten minutes to six. He'd relayed the instructions to Janice, part of the deal. Had she lost track of time? Was John telling her so much, revealing so much, that she couldn't bear to cut him off? Was this, finally, their break? Would John tell enough to—

A shot, from the direction of the winery, and the house. One shot, then silence.

A shot?

Or an explosion, a backfire?

No, not a backfire. A shot. Assume it was a shot, assume the shot meant danger.

Bernhardt turned to face the sound, listening, scanning the road and the trees, and was aware of movement to his left. Yes, it was the barn door opening, dragging in the soft, sun-baked earth. John came first, then Janice. Together, they pushed the door closed as Bernhardt strode toward them. The glance that Bernhardt and Janice exchanged was explicit: concerning the sudden sound of the shot they would say nothing, because of John.

But as Bernhardt came closer John said, "That was someone shooting, wasn't it?"

Bernhardt nodded. "I think so, yes." Then: "Is there much shooting around here?"

"Sometimes they hunt doves. Last time, I went with my dad. He shot three."

Nodding, Bernhardt exchanged another look with Janice, a silent query: Had she succeeded? Reluctantly, she shook her head. Nothing, then, had been accomplished. A hole cut in the fence, a trespasser's risk, and now a shot— all meaningless now, everything risked, nothing gained.

As John turned toward his bike, parked behind a large bush growing close beside the barn, he said, "I'd better go. Maria'll be mad if—"

"Wait—" Voice low, eyes caution-bright, Janice raised her hand. "Wait. Listen. What's that?"

As, from the direction that the dirt road took, winding down to the winery, they heard the sound of an engine.

First a shot, then the sound of a car coming.

Coincidence?

More than coincidence?

"Listen—" Bernhardt gestured to the barn door. "Why don't the two of you get back inside there, for a minute. Just to—" Grasping the door, pulling it open, he let the rest go unsaid.

251

"Come on, John—" Voice cautiously lowered, yet unwilling to reveal the uneasiness she must feel, Janice took John's hand, stepped through the open door, drew the boy inside. Quickly, Bernhardt pushed the door closed. The sound of the engine was louder now, closer. Should he hide? Hold his ground, the protector? Should he bluff? In seconds, he must decide.

6 P.M.

Price braked the pickup to a stop and pointed to a footpath that led to a line of thick-growing trees. "That goes down to the creek. That's probably where they went."

"How far is the creek?"

"Three, four hundred feet. It's that line of sycamores."

"Are we going to take a look?" As she spoke, Theo drew the revolver from her shoulder bag.

"You don't need that."

"If I didn't have it"—she raised the revolver—"your keys would still be in Martelli's pocket." Her voice was flat, her eyes cold. "And you'd be bleeding, not him."

"He was bluffing. He wouldn't've shot me."

"He started pointing guns, not me."

"If he dies . . ."

"He threatened you with a gun, for God's sake. And I shot him. Not you. Me. *Jesus*." The anger in her voice was palpable: blood lust, distilled.

He turned away, released the parking brake, pointed toward a rise beside the stream. "There's a clearing up there."

Traveling slowly in first gear, they rounded a bend. Ahead, on the right, he saw the abandoned barn, decaying in the sun. As they passed the barn he looked for signs of life. Nothing. As he returned his eyes to the road, he saw the revolver, resting on her thigh. Tracking Martelli as he fell to his knees, the revolver had been steady as a rock. Watching her victim bleed, her eyes had been ice. Bright-blue ice.

Killer's eyes.

Lover's eyes—killer's eyes.

Ahead, at the top of the rise, the road ran along the wire fence. He brought the pickup to a stop, set the brake, got out of the truck. From here, the creek was visible for a hundred yards downstream. Was Bernhardt holding John concealed in the bushes that lined the creek bed? This was rattlesnake country. Did Bernhardt know?

Slowly, watchfully, he pivoted, searching for some hint of movement, some sign of life. The full-circle scrutiny ended with Theo, in the truck. She sat motionless, watching him. Theo with her revolver—waiting. Watching him with her ice-blue eyes. Waiting as a killer cat waited, motionless.

As he moved toward the truck, he saw the sparkle of sun striking chrome. The glint came from a grove of oak and manzanita that grew on the far side of the fence beyond the gate. It was a car, parked among the trees and bushes. Had he brought the key ring with the key to the gate? No. Without checking, he knew he hadn't. As he walked to the fence, he signaled to Theo. She got out of the truck, came toward him. He could see the tension in her body. A predator. A beautifully fashioned predator. In her right hand, she carried the revolver as if it were integral to herself.

"What is it?" She spoke softly, avidly.

"There's a car—" He pointed. "It's in that oak grove."

Was it Fowler? Bernhardt? Someone else?

Anyone else?

Were eyes watching?

He looked at the fence: six feet high, topped by two strands of barbed wire. High enough to stop deer. Meaning that—

To his left, ten feet away, he saw an irregularity in the fence.

"Look—" Quickly, he covered the ten feet. It was a flap cut in the wire, three feet across the top, three feet high, bent flush with the fence, to disguise the cut. Bolt cutters had done the job. Premeditation. Planning. Organization. The law?

Would Fowler have done it? As he eyed the minimal gap, he felt his solar plexus suddenly contract. He was giggling. *Giggling.* Imagining Fowler squeezing through a three-foot gap, he was giggling. Secretly. Shamefully.

"Look at this." Theo was pointing at the ground. In the soft, sandy, gravelly earth, the best kind of soil for grapes, he saw footprints. Two sets of footprints, heading from the cut fence to the dirt track, then turning left, toward the creek and the abandoned barn.

"Someone came through here to get him." As she said it, Theo raised her head, looked up and down the road, looked at the outline of the stranger's car: pinpoints of chrome, splashes of orange-painted metal visible through the foliage. She looked down at the footprints, followed their direction with her eyes. "They're still here, somewhere." Her voice was low; her eyes were in constant motion. "These tracks only go one way."

"Bernhardt." Price spoke bitterly. "It's got to be Bernhardt, that son of a bitch."

Not replying, she turned away from him. With the revolver swinging at her side, she was following the footprints, back the way they'd come.

"Get the rifle," she said. "And lock the truck."

6:05 P.M.

As he pulled open the barn door and slipped inside, Bernhardt looked down at the tracks in the dirt; he could see the outline of his Reeboks and the arc of the sagging door dragging in the dust. He drew the door shut and looked for a catch, a bar, something to secure the door. There was nothing. He turned, quickly surveyed the barn's interior, noted a line of horse stalls, a jumble of empty packing boxes, the rusted-out hulk of an ancient truck, oddments of moldering farm equipment.

John and Janice stood together beside a ladder that led up to a hayloft. He went to them, spoke softly to the woman: "They're coming back down the road, on foot. He's got a rifle, she's got a pistol." As he spoke, reflexively, he touched his revolver, holstered at the small of his back.

"That shot—" Janice moved a half-step closer to him, unconsciously seeking protection.

Admitting to his own uncertainty, the first hint of fear, Bernhardt shook his head. His eyes were fixed on the door. "I don't know. It could've been anything." As he spoke, he was aware that John was moving away from them, toward the wall that fronted on the dirt road. The golden light of the gathering sunset came in narrow shafts through the cracks in the wall. John put his eye to a knothole.

"The lookout," Bernhardt whispered, making an effort to smile at the woman beside him. When he'd first met her, hardly more than a week ago, sitting across from an elegant marble coffee table in her expensive hotel suite, she'd seemed remarkably assured, completely in control. Now, wearing jeans that had gotten dirty when she'd climbed through the fence, hair in disarray, with sweat beading her forehead and upper lip, she was a different person: a small, uneasy woman in a strange place. Now she pointed to the ladder. "There's a hayloft, up there. We could hide in the hay."

Instinctively, Bernhardt shook his head. "We'd be cornered, up there. I'd rather face them. Right here." He pointed to the stalls, and the empty packing boxes and the hulk of the truck. "You and John can get out of sight. If they come in, I'll talk to them."

"But the guns . . ."

He smiled. "There won't be a shootout, don't worry. I'm no hero. It doesn't pay."

Trying to answer the smile, she said, "The woman—who is she?"

"She's Price's girlfriend."

Beside him, she stood silently, her eyes fixed on the figure of the small boy, half-crouched, his eye to the knothole.

"Alan—I'm scared. The guns . . . that shot . . ."

He stepped closer, put his arm around her shoulders, squeezed. "Shooting trespassers is like sending people to the gas chamber for overtime parking."

She tried to smile. It was a failed effort.

At the far end of the wall, alien movement disturbed the golden lines of sunshine. Reacting, John's body stiffened; his outspread hands shifted against the rough wood, fingers widespread, tightened.

"They're out there," Janice whispered. "They're right beside the barn."

Bernhardt nodded, moved to stand in front of her as he faced the door.

6:06 P.M.

"They could be anywhere." Theo's voice was wary. "If they're hiding, they could be anywhere."

Price took a fresh grip on the rifle. Had he remembered to set the safety? Had he jacked a round in the chamber? Yes, the safety was set. But was there a cartridge in the chamber, ready? "Just a minute." He stopped walking, rested the rifle butt against his thigh, released the safety catch, drew back the bolt. Yes, he could see the brass cartridge casing. As he pushed the bolt home and reset the safety, the specter of Martelli suddenly seared his consciousness. It was a progression of quick cuts: Martelli half-raising the 30-30; Martelli's face, eyes wide with shock; Martelli falling; Martelli's upper chest, blood-soaked.

Martelli, dying?

Dead?

If Maria or one of the winery workers had called emergency, would he have heard the sound of the ambulance's siren? Yes. In this quiet, open country, sound carried.

"Self-defence," she'd said. Yes. *Yes.* Certainly, self-defense. And kidnapping, too. *Yes.*

With the rifle he gestured to a small pathway that led from the barn on their left down to the stream, on their right. The pathway was grass, not dirt; there were no footprints. "Let's try the creek first. That's where he spends most of his time."

"I think we should've checked out their car."

"Let's check the creek, first."

She made no reply.

At the place where the path intersected the dirt road, across from the derelict barn, he saw another bit of chrome glinting from a thicket beside the barn."

"Theo." He spoke softly, involuntarily. If he had let a moment pass—a single moment, while he considered—would he have said it? Remembering her eyes after she'd shot Martelli, would he have said it?

Instantly, she turned toward him. With the movement, the revolver came up, held at the ready. It was too late now. The second thought had come too late.

He pointed to the thicket. "That's his bike. There, in those bushes beside the barn."

6:07 P.M.

John was about to draw back from the wall when he saw them: his father carrying his deer-hunting rifle, and the woman carrying a pistol.

It was her. *Her*.

The woman he'd seen the night his mother died. The woman who'd come down the stairs from the second floor with his father.

As he watched them come closer, just as they'd come closer that night as he lay on the couch, it all came back: angry voices, the crash of furniture, the sound of fighting, and then the terrible silence, broken only by the sound of furtive movement, and the hushed voices. His father's voice, and the woman's voice.

Murderers.

Murderers.

The word struck him like a hostile hand, so strong that it forced a low moan of pain, brought the sting of sudden tears, doubled him over.

"John—?" his aunt's voice called. Through the blur of tears, he saw her stricken face. She was coming closer. Her hands were on his shoulders. If only she would draw him to her, hug him as his mother used to, his earliest memory.

"John. What is it? What'd you see?"

"It—" He swallowed, fought tears. Suddenly it had all come down to this time, this place, this moment.

Now.

"It—it's her." With great effort, he raised his arm, pointed. "That lady. She was there, that night. The—the night my mommy died. She was there. With—with—"

Could he do it?

Could he say it?

With all the time gone, with the whole world slipping away, could he say it? Here? Now?

"With my—my father. They were both of them there. Upstairs. They—"

"Oh, God. Oh, John."

As, yes, her arms came around him, drawing him close—holding him. Finally holding him close.

6:10 P.M.

Theo pointed to the ground, to the fresh footprints in the soft dirt, to the curving track left by the door.

"That's a child's footprint," she whispered. "That's John. Bernhardt's got John, in there."

"It—it could be the sheriff, though. We don't know it's Bernhardt. Not really."

"The sheriff wouldn't hide." It was a tight, furious hiss. "It's *Bernhardt*." As she spoke, she gripped the door with her left hand, holding the revolver ready in her right hand.

"B—be careful. He could have a gun."

"*Help* me, dammit."

He gripped the door, pulled it open far enough for her to slip through. After a last glance back over his shoulder, one final glimpse of the familiar sun-drenched terrain he was leaving, he followed her into the shadows of the old barn.

6:12 P.M.

Hidden behind the skewed stack of broken packing boxes, Bernhardt drew his revolver, swung the cylinder out. One chamber was empty, insurance against accidental discharge, if the gun were dropped. Before they'd left the car

259

he'd put a half-handful of cartridges in his pocket. With his eyes fixed on the barn door, he took a single cartridge from his pocket, slipped it into the empty chamber, noiselessly locked the cylinder in place. Here—now—the safety theory had inverted. Here—now—the sixth cartridge could mean survival.

From this position he could see both his charges: Janice, crouched behind the farthest horse stall, John kneeling on the ground beside the truck's rear wheel. Janice was thirty feet away from him, John was twenty feet away. It was a defensive triangle, a sixty-second defensive improvisation. He could see them; they could see him. But they couldn't see each other. He was the director, then. Just as, in that other world, his job was to deploy actors on a stage.

But this was real life. This was—

From his far right, fifty feet away, he heard the sound of the door scraping dirt. On the earthen floor of the barn, a slender line of sunlight was widening—widening. A foot appeared, then a leg, a hand gripping a revolver: Theo Stark, moving silently, silkily—dangerously. The female of the species, on the prowl. Followed by Dennis Price, holding a rifle like he might handle a snake.

Outside, at a distance, the rifle would count; the handgun would be useless.

Here, at close quarters, the maneuverability of the revolver could make the difference.

He looked at Janice. Smiled. Winked.

He looked at John. Smiled. Winked. Placed his forefinger to his lips, pantomiming *Shhh*.

Both of them smiled in return. Janice tremulously, John timidly. From where they crouched, concealed, neither of them could see the woman and the man as they advanced: the woman in the lead, searching ahead; the man behind, covering her, his head and his rifle swinging from side to side.

Then, suddenly breaking the silence, Price called softly: "John?"

Bernhardt saw the boy's head come up, saw his lips part, an involuntary response. Quickly, Bernhardt shook his head, raised his hand, once more the director, life or death, now. Confused, the boy frowned, blinked—but remained silent, lowering his head.

The woman and the man had covered more than half the distance between the door and the derelict truck. Another ten paces and Theo, still in the lead, would see John, crouched beside the truck's big rear wheel.

Five paces.

Bernhardt raised his revolver. Should he cock the gun, risk the sound of two metallic clicks? Single-action shooting was more accurate than double action. Slower, but more accurate.

But double action gave no warning, was therefore safer.

He took his thumb from the hammer, raised the revolver slightly, lined up the sights on the woman's head, then lowered them to the body.

Two paces.

A bullet, ripping into that beautiful predator's body— could he do it, pull the trigger?

With his left hand Bernhardt cautioned John, gestured for him to remain motionless.

Moving a single step beyond the truck, inching forward, the woman looked first to her left, toward the jumble of packing cases that sheltered Bernhardt. Could she see him as he crouched behind the boxes, both his eyes and his gun tracking her through a narrow space between the cases? Should he stand up, confront her?

Another half-step, each moment a shrieking eternity, and her head began to swing away from him and toward the boy. All the time was gone—the days, the minutes, now the last seconds, gone. All the—

Suddenly her whole body tensed. Her eyes, he knew, were blazing as, yes, the revolver came up, aimed at the small figure crouched behind the truck.

"Theo." It was his voice, a sound that filled the silence.

His theatrical voice, make-believe loud, make-believe brave. *"Drop it."*

Revolver raised, crouched, she began the turn toward him, committed.

6:13 P.M.

"Theo. Drop it."

A stranger's voice.

Bernhardt, hidden?

Hidden with John? Protecting John?

Price saw Theo's shoulder drop, saw her crouch, saw her revolver swing, tracking the man's voice. The revolver was trained on the stack of broken boxes.

Moving with Theo as she turned, Price raised the rifle, steadied it. Involuntarily, his finger tightened on the trigger. The explosion shattered the silence. The rifle kicked, struck his shoulder, hard.

One explosion.

Another explosion, a second shot.

His?

6:13:02 P.M.

Bernhardt's revolver kicked; orange flame blossomed. The explosion mingled with the shouts, the screams, and the sound of the other explosion. Her blouse was white, her blood was bright red against the white. Holding his revolver in both hands, the approved stance, Bernhardt leaped clear of the packing cases, sprang toward the woman, kicked the revolver from her hand. The pistol struck the front wheel of the truck, fell to the ground. Bernhardt whirled to face the man. Price stood motionless. His eyes were wide, staring at the woman as she sank slowly to her knees. The rifle was pointed down toward the ground at Bernhardt's feet. A single eddy of smoke curled from the muzzle. With his revolver trained on Price's chest, Bernhardt whispered, "Drop the gun, Dennis." As Theo began to slowly shake her head, Price laid the rifle in the dirt and then stepped back. As Theo sighed once and then collapsed, Price lifted his eyes to Bernhardt, saying, "John?"

11 P.M.

John yawned, looked at his bed. His Aunt Janice had turned the bedspread down, the way his mother had done, so very long ago. But his aunt didn't want him to go to bed, didn't want him to go to sleep, not yet. They were waiting for someone.

He looked at his aunt, looked at the TV. It was about a large family that talked too much and laughed too loud. His Aunt Janice had turned the volume down until the voices were only whispers. When there'd been nothing left for him to say to his aunt, nothing left for her to say to him, when only their small, sad smiles were left, she'd turned on the TV, so he wouldn't fall asleep.

Now he looked at his aunt, and saw her watching him. When their eyes met, she smiled a quick, bright smile, more serious than cheerful. His Aunt Janice was worried.

Scared, really. The men downstairs, the cars outside, the flashing lights, the sound of strangers' footsteps—it was all the same as the night his mother died. And his aunt was scared.

Words ran together in his thoughts. Words like *Aunt Janice* became one word. And *Grandpa Hale*, too—the grandfather he'd never know, his mother's father.

And *the night his mother died* all ran together, too: one long, sad word, the word that would never leave his thoughts. It was a word that—

A knock on the door: three light knuckle-raps. A stranger's knock. It was the knock Aunt Janice had been expecting, the knock they'd been waiting for. Quickly, she stepped to the TV, switched it off, then went to the door. She looked back at him, smiled, and nodded. *Don't worry*, the nod meant.

But she was worried.

Plainly, she was worried.

She opened the door to the tall, half-bald man with the thin voice who spoke quietly. But when he spoke, the strangers in the house listened, and nodded, and obeyed. Everyone but the sheriff, who never nodded.

Aunt Janice and the man were talking quietly. Their eyes had gone cloudy. It was the same way everyone had talked at the funeral, the same way they'd looked around the eyes and the mouth.

Had Al died?

Was that what the tall, thin man had come to tell them? When they'd driven from the barn to the house, they'd found Al lying beside the road. Maria had been kneeling beside Al, crying, rocking from side to side as she pressed a blood-soaked towel to Al's upper chest. Soon afterward the ambulance had come, its siren screaming. It had only been a station wagon that was painted white, with red lights on top. So they'd had to send another ambulance for the woman they'd left at the barn.

On *the night his mother died*—those words, again—

there'd only been one ambulance. And when the ambulance left, that night, there were no sirens, no flashing red lights. Only the headlights, sweeping white arcs in the darkness.

At the door, his Aunt Janice and the tall man were finished talking. They nodded to each other as if they were agreeing to something sad. Yes, it was like the two days in Santa Barbara, those final two days: low voices, slow movements, eyes that had gone dark.

Had Al died? He'd been alive when they put him in the ambulance. His eyelids had been fluttering, and his fingers had twitched.

While Aunt Janice closed the door, the tall man stepped forward, smiling down at him. The man was so tall that the ceiling was behind his head, not the wall.

"Hi John," the man said. "My name is Clifford Benson. I'm the district attorney of Benedict County. I'm the one who's got to decide whether we arrest people—put them in jail." As he spoke, the tall man sat on the bed, gesturing for John to sit beside him. Between them the tall man placed a small tape recorder.

"Not the sheriff?" he asked.

"Well, the sheriff makes the first decision, I guess you'd say. He makes the on-scene decision, as we call it. He decides whether someone should be arrested. But then I have to decide whether there's enough evidence to indict someone, make him stand trial, in court. The sheriff does his work first, gets everything secured. Then he calls me." The tall man was smiling at him. "Do you see?" It was the kind of question a teacher would ask. A good teacher, not one of the bad teachers.

"I—I guesso."

"Good. Now—" The man pointed to the tape recorder. "Now, that's a tape recorder, right?"

"Right."

"Okay. Now, I've talked to Miss Hale—your aunt. And I've talked to Mr. Bernhardt, too. And they both agree that they want me to talk to you about the events that transpired—" He broke off, frowned, started again: "About what happened on the night your mother died." The man looked to Aunt Janice. "Is that correct, Miss Hale?"

"That's correct." She spoke slowly; her face was serious. She stood against the far wall, arms folded. She was standing that way because she would say nothing more. Now it was the tall man and the tape recorder—and him. Just him.

As, yes, the man touched the switch on the recorder. The tape began to revolve as the man, Mr. Benson, began to talk: "This is Clifford R. Benson, district attorney of Benedict County, California, at—" He looked at his watch. "At eleven-fifteen P.M. on the night of August thirtieth, of this year. I'm speaking from the residence of Dennis Price, of the Brookside Winery, in Benedict County. I'm interrogating John Price, age seven, the son of Dennis Price and the late Constance Hale Price. Witnessing this interrogation is Miss Janice Hale, sister of Constance and aunt of John. At the end of the interrogation, Miss Hale will make a short statement.

"The subject of the interrogation is the events that transpired at this location on the night of June sixteenth, of this year, and the early morning hours of June seventeenth."

Mr. Benson touched the switch again, stopped the tape. For a moment Mr. Benson didn't speak. As the long, silent moments passed, they sat motionless, looking at each other. Then, quietly, Mr. Benson said, "I know what you told Mr. Bernhardt and Miss Hale a few hours ago, John, while the three of you were in the barn and you observed your father and Theo Stark approaching. I want you to tell me exactly what you told them. If you do—if you tell me the whole story, then that'll be the end of it. Everything will be out in the open after that. There won't be any more lies." Another long, solemn pause. Then, still quietly: "Do you understand, John?"

He nodded. "Yes."

"And will you tell me what happened? Everything that happened?"

Could he do it—nod once more?

Just once more?

11:50 P.M.

"Okay," Fowler said, jerking his chin grudgingly toward the phone. "You can use it, but just for a couple of minutes, no more."

"Is there a phone book?" Bernhardt asked. "I don't know the number."

"Ask Information," Fowler grunted.

He got the number, heard the phone ring in his room at the Starlight Motel.

"Yes?"

For a moment he didn't respond, but instead let the sound of her voice linger. How often, in the past hours, had he thought of her? How often had he longed to touch her, feel her touch him?

"Paula, it's Alan."

"Ah—" It was a soft exhalation: a lover's wordless communion. "God, it's midnight."

"I know. I couldn't phone until now."

"Are you all right?"

"Yes . . ."

"Janice? John?"

"They're fine. Every—" He broke off. *Everyone on our team is fine*, he'd been about to add. At the thought he privately smiled. Did it really come down to a sports metaphor? Was that the American way?

"Listen, I can't talk. I just wanted to check in. But you should go to sleep, Paula. This could take a long time."

"C.B. is here. Do you want him?"

The wry, weary private smile returned. He could imagine C.B.'s frustration, left out of the action. At bottom, C.B. was a bone-knocker.

"I don't need him now. Has he got a room?"

"Yes."

"Then tell him to go to sleep."

"He wants to talk to you."

Bernhardt looked at Fowler, who was glowering. "I can't talk to him now." He turned his back on the sheriff, spoke softly: "Love you."

"Me too you." A pause. Then, intimately: "Be sure and wake me, when you come in."

"Of that," he said, "you may be absolutely certain. 'Bye." Gently, he broke the connection.

As he turned away from the phone, still with his back to Fowler, he saw Benson descending the central staircase that led down to the Price living room. For the last two hours, upstairs, Benson had been alternately interrogating both Dennis Price and John. Price had been held in the master bedroom, the original scene of the crime. John was in his own bedroom, with Janice.

Now, plainly weary, Benson nodded to Bernhardt, then pointed to the front door. Bernhardt nodded in return, following Benson out to the broad verandah. The night was soft and balmy; the moon was big and full, the stars were bright overhead. And, yes, there was the chirping of countless crickets.

"Come over here," Benson said, gesturing to two redwood chairs placed in the deep shadows of the front porch. Wearily, Benson sank into one of the chairs while Bernhardt took the other. Benson glanced at the open front door. Then he leaned forward, cautiously lowering his voice: "I've just come from talking to John—in Miss Hale's presence."

Bernhardt nodded. What came next, yet another sports metaphor, could be the ball game. If baseball was a game of inches, the game of life or death was a game of seconds—this second, and the next.

"It's all settled," Benson said. In his voice, Bernhardt could plainly hear both weariness and satisfaction. The home team, then, had won.

Won.

Through the ache of a bone-numbing weariness Bernhardt felt a kind of lost, wan exultation.

Won.

"John told it to me the way he told it to you," Benson was saying. "Or so Miss Hale states. So I put it to Mr. Price that his account of the events that transpired on the night of June sixteenth was false. Whereupon, surprise, he admitted that he'd been lying. Then he proceeded to blame his girlfriend for everything. So, adding everything together, I'm satisfied that I know how Constance Price died. She walked in on Price and Theo Stark in the master bedroom. A fight started. Theo Stark was probably coked up, or so Price alleges. She picked up the fireplace tongs, which was the murder weapon. Price was involved in the fight, I don't know to what extent. After he realized that his wife was dead, he took Theo down the stairs to put her in her car, get her out of there. Then he'd call the sheriff, report a prowler. But John was sleeping on the couch in the living room. The question was, how much did John see? No one knew, until today—until John told you the whole story in the barn, and then repeated it for me, just now."

"What's Price say?"

"He says that Theo did it. As I said."

"And what's she say?"

Benson shook his head. He let a beat pass as he looked at Bernhardt. Then, quietly: "She can't talk."

"Wh—" Suddenly his throat closed. Thank God, his face was in shadow. "What's that mean?"

"It means that she's got a bullet lodged in her spine."

Speaking with great care, great precision, Bernhardt asked, "Whose bullet? Mine? Or Price's?"

With equal precision, Benson shook his head. "I don't know."

"How many bullets were in her?"

"I don't know that, either."

"Will she die?"

"The doctors don't think so. But it's too early to be sure. They still have to operate. They're taking her to San Francisco, right now."

"If I hadn't shot, she'd have killed John."

"Or so you thought."

"Price thought so, too."

"Or maybe he wanted to shut her up."

Bernhardt decided not to reply. They'd already been over this, in the barn. He'd told the story once to Fowler, then to Benson. They'd questioned Janice separately. Certainly, she'd confirmed his story. As Theo had whirled toward him, revolver raised, he'd fired. Did he need a lawyer? Should he refuse to continue talking, without a lawyer? They'd already put Dennis in a state police car and taken him away. Was there another car waiting? Would he spend the night in a holding cell, not with Paula?

In the darkness of the verandah, in the balmy California night, silence lengthened. This, Bernhardt knew, was the inquisitor's favorite tactic: watching and waiting, observing the hapless suspect as he squirmed under the full weight of the law, cataloging the tics and the false starts, letting the suspect incriminate himself as he tried to wriggle free.

But, another sports cliché, two could play that game. Silence could favor the victim, too. Sometimes.

Finally, wearily, Benson lifted an angular hand, then let it fall. It was an ecclesiastical gesture, a played-out sign of papal absolution.

"Don't worry, Bernhardt. You're okay. Miss Hale's and John's stories match yours, absolutely. Price's story matches, too."

Audibly, Bernhardt exhaled, allowed himself to relax in his chair. Suddenly the night was friendlier, the future brighter.

"Yeah," Benson said, "it's all working out, at least so far. What'll happen when Price's lawyer arrives, that could be something else. Minimum, he'll tell Price to shut up. But for now Price is talking—a lot. His girlfriend, he says, did it all—everything. She killed Constance while Price was trying to separate the two women. She shot Martelli when Martelli tried to stop them from going after John. And she tried to kill John, to keep him from incriminating her. According to Price, he just intended to scare you and Janice Hale off the property, with his rifle. But Theo had other ideas. There's no doubt, he says, that Theo would've killed John."

"When can Theo talk?"

"The doctor guesses it'll be another twenty-four hours, at least. And then nothing more than a word or two. However, as soon as she can respond, even if it's only nodding or shaking her head, I'll be interrogating her. I pointed that fact out to Price, which could be why he started to talk. Maybe he wants to get his licks in first." Tiredly, Benson smiled. "I'd like to think so, anyhow. It'll make things easier." He broke off, closed his eyes, pressed long, thin fingers to his temples. Then: "Of course, if Theo's lawyer has even minimum law-school smarts he's going to turn it all around. He'll say Price struck the blow that killed his wife. He'll say Martelli was threatening them with a rifle, and Theo shot first, before Martelli could. As for what happened in the barn, the lawyer'll obviously say that the light was bad, and Theo thought John was either you or Janice Hale—trespassers. Or, better yet, kidnappers. She'll say she was acting in concert with Dennis, trying to rid him of two interlopers who, they believed, had come to

271

kidnap John, take him off the property through the hole you cut in the fence. She'll say she saw your gun, of course, so she fired in self-defense. And, finally, she'll accuse you of attempted murder."

Ruefully, Bernhardt grimaced. "Thanks a lot." Then: "What about Martelli?"

"Martelli is very, very lucky. The bullet didn't hit any organs, or even break any bones. But it did nick a small vein. He probably would've bled to death if Maria hadn't pressed a towel to the wound. Even at that, when the medics arrived, he was in deep shock and had lost a lot of blood. He'll be fine, though. The bullet went right through."

"Thank God," Bernhardt said. "You'd probably still be looking for Constance Price's murderer if it hadn't been for Martelli. You know that, don't you?"

"Martelli and you, Bernhardt. You're entitled to some credit."

"I'm glad to hear you say it." Bernhardt let a long, thoughtful moment pass as he stared out into darkness beyond the verandah. Then: "Does Theo know Dennis shot at her?"

Benson shrugged. "I'm not sure. If she does know, she didn't get it from me."

Thoughtfully shaking his head, Bernhardt wryly recited, "'The pangs of dispriz'd love, the law's delay . . .'"

Wearily, Benson smiled. "Shakespeare."

Surprised, Bernhardt nodded. "That's right, Shakespeare."

Benson's smile twisted, touched now with nostalgia—and inscrutable regret. "Yale drama," he said softly.

"Oh, God—" Bernhardt shook his head. "Not another actor."

"Worse. An aspiring actor, once. But I come from a long line of New York lawyers."

"So what're you doing in the wilds of Benedict County?"

"I'm not entirely sure. I escaped New York, but not the toils of the law."

"Well, I escaped from New York, too."

"Are you glad you did?"

"Until just recently, I wasn't really sure. Now, though, it's fine."

"Are we talking about the lady registered at the Starlight Motel?"

"You don't miss much, do you?"

"In my job, nosiness comes with the territory. Your job, too."

Bernhardt nodded. Then: "What about John? What happens to John?"

"Ah—" Benson's answering nod was somber. "John—that's the question, now."

"And?"

"It comes back to the toils of the law, I'm afraid."

Aware that he was holding his breath, Bernhardt made no reply. The DA, he knew, was about to render his decision: one mortal man, slightly balding, about to pronounce the words that could mean the world and all its laughter to a small boy named John.

All its laughter—all its pain. Everything.

In the short silence, three men left the house, went down the front steps and got into a highway patrol station wagon. Each man carried a valise: it was the lab crew, leaving the scene. Aside from the cars belonging to Fowler and Benson, all the official cars had gone.

Finally Benson spoke. His voice was crisp: "John's testimony is enough for us to take Theo Stark and Dennis Price into custody. Which, obviously, we've done. Technically—legally—we could lock you up, too, pending a preliminary hearing. However—" Benson waved a casual hand. "However, that's a judgment call. I'd say designating you as a material witness, along with Janice Hale and the boy, would suffice." He looked at Bernhardt, let a cat-and-mouse beat pass. Then testing: "Wouldn't you say so?"

Straight-faced, Bernhardt nodded. "Yes, I'd say so."

"Good." It was the final word, the final protocol. Case closed.

His case, closed.

Should he thank the peripatetic DA? Was that what this little game was really all about?

As if to respond to the query, Benson said, "That leaves John."

Bernhardt nodded. "Yes, that leaves John."

Glancing at the open front door, Benson leaned closer, lowered his voice. "If we go by the book, here, considering that Price is in custody, then the law is clear."

For "the book," Bernhardt knew, he was meant to substitute "Fowler."

"That's to say," Benson continued, "by the book, we've got to take John over to San Rafael, and put him in the Youth Guidance Center."

"The Youth—" A surge of outrage momentarily choked off the rest. Then, incredulously: "The Youth *Guidance* Center?"

Benson raised a cautionary hand. "Wait. Just—"

"The kid makes a murder case for you—incriminates his own father in the death of his mother—and you want to send him to the Youth *Guidance* Center? *Christ!*"

"Goddammit!" Lowering his voice, Benson looked again at the open door. "I said *cool* it."

"But you're—"

"I'm talking about the book. That's by way of reference. A kid finds himself in a spot like John's in, he goes to the Youth Guidance Center. Then a judge decides what happens next. But that's not what I want."

"What about—" Bernhardt spoke softly now. "What about Fowler? What's he want?"

"Fowler doesn't have much feeling for kids. I guess they're too independent-minded for his taste. So—" Delicately, the other man hesitated. "So it's up to me, to do the right thing."

"Ah—" Bernhardt nodded, leaned back in his chair.

"So here's the plan—" Benson glanced at his watch, then made hard eye contact with Bernhardt. As he spoke, briskly and concisely, he ticked off the points on his fingers. "First, John will stay here for the night, in custody of his aunt. He's probably asleep right this minute, in fact. Now, while John's sleeping, Janice and you pack a bag for John. Pack several bags. You know—toys, mementos, things kids like. Then, very early tomorrow morning—six at the absolute latest—Janice and John get in her car and they drive down to Santa Barbara. Where, with luck, they'll live happily ever after—in another jurisdiction."

"You're going to arrange it, are you? This happy ending—you're going to make it happen. Legally, make it happen."

"I'm the District Attorney of Benedict County, Bernhardt. DA's have a lot of power."

"Mind giving me a few details?"

Equably, Benson shrugged. "Plea bargaining. I'm sure you've heard of plea bargaining."

Bernhardt smiled.

"It's obvious," Benson said, "that Dennis Price is an asshole. He doesn't give a shit about John. Never has. Dennis is out for the money—the Hale money. It's equally obvious that he probably wasn't the one who killed his wife. He just doesn't have the stones. Theo Stark, the new breed of woman, is the guilty party. She sniffed a little coke, picked up the fireplace tongs, and went wild. However, because of a combination of weakness and greed—and maybe hot pants, at least initially—Price conspired to conceal evidence of the crime. Which is, as you know, a crime of equal magnitude. So—" Benson spread his hands. "So we do a deal, the great American plea bargain, like I said. Which is to say, if Dennis agrees to turn Theo Stark for us, and if he agrees to let Janice take custody of

John, then we'll go easy on Dennis." As he spoke, Benson smiled, rose to his feet, signifying dismissal, and extended his hand. "See?"

Also rising, also smiling, Bernhardt took the other man's hand. "You're okay, Benson." For emphasis, he nodded, repeating, "You're okay."

THURSDAY
August 31

3:15 A.M.

He took off his glasses, put them on the bureau, slipped
into bed. Beneath the sheet, Paula was naked, lying on her
back. Against the faint light filtering through the drapes,
he could see her face in profile. She was softly, serenely
snoring.

He moved close, touched the flesh of her stomach, just
below her breasts. She stirred, murmured something,
turned toward him. His hand was at the small of her back
now. Against his chest, he felt her breasts. He kissed her
once, lightly.

"Is it all right?" she asked, sleep slurring her words. "Is
everything all right?"

"It's all right," Bernhardt whispered. "Everything's all
right."

"Hmmm . . ."

THE BEST IN SUSPENSE
FROM TOR